A Cyber Affair

By

Lonz Cook

A Cyber Affair

© Lonz Cook 2013

All Rights Reserved

Published by: Elevation Book Publishing
Atlanta, Georgia 30308
www.elevationbookpublishing.com

Cook, Lonz, 1960-
Teri Sampedro -Cantrell Editor
Yanett Hollins Associate Editor

A Cyber Affair by Lonz Cook
p.cm.
ISBN 978-1-943904-03-07(pbk)

BISAC FIC027020
BISAC FIC027030

Acknowledgement

In today's society, people using electronic communications are much more likely to be in a relationship (72%) than those without (36%). Couples who met through friends dropped from nearly 40% in the mid-1980s to less than 30% in 2010. Today, over 40 million people are using dating sites, supporting a $1.9-billion-dollar industry.

Imagine basing your life around a network, decreasing physical contact, and performing a background investigation on the people you meet. Where is the adventure in dating? Well, it's now online. I was approached with many stories of how people met, and those discussions shared a common thread: they met online. This got me thinking, so I asked people a series of questions: How did they get to the point where they desired to meet in person? When they physically met, was it their first time from an initial online interaction? What was their worst and best experience? I heard a lot of stories detailing both good and bad experiences. After my investigation, I concluded that there is a story worth sharing and I compiled their various experiences; hence, the creation of *A Cyber Affair*.

Thanks to my supporters for sharing their personal experiences. I appreciate your input, guidance, and honest feedback for accuracy. To my family and friends, I pray this book doesn't disappoint you and that it maintains your high expectations.

Happy Reading,

Lonz

Contents

Chapter 1

OMG! What the hell am I doing? Tiffany frowned as she sat amongst the passengers waiting for her flight to Las Vegas. She glanced around the terminal, hopeful that someone would read her mind and give her some direction. The gate attendant announced her boarding section. Tiffany rose from her seat, edged through the crowd with her laptop backpack, pulling her carry-on, and got in line. She held her ticket while she moved closer to the gate agent. *Why am I doing this?* She thought while watching eager passengers in front of her hand over their tickets and walk through the door. She stepped to the gate, ticket in hand, and stared. The agent reached for the boarding pass, slid it from her fingers, and scanned it on his machine. "Is this your first flight ?" asked the agent.

"No, it isn't. I'm a little nervous about this trip."

"Don't worry; no one cares what you do in Vegas." He smiled and returned her ticket.

"I hope *he* cares," Tiffany mumbled as she walked through the door. Suddenly the gangway darkened, black as a moonless night. Her hand became moist. The carry-on didn't seem to cooperate. It was as if something was trying to deter her from boarding the flight. Tiffany yanked her carry-on, finally won its cooperation, and walked down the center of the tunnel. The passenger in front of her disappeared into its darkness and conversations behind her went silent. She saw a dim light appear as though the gangway had become a path of torture. Suddenly a bright light near the cabin door led her, as if directing her feet one after the other, deeper into the passageway. She pulled the carry-on and took each step carefully. Her heart pumped like a car engine on a race track. Tiffany walked slower, as if her hesitation could delay the plane's take off. With each step, she heard warning bells.

"Miss, are you okay?" A fellow passenger's voice broke her trance.

"Ah, I think so," Tiffany kept her eyes forward. She saw the fully lit tunnel for the first time, the door to the airplane now directly in front of her. She entered the aircraft with her carry-on in tow.

"Hi, welcome aboard," the flight attendant greeted her.

"Hi." Tiffany smiled and turned right to walk through the economy class section. She looked at the seating chart and glanced at her ticket. "Seat 21C," she read, and walked towards the rear of the plane. Tiffany glanced at the row numbers - 8...9...10... moving further back 19...20... "Excuse me," she said to her seating companion.

"Sure, no problem," He rose from the seat and moved aside. Tiffany lifted her carry-on, grabbed her backpack, and slid through the tight aisle. As soon as she cleared the first seat, the guy moved right in behind her. "I'm sorry." Tiffany looked behind her while dropping her backpack on the floor.

"No problem. I was expecting you," he smiled.

Tiffany pushed her backpack under the seat in front of her, grabbed her seatbelt, and buckled up for the flight. She watched passengers boarding and averted her gaze to look out of the window. Anxiously, she glanced at her watch while butterflies fluttered through her stomach. The idea of having a last chance to escape the unknown tampered with her mind. She watched other passengers board and thought *I can get off the plane right after that guy sits down.* The gentleman sat, but before she could move, the flight's lead attendant announced, "Prepare the cabin for takeoff, cross check and all call." Passengers were instructed to secure electronics and buckle down for the flight. When the cabin door slammed shut, Tiffany realized that it was too late to run.

Tiffany Miles was the only child of strict parents. She wasn't part of a popular crowd in high school, but she loved her circle of friends. Tiffany was average in size and cute, with unique features: curly black hair, a straight nose, and oval brown eyes. She hadn't received much male attention in high school, but when she did date, her parents selected young men from among their church friends. She rarely disagreed with the guys her mom and dad selected for her. The few times she went against their guidance, all hell broke loose and her parents would tighten their control.

Tiffany tried her hand at dating in college. She moved into the campus dorm and there found new freedom to date and explore as she pleased. What she didn't know about dating men became a substantial lesson in reality during that first semester. Some men take advantage of naive girls. She accepted every offer to go on a date from any man who asked. Tiffany was sensual with some and enjoyed the physical desires of others. She didn't know what *not* to do. Her roommate took notice and reeled her in, explaining the differences between dating and being used. Her roommate also started checking out her dates, showing up on occasion to see if Tiffany was following her advice.

Tiffany failed her first semester of college. Her scores were so low that they barely registered in the grading system. Panic set in when reality hit and she realized she'd have to return to her parents' home, since she didn't have anywhere else to go. So instead, she did the next best thing to guarantee her continued freedom: she married Brad Wilkes, her first date on campus and the man who had taken her virginity. She thought he loved her and he was the man she had to have - the guy she felt made her dreams come true. Brad's touch was as soft as the melodies that escape a harp. He had magical fingers that aroused her body in ways unfamiliar to her.

Brad claimed her heart, doing everything he could to ensure she was happy with their relationship. He didn't care about the guys she had dated before him.

They had given marriage a shot, but three years in, the only thing she gained was a husband. Brad didn't deliver on his promise of a good life. Instead, he'd become like a dependent child, always making excuses for his failures. She realized he'd never mature past his college days. It didn't matter what Tiffany did for the marriage; It failed miserably.

***

Dating again in the spring of 2012 meant she had to take a serious chance on meeting Manny outside of Skype. She wanted a positive experience, but somehow fear had her feeling as through she were headed for disaster.

Tiffany recalled horrific stories of women who had undertaken this same journey. Stories of sex offenders, rapists, and physical beatings bombarded her mind. Images of Manny raising his hand against her flashed in her imagination. She thought of him possibly being a stalker, and wondered why she was traveling to meet Manny in the first place. She paused before allowing her fear to affect her nervous system and reminded herself of the many hours of conversations they had shared. *It's no different than meeting a man in San Francisco,* she thought.

Though she had held video chats with Manny over the span of three months, Tiffany wasn't certain if they would be physically attracted to each other. She realized that looks could be deceiving: what's viewed on screen isn't always what appears in person. She wanted the excitement, the candlelight dinners, the slow dance amongst a disappearing crowd, and to feel her heart race at his gentle touch on her lower back. Tiffany imagined every moment Manny as they had been described in their many conversations.

It was a male passenger's voice two seats over, the rolling tongue and spicy mellow tone of his soft delivery, which caressed her ears and reminded her of Manny. Her imagination walked the runway of sensuality over the fantasy about Latin lovers. Thoughts about them managed to sweep her into a frenzy: of how their passion and focus could raise a woman's awareness with every affectionate touch, of their rhythmic movements and suave demeanors, and of their romantic language, designed to match the pace of their victim's heart with a cadence of mystical influences. The thought of Manny made her soul quiver.

She stared out of the window at the ground as the plane taxied to the runway and leaned back for the takeoff. Tiffany thought about her reasons for going and how she had arrived to this point of no return.

She reached for her backpack and pulled out her computer. Tiffany looked out of the window again before she opened the laptop, booted up, and scanned Manny's very first email. He had written: '…I read your profile and find you interesting…' Next she opened a more recent email: '…I'm going to kiss you all over, from head to toe. We'll share ourselves, like we talked about last night.' Her heart fluttered. They had exchanged flirtatious banters during many conversations. 'I can't wait to share our first morning kiss.'

Tiffany clicked on Manny's profile picture and smiled as his appearance gave her a tingle, a twinge, and caused her heart to race. His body, shirtless and sporting swim trunks, was that of a masculine man built with abs of steel and a V-span torso. His arms were defined, and looked perfect for making a woman feel secure and comfortable whenever he held her. Tiffany released a sigh when she looked at his dark eyes, perfect mouth, and caramel skin. She imagined feeling his chiseled cheek next to hers.

Tiffany read one more email and Skype conversation before closing the laptop. She then sat back and imagined their first kiss. Her body felt excited while her mind settled on her decision to invest herself in the coming days.

Tiffany reminisced about the night she had received Manny's first email. It was months earlier and the season was cold and wet, a typical winter. Tiffany looked at the flight attendants who were passing out goodies from their cart and raised her hand to get their attention.

"Yes, can I help you?" the attendant queried.

"Ah, can I get some wine? Red or white, it doesn't matter."

"May I see your ID card?"

"Sure," Tiffany smiled, getting her card from her purse in the backpack. She showed it to the attendant, who scanned and returned the card in one fluid motion. Tiffany bent forward to her backpack to put her card away.

A Cyber Affair

He'd better be the man I think he is. She looked out of the plane's window, realizing that this trip could either be a terrific fantasy or a nightmare in the making. Skepticism kept her grounded. Images invaded her mind, and her body responded. She yearned for a man's touch, and a chance to satisfy the physical stimulation she remembered from men past.

Tiffany smiled, hoping that Manny was a man with good intentions and they would experience the passion he had promised. She knew that with her desire to explore everything about him, going to see him was the right thing to do. After all, the reason she was going to Las Vegas was the belief that Manny was her destiny.

She gazed out of the airplane's window and projected her story against the clouds. She saw her own image on the couch in her living room. It had been earlier in the year when she sat on the couch wearing her winter pajamas and sipping a cup of orange cinnamon tea.

She was surfing dating websites on her laptop; focused, but wary as she clicked on yet another profile. It had become her habit, her hobby, and her goal to find the man of her dreams. She wanted the perfect fit: a man with unique charm and charisma, and she believed her ideal mate was out there in cyberspace in pixels of perfection. Tiffany didn't want a swimsuit model, nor did she desire the metrosexual type that others seemed to admire. She wanted a man with a suave soul and a certain level of sophistication. She wanted magic; the magic most women craved.

Tiffany had enough online dating experience to write a handbook. On web page after web page she saw cute pictures, read appealing write-ups, and enjoyed a variety of music which the men had placed on their pages. Feeling adventurous, she skimmed more profiles than usual in hopes of finding someone who would spark her interest.

Should I click 'like'? she questioned herself. She threw caution to the wind, clicked 'like' and moved on to the next. None of the next few profile pictures excited her, nor did any of their personal profiles grab her attention. Tiffany stopped surfing long enough to read a few emails which she had received from the dating site. One would-be suiter wrote:

Oh baby, you are fine as wine and I want to explore your body. Write me back and let's get things rolling.

She deleted the email. *What a jerk!* The words easily ran through her mind and she clicked on to the next one.

Hi, I saw your picture and read your profile. I'm impressed. You are a sight to behold and I'd like to see if you have time for a chat. I look forward to hearing from you.

How sweet! An email without stupidity or sexually charged comments, she thought, and clicked on his name for a fast peek. When his picture appeared on the screen, she closed his page and cringed. She didn't like to think of herself as shallow, but she didn't find him attractive. She opened another email which contained a simple message:

'Hi, I'd love to get to know you.' Again she read the profile from top to bottom, viewed pictures, and searched for keywords in his description. She clicked the 'Next' arrow and a good-looking man appeared on the screen. *Oh my goodness he's handsome!* ran through her mind. His golden hair shouted remnants of a wheat field before harvest. His bulging pectoral muscles showed through his tight, open, collared shirt, revealing a hairless chest. His smile was warm like the sun; bright enough to warm any woman's heart.

Wait a minute, he looks familiar. She clicked to a web magazine article she had read earlier that evening. *I thought so: it is the same guy. What a shame! He can't put his own picture on the profile. Some guys will do anything to get your attention.*

Tiffany read multiple profiles with pictures she found appealing. She ignored the newly-arrived emails she knew were from men on those dating websites she visited. Instead, she spent hours on newly published profiles on multiple websites well into the evening. There were some guys she liked and other she didn't. When her apartment door opened, breaking her focus, Tiffany watched Valerie enter the living room and at that moment she remembered that they had made plans to go out.

"Hey, girl," greeted Valerie as she walked into the apartment. "Why aren't you ready?"

"I was web surfing and got carried away," Tiffany said.

"Dating sites again? That's why I came to get you, Tiff. You won't find a suitable man in cyberspace."

"You never know, Valerie. Plus, it's fun. There are a lot of men out there."

"Maybe, but you have to find one who's available right now. You need to get out of this house to make it happen. Come on – move it."

"I'm moving, I'm moving. Where are we going, so I know how to dress?"

"It's a good place. Dress like you're going to impress a man." Valerie grinned and followed Tiffany.

Tiffany walked to the bedroom, paused at the mirror, and looked at herself from different angles. She smiled approvingly, knowing she could grab a man's interest. She felt she was still a pretty woman. She appreciated her body, which featured full curves, dark hair, green eyes, and a nose as straight as they come. She smiled, thinking how much she looked like her mother. Tiffany walked into her closet and chose clothes that highlighted her figure. "So where exactly are we going?" she shouted as she stepped into her dress.

"It's a place Orlando told me about."

"Orlando's gay. What do you think we'll find there?" Tiffany put on her shoes, moving to the vanity.

"Straight men. That's why he didn't like it. So for us, that's good news. Now keep moving, or the place will close before we get there."

"I'm moving, I'm moving!" replied Tiffany. "Hey, whatever happened to Joe?" she asked while applying her makeup.

"It didn't work."

"That simple?"

"Just that simple. It didn't work."

Chapter 2

Manny broke from his daily routine of working out at the factory's gym before heading for home after his shift. He worked on the factory's production line stamping metal for calipers. He had taken the job after retiring from the Navy five years ago, just to be closer to his daughter. It was the only decent-paying position in a bad economy and it was perfect for his true objective supporting his only child. His lack of motivation for the job made him consider ending his employment. The work wasn't horrible or stressful by definition, but it was horribly redundant. He realized that this routine was too humdrum in comparison to his fleet days. Employment at the factory was nothing like being underway on one of America's finest Navy ships.

Manny recalled that ship life was from sun up to the next sunrise on any given day. He remembered the group of rambunctious sailors in his section who had kept him on his toes. Each day aboard ship was never a bore, and underway operations were intense during any deployment. He thought about his former life during the last stamp of his machine before his shift ended.

He left the factory for his two-bedroom apartment in the middle of West Palm Beach. It wasn't the fanciest place, nor very appealing, but the location was perfect. The apartment complex did not have a pool, or strategically-placed tennis courts, nor did it have a secure entry gate, but it was decent. His job didn't pay as well as a seasoned Chief Petty Officer, but he managed his finances well enough to live comfortably. Manny, divorced, was supporting his only child in her sophomore year of college. With both his military retirement and his job income, he managed to pay Suzie's tuition.

During his divorce proceeding, Manny had inquired why his ex-wife should escape the responsibility of helping to support his daughter. His resentment never interfered with his charge to provide for his child, but to do it alone challenged his logic. He didn't understand his ex-wife not wanting to assist Suzie despite her financial capability to do so. He felt fortunate to have learned financial management (a lesson he had mastered as the third of four siblings reared in Tamiami, Florida) and the money-saving techniques he had picked up as a sailor.

Manny's appearance had remained the same lean, muscular, and seaworthy -- the looks he had maintained throughout his naval career. His strikingly handsome presence drew attention as he worked on the production line. His physical prowess, dark eyes, auriferous complexion and chiseled cheeks turned women's heads. Often during his shift, he'd catch a lady's lustful eyes gazing at him. And when he shared his suave demeanor - a smile or a muscle flex - or gave a compliment, they fantasized about entering his world.

Manny's cell phone rang as he walked to his apartment. He put his gym bag on the stoop, grabbed his cell from his pocket, and answered, "Hello."

"Hi, I'm coming over. I have dinner," his daughter Suzie informed him.

"No, not tonight," said Manny, "I'm not up to it."

"What's wrong, Dad?"

"Nothing, I just need to be alone. I do love the idea, but not tonight. Maybe we can catch up tomorrow."

A Cyber Affair

"Call me if you change your mind, Dad," Suzie suggested in a melancholy tone before she hung up.

Manny tapped his cell phone off, turned around, and glanced at his desktop computer. He walked to it and pressed the 'ON' button, then went to retrieve a beer from the fridge. He returned to the desk and sat at the computer, feeling homesick for the Navy. He typed the URL for the Navy's website and found the profile of his old ship. Clicking on the website link and waiting for the page to load, his thoughts flashed back to life on the heavy cruiser.

He realized how fortunate he was to have seen the world. His last ship had changed fleets during his tour; it transferred from the Atlantic to the Pacific. This gave Manny the experience of exploring Europe and Asia in a little over three years. *I met some great guys on this ship.* Manny chuckled, remembering a few crazy sailors who had shared his escapades during liberty. *There was nothing like libbo with those guys - good times!*

Before he could move his mouse to another link, an online dating pop-up ad appeared: *Find the right mate; it's only a click away.*

At first, Manny moved his mouse and clicked on the 'X' in the upper right corner, deleting the pop-up. He adjusted his pop-up blocker and moved his mouse back to the Navy's site. He checked out the re-enlistment section of the website, and as he read the first paragraph, the pop-up returned.

He didn't fight it a second time. Instead, he looked at the couple's picture and acknowledged how happy they looked. Manny clicked on the dating site link and the page appeared, blaring of pictures of beautiful people. *Browse without completing a profile*, the site advertised. Manny moved his mouse over to the women's link and clicked.

A full page of available ladies appeared, with profile pictures and a brief bio for each. He clicked on one and read the descriptive write-up. Before he knew it, Manny had scanned over a dozen profiles. He stopped on one profile that piqued his interest. The shapely brunette wearing an orange-colored football jersey caught his eye. He contemplated what would happen if he wrote her a note. Manny clicked on the 'Send a Message' icon, looked at the blank chat space, had second thoughts, and closed the browser.

Chapter 3

Valerie and Tiffany entered the bar, found a tall pub table in the back, and stood next to it. The music blared and folks mingled about the club as if on a treasure hunt. Both women received interested looks as they scanned the room for available men. The patronage population was accommodating. An equal ratio of men to women was a situation that was seldom seen in any dance club on a Thursday night. A couple of men approached them as a popular dance song played. They suggested dancing. Valerie smiled at the guy closest to her, answered "Yes," then moved to the dance floor. Tiffany hesitated, looked at the guy next to her, and thought *Hmmm, he's not so bad.*

"Sure," Tiffany smiled, while thinking *it's only a dance.* The four danced close to each other.

Tiffany turned to face Valerie, raised an eyebrow, and opened her eyes wide while nodding her head to express her surprise at her dance partner's unique moves. When the music mix changed to a slower rhythm, Tiffany's partner attempted to engage her in conversation.

"Hey, I'm Steven."

"Excuse me?"

"Steven," he repeated, tapping his chest.

Tiffany didn't respond because she missed what he was trying to say. *I hate it when people try to talk over loud music.*

Steven moved closer to her ear, grabbed her hand, and in a louder voice asked, "What's your name?"

"Tiffany!"

"Steven!" he replied as he tightened his hand to shake hers. After a short pause he asked, "Do you like it here?"

"I suppose so! It's my first time!"

"Mine, too!" Steven answered as he danced. He followed her eyes and pointed to the tall table near the bar. Tiffany looked at him and decided to talk. although he indicated they should leave the dance floor. She was glad his initial questions didn't include any inappropriate pick up line.

Valerie maneuvered towards Tiffany, caught her attention, and signaled for their return to the table. Tiffany followed, but not before she waved her finger to let Steven know of her exit from the dance floor.

Steven looked for his friend, but noticed that he'd left the floor going in the opposite direction from Valerie. He followed the ladies in hopes of a further conversation with Tiffany, stood next to her, and waved at Valerie as he joined them around the high table.

"Hi, I'm Steven," he introduced himself.

"Valerie," she responded.

"So, Tiffany, what brings you out tonight?" asked Steven.

Tiffany hesitated before responding. She thought of multiple sarcastic comments in reply, but reconsidered and chose to share the truth. "She did." Tiffany pointed at Valerie.

"Oh, I thought you were out looking for fun."

"No, I was happy being at home," Tiffany confessed.

"I'm glad you came out. It's a good thing you did, since you got a chance to meet me," Steven grinned.

"Good one," Valerie laughed.

"Glad you think so. Hey, what happened to Earl?" Steven said, looking around the club.

"I'm sorry to say it, but your friend is a jerk."

"My apologies. It's Valerie, right?" Steven responded before turning his attention back to Tiffany. "What do you do when you're not dancing in a nightclub?"

"She plugs her face into a laptop," Valerie said. "That's why I dragged her out tonight."

"Oh really? I'm a techie, too." Steven's face brightened at the mention of a shared interest.

"No, I'm not a techie." Tiffany said. "I like social interactions, and its fun surfing websites. I'm a dreamer, and the Internet gives me access to whatever it is I might be missing."

"Surfing the web is horrible for you, isn't it?"

"Not at all. If you don't dream, you don't have much of a future."

"True, but what do you do to make any of your dreams a reality?" Steven probed.

Before Tiffany could answer, another high-intensity song began playing. Valerie took Steven's hand, yelling "Hey, dance with me!"

He waited for Tiffany's reaction. When he saw her shoulders shrug, he turned to Valerie and said, "Sure, why not?" - and off they went to the dance floor.

Tiffany stood alone and observed them dance. *Valerie is such a party animal*, she thought, and looked around the club. During her observations she watched people exchanging business cards, laughing, drinking, and socializing in groups or as couples. Tiffany suddenly felt lonely.

When Steven and Valerie returned to the table, Steven immediately refocused his interest on Tiffany.

"I'm glad you didn't mind me dancing with your friend. If you feel like hitting the dance floor, just say so."

"Thanks, I'll let you know," responded Tiffany.

"Now, where were we? Oh, yeah, I remember. What do you do when you aren't in a club?"

"I do a lot of things, but mostly I work."

"What type of work?"

"Floor sales in a department store."

"Nice perks, I bet."

"Sometimes," Tiffany said, and thought to ask Steven what he did for employment. Earl's return interrupted their conversation.

"Hey, dude, I need you."

"Not now; give me a few." Steven turned his attention back to Tiffany.

"Are you ready to dance?"

"Not at the moment. I'll pass. I'm sure Valerie will."

"She said no. Now come on!" Earl insisted.

"Give me a minute," Steven responded as he pulled a card from his pocket and handed it to Tiffany. "Here, give me a call and let's do lunch or something."

Tiffany took the card and smiled. "Thanks."

The girls spent the rest of the evening talking about different subjects while they scanned the club. They danced and talked with other men, but not one man tried to win Tiffany's interest the way Steven had.

Valerie was scanning the crowd and noticed Steven walking towards the exit with Earl, who was flanked by two women, his arms locked around their waists. Valerie tapped Tiffany on the shoulder and pointed to the exit. When she looked, she saw Steven glance towards them, raising his hand signaling goodnight before he walked out. Valerie couldn't wait to ask.

"Are you going to call him?"

"Probably not," said Tiffany.

"Why not? He seemed nice."

"He did, but I think he's a little young."

"He sure can dance well, and you know what that means." Valerie fanned her face with her open hand.

"Yes, it means he can dance," Tiffany said, shaking her head in disagreement.

"Oh, you know, it's more than just dancing."

"Myths, Valerie: myths. We always fall for those damn myths about men. Why can't we simply say he's an attractive guy and leave it at that?"

"Because that's no fun. Dang, sometimes you bore me." Valerie grabbed her purse, took the last swig of her drink, and proceeded to the exit. Tiffany had no choice but to follow: they had driven Valerie's car to the club.

The following day, Tiffany called Steven's number from the business card he had given her.

"Hello," he answered.

"Hi," she paused. "Steven?"

"Yes, this is Steven."

"We met last night," Tiffany said, without identifying herself.

"Tiffany, I'm glad you called," Steven smiled.

"How did you know it was me?"

"You're the only one I gave my card to last night."

She frowned at his response, since she was sure he must have given his card to all kinds of women. She knew Valerie would have been the first to take it, had he offered it to her.

"You said to call if I'd like to have lunch or coffee."

"Oh, yeah! When are you available?" Steven asked.

"How about tomorrow evening for coffee? Where would you like to go?"

"I have a place in mind, but I don't know how far you are from it." Steven waited for a response.

"It doesn't matter. I don't mind meeting you."

"Okay, let's say Cafe Trieste on Vallejo?"

"Yes. How do you know about Trieste? It's a nice place."

"I've been there a few times. I love the atmosphere. How about 6:30?"

"Perfect. I look forward to seeing you."

"Me too, Tiffany. I can't wait to see you."

Chapter 4

It was late night when Manny finally stopped surfing multiple dating websites and focused on one. He found a couple of profiles of interest and decided to write them. When he clicked on one of them, the site asked him to complete his profile description. Manny paused once the form window opened and asked himself *Should I?* while he stared at the screen. A calculated thought ran across his mind. "If I get a response, would it change my life? Maybe. Oh, what the hell ... why not?" He typed in his name and created an online ID. He called himself "Lost Sailor" because of his mood. Manny typed as if his life depended on it. *Maybe it will,* he thought, in response to his own question.

He selected what he thought was an appealing picture for his profile - a perfect beach sunset with just enough sunlight to capture his features and physique. He was proud of being the aging sailor who maintained a youthful shape, and the beach scene seemed appropriate for his profile name. It was nearly three in the morning by the time he completed the profile. Once done, he logged off and went to bed, since the work day always came too soon. Before dozing off, he recalled a few profile pictures that sparked his interest. Manny made a mental note to contact those women.

***

Manny was in the gym but he called Suzie before starting his workout. Her cell phone rang several times and then skipped to an automatic recording. He worried when Suzie didn't answer, assuming it meant trouble, because she always had the phone glued to her hand. Manny continued thinking about his daughter throughout his cardio routine. He called her again, without success. He maintained control over his imagination, trying not to panic or overreact, and remembered the fiasco that had ensued once, when she had been on a date and deliberately did not answer.

He had made a mad search for her and called in favors to get the police involved to find her vehicle. When the police called him, they informed him of her location and the compromising position she had been in with her date. He was furious, but had managed to rein in his emotions, realizing she was growing up. He knew she was developing into a young woman, and those embarrassing experiences were on her path to maturity.

Manny finished his workout and headed home. He wanted to call Suzie to offer her a dinner invitation and maybe let her help him navigate through the dating websites. It was his attempt to make up to her after declining her dinner invitation the previous night. When he arrived at his apartment, he saw Suzie's car parked out front. He rushed inside, surprised that she was in his apartment.

He worried about Suzie and often times his worrying got the best of him. He felt guilty that he had missed so much of her childhood while at sea, yet happy that they had still managed to stay close. He had used every communication tool available, especially the phone and internet. Manny kept his spirit in her presence even though Suzie had watched her mother struggle as a single parent. Not having him around finally got the best of Cheryl. Things didn't change until Manny and her mother, Cheryl, divorced.

Manny accepted Cheryl's fast marriage to George. During one of his visits, Manny talked to Suzie about how her life had changed with her stepdad being involved.

Suzie admitted it never felt the same after her mother remarried. To her, George was doing everything a father would do for a daughter, and she liked him. Well, except for his attempts to replace her dad. She admitted it became somewhat difficult for them to visit when he returned from deployments. Suzie also mentioned how she had eavesdropped on their heated discussions to stop George from adopting her. She was angry with her mom's attempt to phase him out of her life.

Although his apartment was not on a bad side of town, he was still very protective of his child and never took her safety for granted. When Manny entered, the aroma of a home-cooked meal tickled his nose. Loud gangster rap music blared from his MP3 player and he saw Suzie busy in the kitchen. He went directly to his MP3 player on the desk in the living room, changed the music, and then headed to the kitchen.

Suzie turned as soon as she heard the music change. "Hi Dad," she greeted him excitedly.

"Hi," Manny answered. "You're making dinner. How much is this going to cost me?"

"Come on, I don't *always* ask for money."

"I'm not so sure of that," he laughed.

"You seemed a little out of it yesterday. I remember when I was little, you liked eating authentic pizza from Gianelli's. I didn't get here early enough to order one so I made one of Mom's quick dish recipes."

"Thanks for cooking," he smiled, "but I'm okay."

"Are you sure?"

"Yeah, I'm okay." Manny looked on the counter where Suzie normally dropped her phone whenever she entered the kitchen. "Is something wrong with your phone?"

"Oh, it died. I have to get a new one tomorrow."

"Didn't you just get that one a few months ago? You're hard on phones."

"That was five months ago and there are new apps I want to get. Besides, I like the colors on some of the new ones," Suzie giggled, "and the new phones have locator apps on them." She smiled. She had learned how to defuse her dad when she was a child.

"New colors, yeah, good reason to buy another phone," Manny said.

Suzie looked into the oven and grabbed the oven mitts to take out the casserole dish. "Dinner's ready. Take a load off. I'll fix your plate."

"No, I need a few minutes. I have to shower. Would you open a bottle of wine for me? I have something I want to share with you."

"Is it one of your adventures, Dad?" asked Suzie.

Manny walked to the bathroom before answering. He turned on the shower and shouted "Maybe!" just as he closed the bathroom door. The sound of running water didn't allow her to understand his answer. She found a bottle of white wine to open, poured two glasses, and took them to the dining room table.

Manny returned from the shower and entered the kitchen. "Hey, dinner smells good. What is it?"

"It's goulash."

"I can't wait," Manny said, and filled his plate. "Can I fix your plate too?"

"Sure, Dad, thanks."

Manny served up the second plate and took both of them to the dining room. He and Suzie ate their meal and engaged in small talk between bites.

"So, what did you want to tell me... is it another woman?" Suzie asked.

"Yes and no. It's not what you think. I haven't met anyone, well not yet."

"Okay, , I don't get it. Why not yet?"

"I joined an online dating site."

"You did what?" Suzie nearly choked on her goulash.

"Yup, I surfed the internet last night and ended up on a dating website. I hadn't planned on it, but I saw a few attractive women that I couldn't send a message to without a profile, so I joined."

"I can't believe you of all people would join an online dating site. What's going on? You've never had problems meeting women."

"I know, but the women I meet here all seem the same. I'm looking for someone different."

Suzie thought about his last comment and recalled some of the women he had dated since his military retirement. On his second day in West Palm Beach, he met Suzie's English teacher when he picked Suzie up from school. The two adults became close friends, instead of lovers, over time. Suzie hoped Manny would find someone to love because she didn't want him to grow old alone.

Manny stared at Suzie and waited for a response. Puzzled as to why she hadn't answered, he asked again. "What's wrong with wanting someone different?"

"You're right, Dad. You should break the mold. I remember your last girlfriend. She was like the first one after you and mom divorced. I told you she wasn't going to work."

"I remember, Suzie. I remember."

"So, you should do something different, but before you send someone an email, I want to read it."

"No, no, no." Manny frowned, taking a sip of wine. "You'll change everything I write."

"Dad, I only want to make sure you say the right things. You need to come off as above average."

"I hear you, but let me write something before you look over my shoulder. They need to see me through my words and that's not possible if you're writing it."

Suzie smiled. "Okay, you're right. They need to see the real you because I won't be with you on any of your dates. You taught me a lesson when I dated Ed. Remember our disastrous double date?"

Manny chuckled. "Yes, it was awful, wasn't it? I didn't know you hadn't told him I was your dad."

"I did, but I guess you didn't fit the 'dad' mold he had in mind, especially since I spent all my time building you up to Carol and he felt ignored."

"Oh yes, Carol," he added while shaking his head, "she was..."

"...a nightmare!" Suzie finished his sentence.

"I never knew a woman could be so demanding. She reminded me of a hard-ass Chief Petty Officer. She wanted to control every aspect of my life - move into my apartment, have keys to my truck, change my diet and stop me from working out. Most important of all, she tried to limit my time with you. I'm glad we could share that horrible experience."

"Me too." Suzie giggled.

Chapter 5

Steven stood at the door of Cafe Trieste and watched Tiffany approach. He recalled how she had looked the night before. In his mind, she was much prettier. Her hair was combed back in a ponytail and it flowed in the wind as she walked. Her hips swayed, enticing his imagination. *Impressive*, he thought as he observed her approach.

Steven smiled and said, "Wow!"

"Hi. Thanks for the compliment." Tiffany shook his hand and smiled.

"Before we go inside, let me say thank you for coming. I was afraid you wouldn't show up," Steven said as they moved inside and approached the service counter.

"Why?"

"You know, when you try to make a good first impression and it doesn't go very well. It's over before it begins."

"I get it." Tiffany looked at the menu board above the counter. "I'm not sure what I'd like to drink."

"Coffee?" Steven suggested.

"I, um...coffee, yes, maybe I'll have a latte."

"I'm having regular coffee."

When the barista approached, he quickly ordered a medium coffee then stepped aside. Tiffany was disappointed when she realized Steven wasn't quite the gentleman she had hoped. She thought he should have allowed her to order first.

"I'll have a small latte, thank you," she ordered.

Steven looked at the counter of desserts, glanced at Tiffany, and said, "Would you like anything else?"

"No thank you."

Steven pointed to a dessert cake and held up one finger, ordering a slice, and placed money on the counter.

They stood at the counter waiting for their order. Steven looked at Tiffany.

"Tell me, what is it that you do?"

"What do you mean? Are you asking if I have a job?"

"Yes, do you work?"

"Yes, I work at a department store, remember?" Tiffany replied.

"Oh yeah, that's right. You told me last night. It must be fascinating."

Tiffany attempted to understand his comment. She tried to decipher if he was being sarcastic. "It's a job. Not fascinating, but it's ok."

"I'd think it would be fascinating seeing different people."

"True, and sometimes you see people you hope not to see again."

"Doesn't that apply to everyone we meet?"

"I suppose you're right."

The barista placed their order on the counter. Steven grabbed his coffee and cake and waited until Tiffany picked up her cup before walking to a table in the back of the shop. *He didn't say anything, he just walked away*, thought Tiffany, frowning in disappointment. Tiffany followed Steven and sat across from him, then watched him take a big bite of his cake and a slurp of coffee. She couldn't believe his table manners, and watched him inhale an enormous portion of cake as if it was his last meal.

"So, Steven, tell me about yourself."

"Well, I like dancing. I like playing Ultimate, I enjoy water sports, and I like to travel."

"I like dancing and water sports too, but I don't know anything about Ultimate."

"It's a great game. It's like football, but with a Frisbee."

"Really?"

"Yes, one team tries to stop the other from scoring in the end zone. The way you play the game is you throw the Frisbee to a teammate. The guy with the Frisbee can't advance, he has to pass it. They keep doing it until somebody scores. But the defense can intercept the Frisbee at any time and they try to score, just like football."

"OK, I'm not much of a football fan, but maybe you can show me sometime."

"Sure. What I really like to do best is travel."

"What has been your favorite trip so far?"

"I went to Rome one year, and it was awesome. I flew from San Francisco to New York and then caught a flight to Rome. The plane landed in the middle of the night and the airport was still incredibly busy. It was exciting and overwhelming. I had no idea where to go next, so I just followed all of the tourist signs. Thank God, most had English translations on them. You know, some people read about their destination before leaving, but not me. I went without doing any research." Steven paused to sip his coffee and continued. "I ran into a guy who had traveled the Italian countryside. Man, was he helpful. I followed his advice, took the local train into the city, and found a hotel. Did you know many European hotels share bathrooms? I had no idea. And they're co-ed, too! I learned so much from the experience. The next day I got a chance to see Rome. I went to the Coliseum and the Forum. Have you ever been there?"

Steven didn't wait for a response and continued talking. "It was great. You're in the middle of these ancient buildings and you wonder how they lifted those huge boulders or those cement blocks. Astonishing."

"Sounds like you had a great time," Tiffany remarked.

"Yeah, it was awesome! And did you know the streets are like here in the States? You know, it's really not much different from being here in San Francisco. I thought it would be, for some reason." Steven continued talking about his travel experience in great detail. After 40 minutes of rambling, with Tiffany contributing nothing during his monologue, she felt she had given him enough of her time. Tiffany rose from her seat, looked at Stephen, and shook her head. He finally stopped talking.

"I didn't realize it was so late. I've got to go," she informed him.

"I didn't get to tell you about France."

"No, you didn't, and I honestly don't think you will." Tiffany left Cafe Trieste and headed home.

Disappointed, Tiffany entered her apartment, went straight to her laptop, and booted it up, smirking with a thought *At least when these online dating guys ramble in a chat, I can disconnect.*

Chapter 6

After dinner, Manny turned on his desktop and uploaded the dating website. He and Suzie surfed profiles.

"I never thought of online dating," admitted Suzie. "I mean, I've heard some of my friends talk about chat room sites, but it never occurred to me to give dating websites a try."

Manny looked at her with a smirk. "It's because your age group doesn't need help with dates. You know, a college kid has an abundance of opportunities to find someone on campus. People my age don't have that pool of singles to choose from."

"Ah, come on, Dad, you've found numerous Miss Rights."

"No, they weren't right for me. I don't want to end up like some of the guys at the plant. You know: married, they hate going home, and they're drinking themselves into a stupor. It's not worth it. And most women want an engagement ring within two months. I won't do it until I find a woman who makes a great partner."

"Do you honestly think searching online is where you'll find her?"

"I thought about it for hours last night. I surfed and read a few profiles. There seems to be a million women out there. My odds look good. What have I got to lose? I figure it's easier to avoid them in cyberspace than dodging someone local like Katie, for instance."

"Oh yes, scary stalker Katie," Suzie giggled. "She loved you and didn't want to let you go!"

"Loved me!? You can't be serious. We went on two dates. I never touched her. Loved me? Everywhere I went, I felt her eyes on me."

"Yeah, that would get on my nerves too."

"No doubt." Manny clicked on a profile picture and a profile description appeared. "Here's one I saw last night. I was too tired to read about her." He and Suzie read the headline *Soft and Sexy*. "Catchy headline," Manny admitted.

"I think you'd better move on, Dad."

Manny read the description and found out she was a 43-year-old with four kids. The oldest one was seventeen and the youngest was nine months. "Soft and Sexy, alright," Manny sighed.

"You have to look further than a pretty face."

The website's instant messenger dinged and the comment box popped up. They both looked at the message window.

Hi,you, she wrote.

"Should I answer?" Manny asked.

"Why not?"

Manny typed Hi - and waited for a response. It wasn't long before words appeared in the IM (or instant message) box.

You're a handsome man. I'd love to get to know you.

Why are you on a dating website?

He looked at Suzie with a wrinkled forehead and a puzzled expression. "What kind of question is that?"

"She's being very direct without playing games."

"Games?"

"Come on, Dad, don't be so naive. You know what you're looking for online. Tell her you're here to meet interesting people."

Manny followed Suzie's instructions and typed exactly what she said. He received an instant response. Me too, but I want more.

"Wow, this lady doesn't mess around." He thought aloud.

"Most people don't mess around when they aren't looking at you in a face-to-face situation. This is a great way to hide. People can say anything and not mean it at all."

"I hadn't thought about it that way." He paused. "But let me test her with this answer, and we'll see how far she goes in her response." Manny wrote: *I'm looking for a one night stand and maybe if you're good we can go for two.*

Oh, I'm good baby, just say when and where.

Suzie read the IM. "You better be careful what you ask for. I bet she'd be in your bed tonight if you suggested it."

"Who does this over the Internet?"

"Everybody, Dad, from what I hear."

"You think so?"

The IM chimed and another message appeared: What are you waiting for? Tell me how we can connect.

Manny read the IM and said, "I guess I should at least look at her profile." When he followed the IM profile name and clicked on it, her information filled the screen. "Oh my goodness, she's old enough to be my grandmother!" Manny exclaimed as he pushed back from the desktop.

Chapter 7

Following a night of internet surfing (well past midnight), Tiffany didn't get out of bed until after 10 a.m. She put her feet on the floor, rose from the bed, and gazed out of her bedroom window. She thought about the interesting men and the trio of women she had met in a chat room. Tiffany lucked out in the chat room she had chosen. She'd connected with people with like ideas. To her it felt as if they had sat around her kitchen table sharing a pot of coffee.

Her cell phone rang, interrupting her thought. She answered after a quick glance at the Caller ID.

"Hi Valerie."

"Tiff, how's everything?"

"I'm good - getting ready for work. What are you up to?"

"Not much. Just called to see if you've talked to Steven."

"I did, and he's not the one." Tiffany sighed in disgust.

"Why not? He was cute."

"We met for coffee yesterday, and it didn't go well."

"What happened?"

"He talked on and on. I never got a word in edgewise."

"That's it?"

"That's enough. You know, most guys would at least let you get in a word or two. And besides, he was so young."

"No, not most, just some. Those who do are keepers."

"Steven's not a keeper."

"I hear you." Valerie nodded, paused, then asked, "So what time do you get off tonight?"

"Eight."

"Just in time to go out. We're going to have fun."

"No, I'm not going out. It's stay-at-home night for me."
Tiffany made her decision and stood firm.

"Another online date night?"

"No, I stayed up late last night, so I'm crashing early
tonight."

"You're wasting your life online. You're missing out, sitting
at home with your eyes glued to a screen."

"It's better than sitting in front of a boring guy while planning
your escape."

"But at least you see him in the flesh and you can actually
interact. Come on, Tiff, I know you can find someone interesting
in the city," Valerie begged.

"I've got to go, Valerie, or I'll be late for work. Catch you
later."

"Okay, but if you change your mind, call me. Bye."

"Bye." Tiffany placed the cell in her purse and thought that
Valerie's comment rang true. *She's right. I should be able to meet
men in this city.*

Tiffany arrived at her job, checked in, and began her shift.
She helped a few customers with their jewelry selections and had
several big sales. She managed to keep an eye out for attractive
men while she pitched high-priced items. Today, most of the
good-looking guys that came in the store were with women. She
noticed one guy leaning over the jewelry counter, stroking his
moustache, looking at the displays. Tiffany approached, offering
her assistance. Looking up at Tiffany, he pointed at a gem
encrusted seahorse broach. "Can I see this one?" Tiffany retrieved
the broach and placed it on counter in front of him.

"It's for my mother." He picked up the broach and cradled it in his right hand.

"Is it for a special occasion?"

"It's her birthday. Do you think she'd like it?"

"Well, ah…" Tiffany paused, looking at her customer. "Let me show you something else." She walked over to the next case, leaned down, and pulled out a necklace with a cameo pendant. "This is a classy piece. You can't go wrong with something like this."

He put the seahorse down and took up the cameo, holding it by the chain, allowing the pendant to swing. "I like it…it's nicer than the seahorse."

Tiffany focused on his appearance and features. He wasn't the best looking man, nor was he her usual type. "Would you like it in a gift bag?"

"Sure, that would be nice." Tiffany walked to the cash register, entered the transaction, and shared the total price with him. She took his credit card, swiped it, then returned it along with his receipt.

He smiled. "I think she's going to love it."

Tiffany turned to the cabinet behind the cash register with the boxed necklace in her hand. She pulled out a small decorative bag, placed the boxed necklace into it, and returned to the customer. "There's a free gift card that comes along with it. Would a small one do or do you need a larger one?"

"A small one will do, thank you." He smiled.

Tiffany dropped the card in the bag and handed it to him, "It's very thoughtful, giving your mom such a lovely gift."

"Thank you. She's a great lady and deserves a lot more."

"When are you giving it to her?"

"Well, her birthday is next week, but I'm going to surprise her tomorrow at dinner."

Tiffany placed her hand on her heart. "That's so sweet," she said, and thought, *Here is a nice man worth getting to know.* She looked into his eyes. "By the way, I'm Tiffany." She extended her hand.

He took Tiffany's hand and shook it. "I'm Ralph. Nice to meet you."

"Are you seeing someone, Ralph?"

He released her hand. "I'm not at the moment, but I'm..." he looked at the floor as he answered, "...always looking."

"Maybe we can get together for coffee."

"That would be nice," Ralph blushed.

"Let me give you my number." Tiffany took a blank gift card, wrote her name and number on it, then handed it to Ralph. She watched him read it. "Call me," she smiled.

"Okay, I will." Ralph put the card in his pocket and walked away from the counter without looking back. Tiffany watched him leave.

Tiffany arrived at her apartment a little before 9 p.m., opened the door, and dropped her things on the kitchen counter. She walked to her bedroom to change into comfortable sweats and returned to the kitchen, grabbing a can of soda from the fridge before booting up her laptop. When the screen opened, there was a message waiting in her IM box from a guy she had met in a chat room. The message read: You impressed me with your humor. I wish we could chat alone.

Tiffany didn't respond right away. She was trying to remember this person and went back to the saved chatroom conversation to jog her memory. She soon realized it would be too time consuming to find their chat history. Throwing caution to the wind, she responded: Hey, I'm sorry I don't remember you. Remind me who you are.

While she waited for his response, Tiffany went to one of her dating sites and saw multiple emails. She filtered them by scanning for intriguing phrases in the subject line. *No,* she thought as she deleted one after the other. *Nice,* she smiled as she read the subject line *Hi, I'm not good at this.* To her it read humble and sincere. She clicked on the email to expand it and saw the screen name was Lost Sailor. His message sounded hopeful, not desperate.

This is new to me. I read your profile and found you interesting. That's why I took the chance of writing to you. Aren't you tired of empty conversations? If you are interested or if you're so inclined, drop me a line and open a chat.

Manny

Chapter 8

Manny clicked 'send' after reviewing his email a fourth time. "I can't believe I'm sending a total stranger an email. I hope I didn't sound stupid. If she responds – good. If not, oh, well."

Suzie finished cleaning the kitchen and saw Manny staring at the screen. "Is everything okay?" she asked while taking a position behind Manny.

"I sent an email."

"It'll be fine, Dad. Tell me, how does she look?"

"Very pretty. Well, at least to me."

"Let me see, pull her up." Suzie watched San Fran Pearl's profile flash onto the screen. She read the profile description. "San Francisco? Are you gonna go see her?"

"What makes you think I will or that I'll even get the chance?"

"Come on, Dad, I know women. As soon as she reads your profile she'll be interested."

"I don't know, just look at her. I bet she gets hundreds of emails a day."

"Dad, soon you'll get hundreds of emails too. Why did you write her?"

"Look how beautiful she is, and her description doesn't read crazy."

"Don't write again until you hear from her, okay, Dad?"

"Isn't it normal to wait for an answer?"

"Yes, but sometimes you can be impatient. I don't want you looking desperate."

"Desperate. Are you kidding?"

"I'm not kidding, Dad. Be patient. Wait for her response."

Chapter 9

Tiffany read Manny's email a second time, looked at his profile, and liked what she saw. She examined his face with its rugged look, full inviting lips, and seductive brown eyes. Manny's body invited her to imagine running her hands down his chest, feeling the muscles, then circling his nipples with her fingers just before touching her lips to them. She looked at his abs and took a breath before smiling. "Oh my," she said. "I wonder what's hidden in those shorts." She liked the idea of this hot guy writing her in spite of the distance between them. Tiffany remembered that he lived in West Palm Beach, from reading his profile, which for her was a major concern.

She wrote to Manny:

Thanks for the kind email. I'm not sure about starting a long-distance relationship, but I'd love to just chat one day. I'm sure you're interesting.

I hope he'll understand. Tiffany read other emails and checked out profiles. She responded to every local person who piqued her interest and made comments or 'winked' in response. She had high hopes for responses. Tiffany read and wrote emails for hours. She found many interesting people, but one profile in particular caught her attention. The headline read: *Sensible, Fun, Admirable. Give a shout and see for yourself.* His profile picture revealed a handsome man with a metrosexual-style haircut. *At least he's not some shirtless guy with a beer gut.* She read the rest of his profile. *This could be the one, and he's local.* She sent him an email.

Hi, I'm from San Francisco, too, and would like to get to know you. I like your picture. Drop me a line.

She sent her email and noticed a new one in her inbox. She clicked on the link to open it and her first reaction was pleasant surprise. It was a response from Lost Sailor. She smiled as she read:

I agree, I'm not looking for a long-distance relationship either. I have to admit, you do seem interesting. While I was in the Navy, I visited your city and loved it. It was such a beautiful place. I only got to see downtown and its famous pier, but I've heard that other parts are just as nice. I'll get there again one day, and if I'm lucky, you'll give me a tour. I'd like to chat with you and see if we have common interests. Who knows, we may become the best of friends.

She smiled as she wrote: Distant Friends as a headline to her response. *Thanks for getting back to me. I agree with you, a long-distance relationship isn't ideal. But, a friend is always welcomed. At least we realize it's all we can offer, because dating would be difficult. I'd love to chat soon and read your thoughts on dating. Thanks for understanding.* Tiffany clicked 'send' with the thought, *The one guy who seems genuinely nice is over a thousand miles away.*

Chapter 10

"If San Fran Pearl responds to the second email, I might do be better dating online than in person," Manny chuckled. When he was on his ship during off hours, he had used the internet for training and games. Now he was starting to feel that the web would offer him a chance to discover new opportunities. Before long he had three emails from different women, including one from his new interest San Fran Pearl. He read San Fran Pearl's response first. Intrigued by her headline, Manny wrote:

I want to send you my Instant Messenger ID so that anytime you see me online, feel free to drop me a note. I look forward to chatting with you.

Shortly after sending the email, he turned to Suzie. "She responded," he said, smiling. "And she said she'd like to become friends. But hey, that's a start."

"Yes it is. Remember to be patient, Dad, or you'll scare her away. Take it slow."

"We're only talking friendship. What choice do I have?"

"Come on Dad, I know you. You can go from zero to 60 in three seconds."

"Good point, kid, good point."

Chapter 11

Tiffany was surprised by Manny's fast response. She didn't expect another email from him after explaining her feelings about long distance relationships. "It's nice of him to invite me for a chat. It's only a conversation. It can't go anywhere; he's too far away. Miami isn't around the corner." She sighed as she wrote:

It's a charming invitation, and I'll keep it in mind. If you see I'm online, please feel free to IM me.

Immediately after she pressed 'send', doubt surfaced. *Why did I tell him to write? It's just chatting or an email, no harm either way.* Tiffany closed the window and opened a different site. She continued looking through profiles. She found a chat room and joined in on the conversation. Long into the discussion she received a personal chat invitation from Blue Dragon, a member of the chat group:

I find your comments thought-provoking. Please join me in a private chat so I can get to know you better.

Tiffany typically avoided private invitations but, for some reason, she agreed. OK, she responded, and clicked on the flashing invite.

Bluedragon: *Sometimes these chat rooms are filled with despicable people.*

SanFranPearl: *I ignore those folks and only respond to comments like yours. My favorite comments are the blatant propositions, like Hey Baby, why don't you lick my My pole while I kiss your kitty lips. I mean, gosh, is sex the only thing they like discussing online?*

Bluedragon: *That chat did seem vulgar, and I'm glad we left before it got really out of hand. What other chat rooms do you visit? Have we crossed paths before?*

SanFranPearl: *I'm not sure if we have. I'm pretty new at this.*

Bluedragon: *I thought this site was good until a few goofballs entered the chat room. I usually talk about traveling or occasionally relationship stuff.*

SanFranPearl: *I love traveling. You talk about relationships? You must be married.*

Bluedragon: *Actually I am. It's why I ask about it so often. I try to figure out how to interact with my wife. If it weren't for women like you, I'd permanently live in the doghouse.*

SanFranPearl: *You know, I appreciate your honesty. I don't usually chat with married men.*

Bluedragon: *I figure it's better to share my status than mislead you. I'm not after you, San Fran Pearl, I'm here for conversation and friendship.*

SanFranPearl: *Doesn't your wife mind you chatting so much online?*

Bluedragon: *Sometimes she does. But for me, this beats the heck out of watching television every night. I mean, how many shows can you watch for entertainment? I enjoy one on Wednesday night, but most of the time I just sit there.*

SanFranPearl: *Have you told her how you feel about her obsession with television?*

Bluedragon: *I have, but it's ignored. I've learned not to fight about it and to use this time to surf or chat on the internet.*

SanFranPearl: *Well if you don't find chats, what do you do?*

Bluedragon: *I look for things that might interest me. I found one website giving tips on how to repair home appliances and* another one on home renovations. *I watch training videos and visit travel sites. Those are my favorite. Did you know you can view a foreign city from a satellite camera from your laptop?*

SanFranPearl: *No, I didn't.*

Bluedragon: *Here, use this link.* He provided the URL (uniform resource locator) link to the webpage to Tiffany. She hesitated to click on it since the last time she had clicked on a link someone sent her, it was a virus download. Tiffany wrote: *Don't give me the link, just give me the site name and I'll look it up.*

Bluedragon: *You must have had a bad experience with a virus, LOL (Laugh Out Loud). It's okay, I understand.* He gave her the name of the website. She googled it and saw his information was legit.

SanFranPearl: *Sounds like a great site. You should take your wife to see some of these places.*

Bluedragon: *If I can ever get her away from her television shows, I may just do that.*

SanFranPearl: *Well, I'm sure you can persuade her. Just plan a trip and don't share it with her until you have everything set. I admire men who take charge and do things for me without my input. You know, I'd give anything for a man to make me feel that special.*

Bluedragon: *I've heard that from my wife, who stays glued to that box.*

SanFranPearl: *Sounds to me like she's waiting for you. Go for it and make sure you take lots of pictures.*

Bluedragon: *I will. I'll keep you updated on my progress.*

SanFranPearl: *Sure, that will be great. It's nice chatting with you.*

Bluedragon: *Same here, we'll keep in touch. Thanks.*

They closed their chat windows simultaneously. *At least he was honest about being married. It's sad that a man with outside interests is stuck with a woman tied to a television set.* Before she could type in another URL, a flash notification appeared announcing a new email from Lost Sailor. She opened her email and selected the awaiting message.

Hi Again,

I recently had an interesting chat with someone and wanted to share it with you. SoI hope you don't mind. It was the conversation from hell. I didn't know people use these websites to be so vulgar and aggressive. Believe me, I'm no prude, but what happened to finesse? When did I miss dating turning into how fast can we get in bed? This woman made me appreciate the finer points of conversation. Can't wait to read your thoughts.

Manny

Tiffany smiled after reading Manny's email. She just had the same conversation with Blue Dragon. She responded:

Manny,

It's mindboggling: we're experiencing the same type of behavior. I left a chat room for that exact reason. The conversation went south and got dirty. It's almost as if people want to live their fantasies online with total strangers. Maybe that's the attraction. Like you, I find it quite despicable.

As far as modern dating rituals, the race to get in to bed isn't anything new. Unfortunately, finesse is a disappearing quality. You haven't dated much lately, have you?

A Cyber Affair

Tiffany

Tiffany pressed 'send' and returned to surfing the net. She found a favorite site and clicked 'yes', 'like', or 'flirt' on certain local profiles. Although she received invitations to chat, she decided to ignore them and turned in for the night.

Chapter 12

Manny woke at 6 am to his clock radio. He found a music station that got him moving out of bed and onto the floor for a set of push-ups and sit-ups. Exercise had been his morning routine since retiring. Manny showered, dressed, packed his lunch, grabbed his gym bag, and left for work. His mornings ran like clockwork.

Driving to the factory, he felt rejuvenated from his morning routine and was thinking about his new experiences on the internet. It was much easier writing to women than making a cold approach on the street or in a night club. He enjoyed the mental stimulation but did not think much of the sexual overtones he encountered.

During a break, he mentioned what he'd seen and read on the internet to a few co-workers, and told them how surprised he was how women were as aggressive as men. The guys laughed as they, too, admitted to horror stories of their online experiences. One guy told of his catfish (or 'fake bitch') story where the woman was nothing near the beauty she had professed to be. He had driven three hundred miles to a motel, excited for the chance to measure her oil level.

Once at the motel, he'd set up the room with roses and a dozen lit candles and placed edible condoms in the shape of a heart on the center of the bed. He had stripped to his heart-print, silk knickers and played his favorite country song while he sat in a chair waiting.

He said he'd nearly given up two hours after their agreed rendezvous time when, just before he blew out the candles, there was a knock at the door. He raced to the door and swung it open only to find a large guy with a long beard wearing a flower print dress standing there with a smile as big as the moon on his face. The crew busted out in loud laughter. Some of them laughed so hard that they were nearly on the floor in tears.

Manny shook his head. Being a retired sailor, he had experienced several cultures where women were aggressive, but mostly it was because of their social status or living environments. He didn't believe that was the case in America, yet the internet showed a different reality. He didn't understand why so many women wanted to get into sexual conversations with total strangers.

Manny left work after visiting the gym. On his way home, he decided to stop at a grocery store and pick up a few items. While walking down an aisle, he bumped into a lady. His apology opened the door for conversation. Within minutes, his new acquaintance had given him her cell number and a smile to remember.

Once home, Manny put his grocery items away, jumped in the shower, and dressed for the evening. It was his weekly dinner night with Suzie, their custom when she didn't have a boyfriend. The weekly dinners helped their father-daughter relationship. He had already missed too many of her younger years.

Now that he was retired, Manny fought to strengthen their relationship which had been weakened by her mother's negative influence. The dinners helped, and besides, he liked sharing time with her. After his shower, he called Suzie. "What time are we getting together?"

"Dad, did you forget?"

"Yes, that's why I'm asking. What time are we meeting?"

"We said 7, Dad, and I have a surprise for you. I think you'll like it."

"No way, Suzie, I know better. Your surprises usually cost me. What's the surprise and how much?"

"Come on, Dad! It's nothing bad and there's no money involved. Give me a chance."

"We'll talk about it over dinner. See you in 20 to 30 minutes."

"Love you, Dad."

"Love you too, Sweetie."

Manny dressed and rode his 2008 Benelli BN6000GT motorcycle, a bike he had fallen in love with while living in Naples, to the restaurant. He arrived, parked his bike, secured his helmet, and walked to the entrance. Manny saw the reflection of two women in the mirrored glass paneled insert of the door.

He turned to look and noticed it was Suzie, and she wasn't alone. A well-dressed woman accompanied her. She wore a tasteful, blue form-fitting dress that revealed her figure. Her hair was short, in a complimentary style, making her face slim and youthful, with features that met Manny's basic requirements.

"Hey, Baby Girl." Manny held his arms out for their usual hug.

"Hi, Daddy," she answered. Suzie turned to introduce her friend. "Daddy, this is Camille Peters. Camille, this is Manny Perez, my father."

"Hello, Camille," Manny said as he reached for the traditional handshake.

"Hi Manny, nice meeting you," Camille said, taking his hand with a firm grip.

"It's nice meeting you too." Manny released Camille's hand and opened the door for them to enter the restaurant. He looked at Suzie as she passed, raising his eyebrow. Camille led the way towards the hostess. Manny touched Suzie's arm, before leaning to her ear to whisper, "I hope the restaurant doesn't mind adding one more to our reservation."

"Don't worry, Dad, I called ahead and added Camille."

"How thoughtful of you." Manny smiled at his daughter. Suzie poked Manny and rolled her eyes. They followed the hostess to their table. The table was set for three. Suzie deliberately chose the setting that would allow Camille and her father to sit next to each other. Manny pulled out a chair for Camille and waited.

"Thank you, Manny," Camille said, and smiled. "It's pleasant having a gentleman at dinner."

"You're welcome." Manny smiled and walked over to his chair. "How do you ladies know each other?" Manny asked while taking his seat.

"I own a coffee shop not far from the campus. And Suzie became one of my regulars. One day she came into the coffee shop during the busiest hour. She didn't ask for my permission before volunteering her services. Thank goodness she jumped in, because I had a staff member no show. I was so impressed that I offered her a job. You did a great job raising her."

"Thank you, Camille, but I can't take full credit for her manners," Manny admitted. A waiter approached the table and announced the specials of the day. After listening to him, Manny allowed the ladies to order. After the waiter left, Manny broke the awkward silence.

"Camille, how long have you had your coffee shop?"

"Over a year," she replied. "It's the best thing I've ever done. I love the independence."

"So you met Suzie and were impressed by her kind heart."

"Yes, she's a charmer, and I'm so grateful to have her. You know, when I first offered her the job, she wouldn't take it."

Manny looked at Suzie. "You were offered a job at the coffee shop and didn't take it?" Manny frowned in surprise, as he had always encouraged Suzie to work for her spending money.

"Dad, don't have a coronary," Suzie smiled. "I'm working there now."

"I guess we'll see less of each other unless I…" Manny caught himself before making a harsh remark and getting into a heated father-daughter discussion in front of Camille.

"Dad, the class load I'm carrying right now doesn't allow me to see you most weeknights anyhow."

"Yes, I know, Sweetie…umm, we'll work it out." The waiter returned with a pitcher of water and poured each a full glass, then left. Manny looked up at Suzie before he glanced at Camille. "So, Suzie, you're enjoying coffee these days?"

"Actually, no, Dad, I don't drink coffee. but I like my job because I get to see my friends more often."

"That's good to hear." Manny winked. "Camille, how do you like being around these college kids?"

"The kids keep me young and the business strong," explained Camille. "You know, Manny, your daughter is a great employee, and is always eager to work whenever I need her. She's a hard worker."

"She's always been like that," Manny smiled. "She's always been amazing at everything she does. I remember once during a deployment, I called and she told me about her dance class, gymnastics, and all of her student counsel work. She was impressive at age ten!"

"A busy young lady," Camille commented.

"Dad, I invited Camille to dinner to meet you. She's your surprise."

"Yes, she is," Manny smiled.

"You didn't tell him I was coming?"

"Nope," Suzie explained. "He's always okay with having one more for dinner. I usually bring a friend or a boyfriend, so I knew he wouldn't mind."

"You know, I like this a lot better than one of her boyfriends," Manny laughed.

"Dad, be nice."

"I'm just saying some of those young men were…"

"A father stressing his expectations of the men you choose to date. Suzie, be glad you have a father who loves you enough to teach you those important characteristics," Camille advised.

"I guess that's tough for you, Dad. I mean, me trying to find the right guy. Am I right? I mean, we think we have the right man and get surprised when we start dreaming and our dreams shatter. It's tough."

"Depends on what you call tough," responded Camille. "I see your point, but every woman handles disappointment differently. I, for one, didn't see it as painful."

"Dad, Camille was married to a sailor. I told her you are a retired Navy Chief."

"Wait - I didn't come to dinner to meet a sailor. I came because she asked me to dinner and said you were coming. I thought, why not?"

"I'm glad you're here, Camille." Manny looked at Suzie.
"What else did you tell her about me?" Manny lifted an eyebrow.

"Enough."

Throughout dinner the conversation was easy. Over dessert, Suzie and Camille entertained Manny as they spoke of incidents at the coffee shop.

"Where is this coffee shop? I'd like to visit it one day," he asked after taking a bite of his key lime pie.

"Sunset Drive in Coral Gables," Camille responded.

"Dad, it's really close to campus. Everybody loves it."

"Is that so? What's the name? Camille's Coffee, or College Caffeine?" asked Manny, smiling at his guess.

"Cupcakes and Coffee, Dad. If you'd increase my allowance, I could get more than the house special." She turned to Camille. "Oh, no offense."

"None taken. I get your drift." Camille let Suzie know that she understood.

"Good try, kid." Manny looked around the restaurant, which gave him time to pull his thoughts together and change the conversation. He noticed Cheryl, Suzie's mother, and her stepfather George approaching their table.

"Incoming." Manny touched Suzie's arm and nodded towards Cheryl and George.

Suzie looked in the direction where Manny nodded. "Mom, what are you doing here?" Suzie stood to greet her mother with a hug and a kiss on the cheek.

"We were having dinner and George saw you guys, so we decided to say hello." Cheryl glanced at Manny. "Hello, Manny."

"Cheryl, George," Manny replied with a stoic face. Once the greetings ended, an awkward moment lingered until Suzie remembered Camille and said, "Mom, this is my friend, Camille. Camille, this is my mother, Cheryl Davis."

"Hi," said Camille as she stood and greeted Cheryl with a traditional handshake. "It's very nice meeting you."

"Lovely setup - you three. I guess Manny needs help getting dates these days," Cheryl huffed.

"Mom…please."

Manny took a sip of water, placed the glass on the table, and took a relaxing breath before facing Cheryl. "Most married women respect their marriage vows even when they're lonely. But not the selfish and self-centered: she finds a man to fill those lonely moments during her husband's deployment instead of waiting for him." Manny tried to keep his tone pleasant.

"Manny, let it go. She's my wife now," George proudly proclaimed.

"I'm glad she's your wife, George. Don't let your guard down for more than a week or she'll replace you, too."

"I don't want to entertain this discussion. Cheryl, let's go, Baby," George said.

Cheryl kissed Suzie on the cheek and turned to follow her husband. "He's an ass, George. Ignore his remarks."

Manny, Suzie, and Camille watched George and Cheryl leave. Camille looked at her plate and mumbled, "You have interesting parents, Suzie."

Suzie was embarrassed, "Yes, interesting, because Mom holds a grudge when it comes to Dad."

"Really. I thought your parents were rather cordial," Camille said.

"Cordial?" responded Suzie with a gasp.

"Yes. I've seen worse." Camille patted Suzie on the shoulder.

"What is worse than your parents not getting along? I should have attended Florida State so I wouldn't have to see you two fight all the time." Suzie said.

"That would have been fine with me, kiddo," Manny smiled. "I always told you it's a better school."

"Dad, how many times do I have to tell you The U is forever? The University of Miami will always be in my heart. I'm glad I chose it," Suzie reminded him with a look of disdain that Manny knew so well.

"Do I sense a little school rivalry?" Camille nodded as she smiled, glancing at one and then the other.

Suzie and Manny both smiled at their inside joke and simultaneously answered "Yes," and then, like kids, they began to argue about why their school was better. It was a dueling contest. The two of them entertained Camille with their stories. It was an hour later when Manny looked up and saw the waiter hovering with the check folder in his hand. "Sir, will there be anything else?" he asked.

Manny looked at Camille and Suzie for a response. "No, I don't think so." Manny grabbed the folder and glanced at the bill. He pulled out his wallet, placed a credit card in the folder, and handed it to the waiter.

"Thank you." The waiter took the folder and left the table.

"This was fun." Camille smiled at Manny and touched Suzie's arm. "We should do this again."

"Yes, we should. If Dad's okay with it."

"I enjoyed the company, and doing it again would be nice."

The waiter returned with the folder and placed it on the table. Manny signed the check and put the credit card back in his wallet.

A Cyber Affair

He stood up from the table, put the wallet in his pocket, and moved to pull out Camille's chair as she rose. "Thank you."

"No problem." Manny walked next to Suzie and put his arm around her. "Next time, no surprises," he whispered. He kissed her on the cheek. "Let me walk you to your car."

Suzie led the way to the exit with Camille following and Manny walking in her shadow. He looked around the restaurant, scanning for Cheryl in hopes there wouldn't be another unpleasant interaction.

Manny arrived home, dropped his coat on the couch, and picked up the phone to share his dinner experience. He'd had fun tonight and wanted to tell someone. He ran through a mental list of friends and realized that nearly everyone he thought of was either down for the night or away at sea. He walked to his desk, set his phone on the charger, and booted up his desktop, then went to the kitchen and grabbed a beer from the fridge. He sat at his computer and clicked the shortcut for his email. After logging in, he selected 'compose' and wrote.

Tiffany,

I hope you are having a pleasant evening. I had a great night and I hope you don't mind me writing about it. I had an experience I'd love to share with someone.

Since we're new acquaintances, I thought sharing our life experiences would be an interesting way of getting to know each other. Maybe you can share something going on in your life. I'd love reading whatever you send.

Tonight, I had a blast with my daughter, Suzie, and her boss/friend Camille. Suzie is a sophomore at the University of Miami, and Camille is a coffee shop owner around my age.

Funny thing is, my daughter introduced us because she thinks I'm lonely, which is far from the truth. I'm an active person, and I don't allow loneliness to set in. Dinner was fun and Camille and I seemed to hit it off. We didn't make any future plans, but I think I'll drop by her coffee shop.

Do you think tomorrow is too soon? She seemed interesting and, I admit, she is an attractive woman, but in that environment and company, I couldn't gauge if she liked me enough to date me. I believe her first impression of me was favorable.

Okay, I've shared my experience and would appreciate any advice you'd give me. I get a lot of tips about women from my 19-year-old daughter, but what does she know about dating in your 40s?

Manny

Chapter 13

Tiffany put her dinner plates in the cupboard while analyzing her friendship with Valerie. She realized that listening to Valerie wasn't always right. Tiffany knew Valerie's intentions were in her best interest, however, there were times when she went too far, such as on the multiple occasions when Valerie would strike up conversations with guys she found interesting and invite them to meet Tiffany.

Not many of those men fared well with her, and with one introduction, the guy was a total sleaze-ball and ended up being a stalker. He lacked the mind-set, much less the attitude, for dating a mature woman. When Tiffany asked "Why him?" after discovering how crazy he was, Valerie shrugged her shoulders and answered, "He seemed ok in the short conversation we had. Besides, you needed entertainment. I thought he'd at least be fun."

Valerie entered Tiffany's apartment, a warm, cozy two-bedroom nestled in the confines of the city, and announced herself as usual. "Tiffany!"

"Before you ask, I didn't call the guy you suggested."

"What happened? I thought he was pretty nice."

"First of all, I was busy surfing online. And to be honest, I get more from people online than from your blind dates."

"It's because you're afraid of real people," Valerie sighed in disagreement. "I don't understand why you're on the computer so much."

"It's entertaining and fun. Don't you get it? You can travel the world with a click of the mouse."

"Wouldn't you rather travel in person and not use your imagination so much?" asked Valerie.

"When you find people sharing a lot of their experiences, it's better than a movie. And it's right at your fingertips. I talk to all sorts of people."

"But you're still alone."

"Only when I'm offline."

Tiffany moved to the coffeemaker, poured coffee into two mugs, and handed one to Valerie. "Let's go into the living room."

"Yeah, sure."

They walked to the couch with their cups in hand and sat on the sofa. Valerie faced Tiffany and said, "If you want someone local, you have to focus here. If you target your online search to a local area, maybe, just maybe, you'll find someone."

"I do focus locally when I consider a date. But that doesn't mean I don't interact with people from all over."

"What happens when you log off? Online friendships fill a lonely heart only for a short time," Valerie sighed.

"Don't I know, don't I know." Tiffany frowned, remembering the disappointing online interactions with some local men she'd chatted with. It was unnerving how a great number of men didn't care about being honest, or how they avoided getting to know her before trying to lure her into a sexual conversation. Other local online men had failed to spark any interest.

"You know, Valerie, it's not like I'm searching for a hunk of a man, a perfect model, or gorgeous actor. I want a decent guy who carries himself well. Isn't there one available in San Francisco?"

"They're here, trust me. I know they are." Valerie sipped her coffee.

"So why is it so difficult for me to find one?"

"You're looking in the wrong places. Online isn't it. Maybe we should try the grocery store."

"Haven't we tried that before?"

"Well, yeah, but you never know."

"I'm not shopping every day."

"You're online every day."

"Good point. But I'm not online only to find men. I'm online for different reasons and sometimes it's just for a great conversation," explained Tiffany.

"As focused as you are online, I wonder if you're as hard to please there as you are in person. I'm almost at the point of giving up on you."

"Really, Valerie?" she paused. "Not that I don't appreciate your effort; but come on, some of those guys you introduced were...well...let's just say, you not helping might be a good idea."

"If I didn't know better, I'd say you're being harsh with me." She clasped her hands, frowned, and then smirked. "But I love you the same and yeah, I'll stop trying to take care of you. If an interesting man shows up, I may have to keep him for myself. And I'll have to remember that you will find your own guy."

"Thanks for understanding. That's why I love you." Tiffany rose from the couch and raised her coffee cup. "Want a refill?"

Valerie looked at her watch. "No, I've got to get going," she said, and placed her cup on the coffee table. "I've got to get to the store. I'll catch you later. Listen, you've got to get out of the house and start living."

"Yes, get out of the house. Have a nice day, and I'll talk to you soon," Tiffany said as she watched Valerie leave. Tiffany walked to the kitchen and opened her laptop on the kitchen table. She pressed the button, turning it on before returning to the living room and grabbing Valerie's cup from the coffee table. She placed the cup into the sink on her way to the kitchen table and sat down in front of the laptop.

She clicked on a dating site from her 'favorites' drop-down menu and logged in. The site gave her notifications of multiple new messages. Tiffany surfed through their subject lines, ignoring flirts altogether and sidetracking any marked 'I'm interested'. She scanned the list and saw that her new friend Manny had sent a message. She opened it and read his note. She thought about her response before composing her reply.

Hi Manny,

Thanks for sharing your experience with me. It's important that you visit Camille very soon. Women love men who follow up. You could take her something, but not flowers. How about a package of specialty coffee or chocolate coffee beans? You can't go wrong since it's based on what she does. I know I appreciate any gift I can enjoy or use immediately.

It's nice you're doing this so early. I've never had a man make such a fuss over me. Here in San Francisco, I haven't found that guy. Oh well, I guess I have to keep looking. Let me know how it goes.

Well, your daughter seems sweet. It's cute that she's looking out for her daddy.

Please let me know what happens, and I'll give you an update on my search for Mister Right.

Take care,

A Cyber Affair

It wasn't long before Tiffany found a profile that captured her interest. She checked the guy out from every possible angle. She Googled his profile name and searched for any possible connection the guy could have to other dating sites. When she found a few of them, she joined the sites to see if his presentation was consistent; a lesson she had learned after a bad experience.

Previously, Tiffany had met what seemed to be a down-to-earth guy. She chatted with him on multiple occasions and felt hopeful. Before she could suggest meeting her new interest, she stumbled onto another dating site of which he was a member. Tiffany didn't see a problem with him using the same picture on all of his pages, but she was shocked at the comments other women had left for him.

It was then that she saw where a few of them had linked his profile to the 'Shameless Bastards' website and described him as an extreme liar and pervert. She read some of their accounts about their interactions with him and wasn't about to second guess their impressions.

Tiffany found him in the chat room where they usually conversed. As soon as her name appeared, he pounced into action.

Betterthan8: *Hey SanFranPearl, good seeing you online, babe.*

Tiffany, remembering the comments she read from those other women, was anxious to start her interrogation. She placed her fingers on the keyboard and words rolled onto the screen that were reflective of her newly-found information.

SanFranPearl: *I'm doing okay...So, I found your profile on multiple dating sites.*

Betterthan8: *I'm on a lot of sites, but as soon as we get together, I won't need them anymore.*

SanFranPearl: *Is that what you told those other women?*

Betterthan8: *What do you mean?*

SanFranPearl: *The women who called you a liar and pervert.*

Betterthan8: *Those women lied.*

SanFranPearl: *How can multiple women say the same thing and all be lying?*

Betterthan8: *Because, unlike you, they didn't stand a chance to get with me.*

Tiffany exhaled with a short grunt while tapping the table with her fingers on each side of the laptop. She looked at the ceiling in search of a thought, as if she had a person changing cue cards. She glanced at the laptop, set her fingers on the keyboard, and typed her message with as much kindness as she could muster.

SanFranPearl: *You'll never get a chance with me. I don't do shitheads.*

Before long, room members saw his hasty retreat from the chat room. Tiffany clicked the chat room box's exit button and closed the window. She closed the laptop and walked to the bathroom, standing in front of the mirror and staring at her reflection.

Then Tiffany laughed, covered her mouth, and shook her head, recalling how Betterthan8 played on a woman's vulnerability. She ran warm water in the sink, held her hands under the faucet, and splashed her face before toweling dry and walking back to the living room couch.

She pulled the laptop from the coffee table, opened it, and tapped the mouse pad, awakening the screen. Tiffany then typed the URL to another dating website. She read each profile and confirmed the guys' location following her new strict rule of "locals only".

It was her dream to connect in San Francisco as she was opposed having a long-distance relationship. Her marriage to Brad had failed her in ways she hadn't understood then, but now, on those lonely nights, she missed having a companion. She remembered being spontaneous; enjoying long nights of conversations or heated debates that stimulated her mind.

Tiffany yawned, covering her mouth with her hand, flashing back to a moment when she'd reached for her husband just to pull him closer, feeling his warmth and smell his fragrance. She looked left and didn't see him there sitting next to her on the couch. Her body yearned for a touch, the graze of a hand against her cheek, an arm around her shoulder pulling her closer, and the perfection of rhythmic breathing and the kiss upon her lips made for one reason…love.

Tiffany blinked at the dark laptop screen in disappointment. She wanted a live body; someone to keep her sane. Her desires increased once she touched the keyboard, awakening the laptop and the screen to its full color and brightness. She saw a cover picture of a man on her screen and her mind imagined what she'd experience in the wee hours of morning. It was one of many moonlit, breathtaking moments, when love was the practice of entangled hearts.

"I need him here." Tiffany dropped her head. "I want him next to me." She closed her eyes, took a deep breath, and fantasized about a romp in the hay. Her body responded to a flash of what she had experienced with Brad: though he had been a disappointment, at least he satisfied her physical urges. There were times when Brad had filled what she now knew to be empty moments.

Tiffany returned to her reality when the light of the laptop went dim. She tapped the keyboard, reawakening the screen, touched her URL space bar, and a dating website appeared.

"I am not traveling to a man, no way." She shook her head, leaving the great-looking man for a landing page. Her idea was that traveling outside of San Francisco was a serious risk. She looked at the website, touched her search engine, and pictures appeared from her saved query selection. After Tiffany scanned the list from her selection, she wrote an ice-breaker email.

Hi Stranger,

You have an interesting profile and you're posted on multiple dating sites. I'm curious how having so many profiles works for you. Maybe we're searching for similar things. Drop me a line. I hope we get a chance to talk. I'm open for a conversation; what about you?

San Fran Pearl

There. I hope its good enough for a response, she thought, and continued thinking. *It's easier writing an introduction than having an unattractive man approach me on the street. What can he do? Here, it's simple: either he responds, or he doesn't. This is so much easier.*

Tiffany relaxed and was happy with her actions. She stood, walked to the mirror, and evaluated her reflection. She sucked in her stomach, turned to the side, and relaxed her body as she watched it take on multiple shapes.

"What if he responds? I'm not even close to being ready to go on a date. There is no way I will impress a man, looking like this. Who am I fooling?"

Shortly after she profiled herself in the mirror Tiffany decided to start a workout regimen. It was her third attempt at staying fit. The battle against aging and fighting a skirmish with a strict diet was normal for her self-preservation.

She had never worried about her weight as a young woman, but now it was a major concern. She knew that for her to impress anyone, she would have to improve her appearance. Tiffany decided to take a huge step towards regaining her youthful figure and vowed to use her gym membership. Tiffany sighed about her best intentions as she returned to the laptop.

Tiffany surfed dating sites in search of more profiles. Each guy's looks held certain values and some of their content was amusing. The more men she found matching her interests, the more her basic qualification rules disqualified them. Distance was strictly a no-go and those who declared they were local didn't seem to live close enough.

In the Bay Area, there were not enough guys available within a twenty-mile radius. Tiffany was insistent about locals only, so she expanded her age range from 40-50 to 35-52. There were quick responses and invitations which she ignored because the guys didn't suit her. It was her drive to find someone - a special someone - to share every moment. She wanted a person who complimented her life.

Being married at a young age hadn't helped Tiffany. Her forever-mate had neglected her need for a fulfilling relationship.

She had thought her husband Brad was the love of her life, but it wasn't a partnership, by any means. It was more of a mother–son relationship. Brad was not the man she needed him to be. He had never made an effort to fulfill her emotional needs, even in the short time they dated and rushed into marriage.

He wasn't respectable enough to keep his hands off other women. And although he begged for her forgiveness, he failed to get back on track even after admitting to the deeds. After multiple discoveries of infidelity, their marriage became Tiffany's nightmare. She feared diseases and unwanted pregnancies from his wild excursions.

Finally, she discovered their finances had been derailed by the money he'd spent on other women. She made a second effort to fulfill her dream of a happy marriage and took on additional jobs to keep the family afloat. She tried everything possible to make her marriage work, but when he broke the last straw, spending the dollars she sweated to earn on another woman, she ended the marriage and felt losing a battle was better than living with unwarranted pain. She thanked God for not having had children with Brad. Tiffany felt it was better not having any ties with her ex-husband. Her memory of a failed marriage made her sad, but it also sparked a desire for more in her next relationship.

Tiffany turned in, after reading a large number of profiles. She was happy with her newly-made list of eligible bachelors to explore another evening. She felt life would change after finding a local man to date. She smiled before closing her eyes.

Morning came quickly. Tiffany woke without her alarm, opening her eyes at a time when the sun had not yet crested on the horizon. She rose from bed, got herself together, and began her day. Thinking about her life made her restless, and she walked to the kitchen in a daze. She stood next to the stove and thought about having a man to love, a man to share the early morning sunrise, and someone with whom she could turn herself into a fireball of heated passion. She started to make coffee, but as she pulled the coffee can out, she remembered this was her day for an early start time at the store. It was her storefront day, and she had to be there by nine.

Since it was early morning, Tiffany decided to stop somewhere along the way and have breakfast. It was a break from her routine, because she seldom left home so early. She chose a route to a little diner not far away before catching her bus to the downtown cable car.

Though she thought the streets were safe, it wasn't her norm to walk in public before commuters appeared at the local bus stops. She felt safe in large numbers versus walking practically alone. While she waited at the bus stop, she greeted a few neighbors and even spoke to several strangers.

A tall gentleman standing in the group caught her eye. He was slim, well dressed, and mature, with an aura of wisdom about him. Tiffany found him attractive and she covertly searched for any sign of his relationship status, looking at his hands and work bag for any hint of a woman's influence. Tiffany moved to the far side of the crowd and watched him. When the bus arrived she heard a group of neighbors in a conversation. Tiffany caught part of a comment: "…he's new around here," a woman boarding the bus said quietly. Before Tiffany could turn around, the tall gentleman was behind her and she stepped to tap her electronic bus fare card.

"So I'm the new guy. That sounds like I'm a kid going to school after moving to a new neighborhood," he said.

"To us regulars, you're a fresh subject we can talk about," Tiffany responded as she paid the bus fare and moved to an empty aisle seat. The gentleman followed her and sat in an aisle seat one row behind and across from Tiffany.

"I'm Tom Stetson, by the way." Tom reached over to shake Tiffany's hand. She obliged and responded, "Tiffany Wilkes."

"Nice meeting you, Tiffany. I must ask: do you always look so great in the mornings?"

"I..." Tiffany hesitated and looked at Tom's ringless hand again before she answered. "I always try to look my best before leaving home. You never know who you'll have to impress." She faced forward, expecting the conversation to end.

"Impress?" asked Tom.

"Yes, impress. You only get one chance for what I call "making the impact"."

"Impact! I haven't heard anyone use that word to describe a first impression. Why impact?"

"Well," Tiffany turned to face Tom as she answered, "most people say the first impression is everlasting. Over time, I've realized why. I think it's an impact, because it forces people to think and respond. So, the greater the impact, the better the response."

"The greater the impact, the better the response...hmm, you have a wise outlook."

"Yes, what an impact!" Tiffany smiled at her wit. She saw, by his facial expression, that Tom was impressed with her thoughts. Normally Tiffany wouldn't talk to a total stranger, but Tom seemed like a gentleman.

"So what's the deal, Tom? Are you married or single?" Tiffany got to the point. She looked into his eyes for an answer and then glanced at his left hand. "Well, I'd bet you're married."

"I am. How did you arrive at that conclusion?"

"I looked at your hand and didn't see a band or a cheater's ring. I didn't see anything giving it away. But, I've noticed in general, married men usually have a kinder way of conversing."

Tom looked at his hand before responding. "Yeah, dang, I left without my ring. She's going to be pissed," he chuckled. "Usually my hand gives it away. I'm proud of my commitment. Nothing in this world is greater than having an excellent woman. I guess we married men aren't good at making a personal acquaintance."

"Your ring would be a total giveaway," Tiffany smiled, turning to face forward and adjusting her purse in her lap.

If only he were single…well, I better leave well enough alone.

The bus stopped at the next route pickup. Tiffany let her imagination fly as images of Tom flashed into a fantasy. She saw a vivid picture of a delightful, scented field of waist-high wildflowers, a clear blue sky, and a patch of trees near a stream. She imagined Tom holding her hand while they walked in the field, laughing as they approached a large tree with extended branches in full bloom that blocked the beaming sun. Tom embraced Tiffany and kissed her sweetly. She felt the strength of his arms around her. She enjoyed the touch of his toned torso next to hers. And she felt his power to melt every ounce of her will.

Tiffany gave into him, much as a vine of a weeping willow swaying with the force of the wind. He pulled her closer and enjoyed the shortness of her breath. She imagined his heart beating next to her breast, and she enjoyed the pounding excitement he brought to her body. Tiffany looked into his face and saw him staring back as if he was searching for heaven in her eyes.

The bus bell rang for the next stop, snapping Tiffany out of her daydream. She watched Tom exit the bus. Her thoughts vanished, yet she wished for the opportunity to share her daydream with him.

Shortly after Tom got off the bus, it arrived at Tiffany's stop. It was a short walk to her job. Along the route, she walked around Union Square's beautiful statues and artwork, with its touching structures. She smiled every time she passed that concrete haven for early morning coffee enthusiasts who purchased drinks from the few vendors within the square. Tiffany observed how comfortable and easy-going those   drinkers were. She envied their relaxed looks, drinking in the morning with the city coming to life.

She had dreams of waking early as the sun rose, commuting to the square, and, like those who were already there, sipping the morning's steamy drink while watching workers invade the city. Tiffany stopped at a restaurant on the far end of the square, ordered a bagel and coffee, and enjoyed her morning amongst the easy-going drinkers as she joined their ranks.

After breakfast, Tiffany walked around Union Square until it was time to start work. She entered the store, went to her locker in the employee break room, stored her purse and jacket, clocked in, and reported to her assigned position. It was early for her, since she normally had the afternoon shift. Early morning hours in the store were usually peaceful, but today it was busier than any day she could remember.

The difference between the shifts was in the meticulous preparation and clothing presentation – restocking shelves and hanging new clothes on racks, then pricing items -- during the morning shift, versus the less hectic afternoon shift with its focus on customer interactions. She realized that customers were more interesting than merchandising.

It was near her lunch break when she noticed Tom. He entered the building from Union Square, stepped downstairs, and walked directly to her counter. It felt like the winds of change were pushing Tom towards her. Before Tiffany had a chance to greet him, he looked down at the perfume display counter where she had replaced a coworker who had gone on break. "Do you have this ring in a size nine?"

"That isn't real, sir. It's a giant plastic replica and it goes with this perfume display." Tiffany smiled, waiting for laughter in Tom's response.

"Really?" His face twisted in an awkward smirk, then he lifted his head and saw the smile in her eyes. "How's your day so far?"

"Great! What a pleasant surprise. I didn't expect to see you again."

"I was near the store and I saw you from the window."

"Spying on me?" asked Tiffany.

"I wouldn't say spying," he smiled. "I'd say "admiring" is a better description."

"You're dangerous. You know we're off-limits."

"Who says this is going anywhere?"

"I wouldn't consider it going anywhere. It's nice of you to drop by and say hello. I guess I'll see you on the bus later today?"

"How about having coffee with me during your next break?"

"I don't think so, but it's nice of you to ask. I'm serious about not getting involved with a married man."

"Thanks for the honesty, but I'm just offering conversation."

"Conversations can be the first step."

"Not if we're on our p's and q's. There's nothing wrong with innocent conversation, unless you have other thoughts."

"I have to get back to work. We can chat another time. Have a wonderful day, Tom."

"I'll see you around." Tom gave an old-fashioned wave before leaving.

Tiffany's workday ended without the shift leader asking her to work late. She clocked out, got her things from the locker, and headed to the bus stop. Before she escaped the building, Valerie caught up with her. "You and I have plans tonight."

"No, not again, Valerie; not again."

"Come on, it'll be fun."

"Who's it with this time? Are we meeting them there or am I meeting a blind date and your guy is picking you up to meet us later? Last time we met at a club."

"We're meeting them. Remember the coffee shop you went to for your date with Steven?"

"It wasn't a date." Tiffany walked towards the store's exit with Valerie walking alongside her. "Besides, why go there, of all places?"

"It's got the right stuff. We can enjoy watching guys come in and we can escape if we need to. You know, why give your all to a man you really don't know?"

"Why go if we're going to meet dates? Wouldn't you think it's better that we go there alone and take a chance on new guys instead of meeting your friends there?"

Valerie shook her head left to right while responding: "Because "chance" never works."

A Cyber Affair

"Call me. I'll be ready."

"I didn't tell you what time."

"No worries. I know what time you get off. And I'll be ready. Just call me to make sure I still want to go." Tiffany didn't wait for a response; she left the store and walked into pedestrian traffic, traveling on a direct path to the cable car stop, jumping on the next trolley towards home. During the ride, she noticed there were a lot of tourists on the cable car. Tiffany giggled as she took an open seat.

A minute into the ride, she grabbed her cell phone and noticed an email notification on her screen. She read her email:

San Fran Pearl, what a name. I bet you're just as you described. I saw your profile picture, read your quick note, and find you one interesting soul. I'd love to chat and see if we can create opportunities for a future. Please tell me your picture is actually you. I just have to know.

As you referred,

Stranger ☺

She smiled at the cute email but decided to wait until she got home to respond. She wanted a chance to review his profile again. She wanted to make sure 'Stranger' was someone with whom she would like to continue a conversation. She noticed that the next email was from Manny.

Hi Tiffany,

Nice of you to reply. I like seeing your emails in my inbox. It's a good feeling knowing someone is thinking of me.

I decided to visit Camille's coffee shop near the college. It was packed with kids. My gosh! Those college students looked so young. They reminded me of new recruits from my Navy days. I mean: not quite fresh out of diapers, but more like little tykes playing dress up or make-believe with guns. Oops, I digress.

Camille was interesting, to say the least. She runs a nice shop, and it seems to do well. When I entered the place, she barely recognized me. I took that as a "bad sign," and nearly turned around. But then my daughter yelled "Dad!" and when she greeted me, at least there was a smile.

She quickly took me aside and led me to a table. It wasn't like there were many places to sit, but her interest in my seating led me to believe I was at least special. I took your advice and gave her a copy of <u>Coffee Barrister's Book of Drinks</u> and a special blend of coffee. I thought I had made a good selection. That was, until she looked at me with a raised eyebrow. In haste, I second-guessed my selection. She left the table, pointed to the bar, and said she would be back.

She placed a cup of coffee from one of the book's recipes in front of me. It smelled great. She smiled as she turned around after placing the cup down to focus on her business. It was a busy time, so I stood up and offered to help her in the shop, but she insisted that I was a guest.

I sat there for over an hour and although my daughter visited my table a few times between customers, Camille never returned. She waved periodically, instead.

She kept up a pace that usually youngsters would keep, going from table to counter and pressing the coffee machine for orders she received. When she stood at the counter with another customer, I approached her and insisted on paying for the coffee.

A Cyber Affair

Of course, Camille didn't want me to pay, so I left a few dollars anyway before walking out. I saw her smile as I left the shop, but something was missing. Even though I took your advice, I felt as if I hadn't made the connection I'd hoped for.

I hope you're having better luck at this dating game than I am. Even though many aren't the Prince Charming you seek, at least men are eager to kiss you. Let me know how you're doing when you get a chance.

Your friend,

Manny.

Tiffany put her phone back into her purse before she stepped off the cable car. She walked to the corner bus stop and waited for the next bus. Within minutes, Tiffany was on a bus and continuing her journey. When she got home, she grabbed her mail and saw a pink slip for an undelivered package.

Tiffany placed her mail on the kitchen counter, booted up her laptop, and quickly responded to Manny's email. While she wrote, she couldn't stop thinking about the pink slip. She loved getting gifts. After sending her response, she changed into comfortable clothing, grabbed the slip, and hurried to the post office.

Chapter 14

Manny drove north from Camille's coffee shop, right after sending Tiffany an email from his daughter's laptop, in time to beat rush hour traffic. He had learned, while living in South Florida, that traffic congestion infiltrated the streets and bi-ways of Miami during certain times of day. While he enjoyed his bike, he relished the feeling of freedom with the wind as opposed to the torment of riding in the middle of rush hour traffic.

It wasn't long after Manny left Camille's shop that he had the idea of extending an invitation to dinner and a night of dancing. He thought that their first outing wasn't bad and his recent visit to her coffee shop didn't turn him off. He passed the first Fort Lauderdale exit and decided to explore the beach and locate a party destination to show Camille.

Manny drove back to his apartment by Highway 1A-1 and rode down Atlantic Avenue, watching beachcombers enjoy the sun. It was the right time for tourists which gave him plenty to view, a welcome break from his busy work schedule. Manny escaped the large crowd by finding a parking space further north. He then strolled on the beach, watching people and glancing at an ocean freighter in the distance.

Manny walked north along the beach and decided to sit in the sand. He thought of how he had blown it with Cheryl. He remembered how, when they were first married, she had been spontaneous and sensuously exciting. He smiled, remembering how Cheryl could whip up a meal from nothing and how she had not minded their struggle on a 3rd Class Petty Officer's pay. He then frowned, thinking of his long deployments and the beginning of their ending. Cheryl's will and patience had shortened and her entire life wrapped around Suzie. The little girl became her only focus. Manny's homecomings felt like interruptions to Suzie's schedule.

A year of fighting with Cheryl during two overseas missions and Manny's training schedule was the last straw for their relationship. Manny remembered his last homecoming, when Cheryl wasn't at the pier and he had to call a cab to get home. Cheryl had jumped off of the military deployment widow-wagon and decided she could raise Suzie alone.

Manny picked up a seashell, looked at it, and tossed it towards the oncoming waves. He remembered that Cheryl could not live in Norfolk, but she was good enough to stay near the naval base after they legally separated so that whenever Manny's ship was in port, at least he could spend time with Suzie. Manny stood and brushed sand from the seat of his pants. *My next relationship is going to be different.*

Manny returned to his bike and headed towards home. He ventured north to West Palm Beach, where he spent most of his days. Just a few miles from home, after passing a strip mall in the center of town, Manny noticed an Italian restaurant named *La Sirena* with a charming entryway. Piqued by curiosity and a prodding appetite, Manny turned into the parking lot and parked in front of the restaurant. Once inside, he looked around and immediately decided to make this the spot for a date with Camille. But before calling her to reserve the date, he thought to try a random dish from the menu.

The hostess greeted Manny, escorted him to a table, and handed him the menu. Within minutes of being seated, the waiter placed a glass of water on the table and took his order. Manny observed the restaurant's décor and admired how the owners had created a classy environment and supported local artists by displaying their paintings, as well as featuring stained glass murals on many of the windows. The restaurant also exhibited metalwork as table décor, as well as serving bread in metal breadbaskets made by local crafters. All of the items had discretely-placed price tags on them.

Manny was known as a chef by his family and friends, and Italian cooking classes helped him evaluate the food's authenticity. He knew it took focus and finesse to cook most Italian dishes. Manny had been stationed in Naples, Italy; and on days he didn't eat in the mess hall, he went to local family-owned restaurants.

When the waiter returned with the meal, Manny knew it had been prepared well. The aroma and its rich body intoxicated him; he was like a wine connoisseur sticking his nose in a wine glass. He looked at the colorful presentation and it reminded him of Flora, the nice old lady who ran his favorite spot near the base. He smiled as he picked up his fork. He thanked the waiter and without hesitation, took the first bite.

Manny evaluated each bite as if the meal was in a competition for the best Italian food in Florida. He laughed, remembering the dish with each bite, and he mumbled the names of the flavors he savored, remembering the cooking classes he had taken in Naples. When he finished, he called Suzie. "Hi, Baby Girl."

"Hi, Dad. What are you up to?"

"Not much, but I have an idea and I wanted to run it by you."

"Okay, what is it?"

"I think I should ask Camille out for a date. Is she seeing anyone? I don't want to overstep my boundaries."

"Dad, would I introduce you if I knew there was someone else?"

Manny paused before answering. "No, Baby Girl, you wouldn't. I'm going to ask her out, so don't say anything."

"Make sure it's Saturday night. Her Fridays are real busy. She lets students share open mic poetry and sometimes there's a guy who plays his guitar. It's really fun. You should come by one of those nights."

"Sounds interesting enough and I may do that one day. Yeah, me and a bunch of college kids - as if I would blend in that crowd." Manny turned the conversation back to his focus. "Right now, I'm at an Italian restaurant in West Palm. Do you think she would like Italian? It's really a neat place."

"Remember, Dad, she's a sweet woman."

"What's that supposed to mean?"

"I'm just saying." Suzie giggled, as she knew to end the call before Manny got into her smart comment. "Bye Dad, love you."

"Love you, too." Manny disconnected the call, looked at the check, and placed his credit card on top of the leather holder. *She's a smart kid, and I bet she's scared I'll pull Camille away for a wild time and maybe break her heart in the effort. Damn, does she know me or what?* The waiter returned and offered dessert. Instead, Manny gave the waiter a message to take to the chef. "Please share my apologies to the chef. I assumed they wouldn't have any idea how to cook authentic Italian."

"You want me to apologize for you?"

"Please do. I'm usually a food critic, but man, was this good. It's like we attended the same cooking classes in Italy. Can you please tell him thanks for a wonderful meal?"

"I'll do it right away. Would you like anything else?"

"No, I think the apology is enough. Thank you."

After the waiter left, Manny looked at his watch, stood from the table, and took another look at the place. He nodded in confirmation that it was the right place to impress Camille. He walked to the bar just as the waiter returned with the credit card slip and, to Manny's surprise, with the head chef in tow. He greeted the chef with a handshake. "Man, your cooking took me back to Naples."

"Thanks, I appreciate the compliment. Naples is where I learned to cook."

"Really?"

"Yes. Rick Armando," the chef smiled as he took a seat at the bar

"I'm Manuel Perez, but most call me Manny."

"Nice meeting you, Manny. Have a seat." The Chef pointed at the bar stool next to him. "You said you took cooking lessons in Italy. When were you there?"

"During my Navy years. I was stationed at the air station in Naples in the early 80s. You know, I had to find something to do besides hanging out in bars. After visiting all the historical sites I could take in, it was either attend college or find a hobby. I took up cooking."

"Funny, I was there as a sailor, too. Not in the 80s, but from '01 to '03. I did the same thing for the same reason; it's a small world."

"Yes, very small. Is this your restaurant?"

"No, I'm the head chef, not the owner. The owners are very good people, and they've always treated me with the utmost kindness and respect."

"I guess working here is nothing like being in the Navy."

"No comparison. You know, there are times when I miss those days in the fleet, but then I snap back to reality. I remember being underway on a carrier, and it felt like we would never get home. If it didn't fill me with anxiety, I would have stayed beyond six years. I got off that ship and became a land lover. The best decision I ever made."

"How did you end up in West Palm Beach?"

"At first I followed a lovely woman here. Then I fell in love with Ft. Lauderdale. A couple of years later I took a chance and started looking for a job as a chef. After meeting the owners, working here was smoother than Neapolitan ice cream. How about you?"

"I retired from the Navy a few years ago. I took a job in South Florida to be close to my daughter."

"Family first. That's good."

"Listen, Rick, can I ask a favor, sailor to sailor?"

"Sure."

"I'm setting up a date with a special lady. I'd like to bring her here. Would you mind creating a dish off the menu?"

"Sure, throw it at me."

"It's authentic Naples Campania – I was thinking of Maccheroni Ai Quattro Formaggio, salad and maybe some of that Neapolitan ice cream you just mentioned. I know she'll love it."

"Yes, an easy dish, and when it's done right, it's awesome!"

"Nobody can hate this meal."

"As a fellow sailor, it's covered. No problem."

"I'll call you with the date. I haven't asked her yet."

"She'll come. A sailor's charm always works. Just give me a day's notice for shopping, okay?"

"You got it, Rick. I appreciate the support."

"No problem."

Manny gave him a gentleman's hug as they shook each other's hand and their shoulders touched.

"Here's my card, Manny. Give me a call when you're ready."

"You've got it." Manny waved at the waiter and exited the building. Before he mounted his bike, he called Camille at the coffee shop. "Hi, Camille."

"Manny?"

"Yeah. Look, I know you're busy, so I'll get right to the point. I was hoping you'd be free to go out to dinner with me on Saturday."

"Saturday is perfect. I'm so glad you didn't ask for Friday."

"Suzie warned me."

"Good. I love your daughter."

"She's fond of you, too. So on Saturday night I can pick you up around 6. Is that okay?"

"Early dinner?"

"No, there is a special place I would like to take you, and it's about an hour's drive from your shop."

"Six is good. I'll be ready."

"Awesome. Talk to you later?"

"Please, and I hope you don't wait until Saturday to chat again."

"I don't plan to. I'll call you again soon." Manny ended the call and smiled as he returned to the restaurant. He went back to the bar and asked the bartender to give Rick a message. "Tell him Manny said it's on for Saturday night at seven."

Camille stayed on his mind during the entire ride home. He planned activities they would do that Saturday night and thought about how they could spend future extended weekends together. His mind jumped to the eventual arguments he usually got into with women. Manny knew that sometimes he wasn't too quick to trust women, and by doing so, he frustrated them with his short temper. He vowed to watch that behavior this time. He arrived home, booted up his laptop, got a beer, and sat at his desk. He logged in and surfed the websites he routinely visited. Manny checked his email and saw a note from Tiffany, so he clicked on it.

Manny,

It was a lovely email you sent. I'm glad you decided to see Camille. Maybe it's only me, but today was different. I didn't mean to be, but when I met this guy on the bus, I was aggressive. No, I'm not always aggressive, so don't ask. LOL. He was kind of cute. I started a conversation and discovered that he's married. From the way he joked about being married, it didn't sound like it was the best.

What bothers me about Tom is that he visited my job and asked me out for coffee. I didn't think I led him on, so he surprised me. I didn't go with him and I reminded him that he's married. I had to let it go because this woman has morals; I don't date married men. I don't want to cause any drama in anyone's life, especially mine.

Why do you think he asked me to lunch? He claimed it was to start a friendship. I'm uncomfortable becoming his friend, so we only talked while riding the bus to Union Square. I would be glad to be friends, but only if it were with both him and his wife. Just being with him could be dangerous, and even more so since I enjoyed his conversation.

I know I did the right thing by not going for coffee with him today. Should I cut all ties, including conversation? I'd like your take on it.

Looking forward to your response,

Tiffany

Manny laughed and contemplated his response. *Why would Tom press Tiffany? He's looking for one of two things: a sexual excursion or a true friend.* Manny pushed the chair back from his computer desk, looked around the room, and saw a photo of Suzie as a child. He had traveled everywhere with that picture - every deployment and every OCONUS (Outside of the Continental United States) base. He kept the picture in his sea bag; a reminder of happier times. He would stare at her face as if she were the angel of wisdom, and usually she was. Manny rolled his seat back to the desk and typed:

Tiffany,

Glad you asked about Tom's intentions. It seems he's being honest with you. A man with dishonest intentions wouldn't share the fact that he is married, unless he's looking for sympathy. Then he would tell you his marriage was failing or he'd list their hardships. Was he asking for a date? Has he talked about introducing his wife to you? If so, it's probably just a friendly effort.

A Cyber Affair

I decided to ask Camille out for dinner this Saturday. Suzie suggested Saturday, as it's a slower night at the coffee shop. I will share what happens after it's over.

Good luck with Tom. I'm sure he's just being kind and if he isn't bringing the wife, stand clear of the fodder.

Manny

After clicking 'send', he left his desk, grabbed another beer from the fridge, popped it open, took a sip, and went out to his patio. He watched the day end with a flashback to his naval experience where he'd watched as the sunset turned to darkness on the main deck aft. He remembered how the ship's propulsion gave him comfort and provided a moment to escape in his solitude.

Those were times when his thoughts were clear. Even though he loved the life he had with him and Suzie, he admitted missing the camaraderie of his shipmates. He always said sailors were more like family than working compadres. Those guys had helped him through his divorce. It was during a long deployment in the middle of the Atlantic, after a mail run when Manny received a confirmed delivery package from Cheryl's lawyer. That's the moment he learned that the adage 'absence makes the heart grow fonder' wasn't true. Manny had seen other sailors go through breakups, but he'd never thought that it would happen to him.

When he was promoted to Chief without a pay raise, he achieved a naval milestone. But his military investment didn't help him avoid being lonely and his promotions didn't measure up with the increased financial support needed to assist her in raising their only child. In Cheryl's explanation letter outside of the lawyer's package, she complained about raising Suzie alone.

It was too much work for one person. In the same letter she mentioned George. It was her way of saying that she wasn't alone anymore.

He sat out on the patio, staring into the darkness and listening to the night. He heard laughter and conversations. He finished one beer and drank another. Manny allowed his mind to wonder about the many nights when he had liberty in various ports. He envisioned Saturday night's dinner and imagined what he could do to impress Suzie, since she had made such an effort to introduce him. It wasn't like she hadn't set him up before, but this time she had actually introduced him to a woman whom he felt had some substance.

Manny thought about the importance of keeping his daughter in his life, especially after they rebuilt a connection when the divorce became final. He had watched his peers struggle with kids, and saw some sailors with ideal marriages, but was sad to admit that most of the men and women in his crew were estranged from their children. He was keen on those who somehow kept it together.

Manny supported Suzie at every opportunity during the last years of his naval career. He did everything he could, attending shows, watching her practice gymnastics, or attending sporting events to watch her cheerlead despite Cheryl's constant attitude and her attempts to block their bond. She was always negative and discouraging.

It wasn't until Suzie's senior year of high school when their bond finally came together. His daughter recognized her mother's blocking behavior and how her mother tried to make her stepdad the only man in her life. Suzie fought Cheryl's attitude and actions by making her dad the highlight of her life. She told her mother about living with Manny, which caused a breakdown of their relationship.

If it weren't for changing schools, restructuring her after school activities, and new friends, she would have moved immediately after prom. Fortunately, her growing independence trumped her mother's ploy as she drove her car to see her father more often until her graduation. From then on, both Manny and Suzie continued nurturing their relationship.

Manny decided to turn in for the night. He went inside, straightened up his apartment, turned off his laptop, and went to bed happy. He felt wonderful about how he and Suzie had overcome obstacles and remained close. Manny acknowledged that only one more thing would make his life complete and that was finding his true companion.

It was Saturday afternoon when Camille looked at her watch and realized that Manny would be there before long. She yanked off her apron and handed it to Suzie.

"It's all yours," she giggled girlishly.

"I thought Dad was picking you up around five or so."

"Yes, he is, but I'm going to get ready."

"It's only 1. Don't you think it's a little early?"

"No, not for the pampering and preparation I want to do." Camille winked and smiled as she started towards the door. "Call me if anything unusual happens."

"Okay, I will." Suzie finished serving customers and, during a slow period, she called her dad. When Manny answered the phone, Suzie skipped right past "hello". "Dad, you can't blow this date tonight."

"Suzie, come on. I'm an adult. I think I can handle Camille."

"She's so excited, and I don't want her to be disappointed. She's getting ready now. She left the coffee shop nearly an hour ago."

"She's excited." Manny smiled and said, "Good, because so am I."

"No, you don't. Not tonight, Dad."

"What?"

"You know, come on…be a gentleman and leave those crazy port stories out. She's a nice woman. Don't do those crazy Navy things you told me about."

"I told you about those events for your protection. You know that even old men can be mischievous," he laughed.

"Still, it's Camille. Just don't get crazy or overdo it. Dad, I really like her."

"I like her too. I asked her to go out, didn't I?"

"Okay, you asked her out … I just don't want you to blow it."

"Did it ever occur to you that she may blow it with me?"

"That really hadn't crossed my mind, Dad. I hope you two have fun tonight. Love you!"

Suzie disconnected before Manny could respond. He reflected on the time he had dated the teacher his daughter was fond of. Manny and the woman had gone to a pool hall, the kind that seemed okay on the surface. During the pool game, he noticed guys gawking at his date and Manny, in a huff, had asked if they would like to buy her time. Of course, the date didn't like this comment and when one guy approached and touched her, Manny punched the guy and swung his cue stick, hitting another man who was standing nearby. The cue broke across the guy's body and a splinter jammed into his date's thigh.

He heard her painful scream, but did not respond to her cry. He kept his attention on the fight and swung his fists as if their lives depended on it. Manny thought that someone would join him against the greater number of foes, but the crack of a pool cue over his back signaled the painful realization that he was alone. He realized there were no other sailors or shipmates around to jump in and assist.

When the police and ambulance arrived, Manny and his date were outside of the club and both of them appeared to have gotten the worst of it. The woman had to get stitches after having the broken cue splinter removed and she never spoke to Manny again. Suzie was embarrassed and apologized for her father's behavior. She didn't speak to Manny for a week because his date was the first of his girlfriends that she had liked.

Manny laughed at this memory, then looked as his watch. He wanted to make a great impression on Camille, so he walked to his closet and gathered his coolest jeans, a stylish shirt and a leather vest. He placed those items on his bed and imagined how he would look. As he envisioned his look and pondered his selection, reality sank in, and he knew Suzie was right. He put the clothes back in the closet and started over. He reminded himself that he was no longer a young, wild man who sailed the seven seas.

He pulled a cotton blazer, a nice plaid patterned V-neck shirt, and a pair of nicely creased black pants from his closet and laid them on the bed. He grabbed a black belt and socks that matched his pants. Manny looked down at the classy loafers he occasionally wore and decided to add them. Satisfied with his choices, he hopped into the shower. By the time he'd gotten dressed, he was surprised at his own transition from biker to gentleman.

Manny walked to his living room, glanced into the office, and decided to share his experience with Tiffany. He sat at his desk and waited for his computer to boot up. He clicked on his homepage and logged into his email account and wrote:

Tiffany,

I hope you're doing okay. I was getting ready for my date with Camille and decided to write. I had forgotten that making a good impression was such a serious job! I mean, what I did getting ready for this date was like preparing for an admiral's inspection. I guess the details will make the difference between a great evening and just a good evening. I am eager to get there, so wish me luck. I'll let you know what happened when I return.

Enjoy your night,

Manny

Manny clicked 'send' and shut down the computer. He looked at his watch and decided the slow drive to Camille's place was worth it. He walked to his bike and pushed it into the garage, then stepped into his Dodge Ram-Charger truck. He drove to South Miami, arriving half an hour earlier than planned. Manny called the chef at the restaurant to make sure of his timing and reconfirmed their arrangement. It was a habit from his Navy days to always check on the details of any plan.

Perfection was his goal when impressing a woman. When he parked the truck, he sat in front of the coffee shop surveying patron traffic and watching Suzie through the window. He was proud of his daughter. She had become a responsible young woman. He got out of his truck, approached the door, and smiled when Camille recognized him.

"Are you coming in or are we leaving early?" Camille smiled as she stood in his path.

Surprised by the question, Manny looked at his watch and said, "I can come in."

"Good, I need a few more minutes before I'm ready."

"You look great to me." Manny grinned with intent and watched her walk to the coffee shop counter. He followed her and took a seat at a nearby table. Suzie, hearing her father's voice, prepared a cup of coffee and brought it to him. She sat across the table and gave him the eye. "Remember, she's special," she whispered.

"Suzie, are you going to coach me on dating?"

"I know you, Dad, and I know how you can get, so please be on your best behavior. Save the wild stuff until after she's gotten to know you."

"We're not going to do anything wild tonight. Look how I'm dressed - and I picked a fancy place, too."

"I feel a little better knowing you aren't going to a bar."

"Who said we weren't going to a bar?" Manny laughed. He touched Suzie's arm. "Stop worrying…there are classy bars, you know."

"Yeah, well, promise you'll let her choose the bar. Please, Dad?"

"Okay, okay. I'll let her choose the bar." Manny sipped his coffee and winked as he set the cup on the table.

"Nice." Suzie rose from her chair and stood next to Manny before kissing him on the cheek and returning to work. She smiled at the next customer and took his order. Manny stood up from his chair when Camille approached.

"Okay," she smiled. "Are we ready for a good time?"

"You look gorgeous. I love your style, it's real classy." Manny took her hand and spun her around as if they were swing dancing. "If only I had known earlier, I'd have worn something more appropriate; maybe put on a tux."

"No, silly, you look handsome," Camille blushed. "I see where Suzie gets her good looks." She turned to the door, leading Manny to an escape. "I hope we're not riding your bike."

"I didn't think the bike would be fitting for our date."

"I'm glad. Suzie told me about the wild streak you've had. I'm not afraid, but you know, first impressions without a chaperone are just as important as with one," Camille chuckled.

"Well, let's get the impression started. Please, after you." Manny waved his hand towards the exit. They walked to his truck, and he opened the passenger door. He secured her door and quickly went around to the driver's side and got into the seat. He smiled at her as they started on their way.

After a few miles of silence, Manny asked Camille about some of her likes and dislikes. Camille answered candidly until they found a common subject of conversation for the remainder of the ride. He parked in front of the restaurant.

"I hope you like Italian."

"I do."

"Good. I gambled on this cuisine. I know you'll enjoy it." Manny got out and opened her door, offering his hand to help her out of his truck. "Did I tell you how lovely you look tonight?"

"Yes, you did - for the third time," she chuckled.

"Good. I want you to know how much you impressed me the first time we met."

"Did I?"

"Of course, but I didn't tell you because we had company."

"I remember."

Manny pointed to the front door of the restaurant and before he stepped towards it, he signaled for her hand and slowly pulled her closer. "I want everyone to know you're with me," he smiled, looking into her eyes.

Camille returned the gesture and tightened her grasp on his hand. She moved closer to his ear and whispered, "I am."

They entered the restaurant and Manny gave the hostess his name.

"Come with me." The hostess led them to their table. Manny pulled out Camille's chair before taking his. He sat down as the hostess introduced their waiter, who handed them their menus, then excused himself to attend to another table. Camille looked around the restaurant. "This is nice, very nice."

"I'm glad you like it. I hoped you would, because it impressed me. Wait until you get a chance to try the food."

"What's on the menu?" She opened it and quickly scanned the first page.

"Actually, you don't need the menu. I placed a special order with the chef. He and I attended the same cooking school near Naples, Italy. I asked him to make a very delicious dish for us, local to the region."

"Really?"

"Yes, really. I hope you'll like it."

"I do, too. I'm famished."

The waiter returned with a wire basket of bread and placed it on the table, then asked for their drink orders. Before Camille could order, Manny asked for a bottle of Greco di Tufo, a white wine from Naples, and then told the waiter to tell the chef his sailor buddy had arrived. The waiter left.

"I know you're going to like this wine. It's a favorite because it's the right bouquet, from the most perfect grapes in the region. I fell in love with it years ago."

Camille looked at him. "You know, most men aren't that crazy about wine." She took a piece of bread and placed it on her saucer. "I mean, none of the men I've dated ever cared about wine. You're overly excited about this bottle."

"I am?"

"It seems that way. For your sake, I hope it's good." She frowned as she tore off a small piece of bread with her hands.

The waiter returned with the wine bottle in a bucket of ice. He poured a small amount in a glass and had Manny sample his selection. He explained the year and winery location when Manny took a sip.

"Perfect: just as I remember it." Manny nodded as he sat his glass on the table.

"Camille, even if you prefer red wine, this white is fabulous."

"We'll see. I don't usually like whites."

"But this one is…well, you'll see."

She took a sip after the waiter poured her glass. Manny waited for her response.

"Not bad." Camille sipped from her glass a second time. "Not bad at all," she added. "I'm surprised it's not sweet."

"You have to trust me."

A Cyber Affair

They continued their small talk, finishing where they had left off in his truck. Camille had finally started sharing her life experiences when the waiter came with their meals. Once the waiter placed Manny's dish on the table, Camille looked up. "Can I have a menu?"

"What's wrong?" Manny was surprised. "You haven't tasted anything."

"I don't have to. I can look at the sauce and see that it has a lot of cheese."

"Well, it's cheesy because it's a southern Italian dish with four cheeses."

"Except for one thing." Camille frowned as she opened the menu the waiter handed her. "I'm severely lactose intolerant."

"I didn't know."

"You never asked."

"Forgive me for not asking." Manny gave her a blank stare. "You're right, I should have asked. It would have been more impressive had I known of your intolerance."

"I would guess you're right," Camille looked at the menu. "You would have impressed me by asking more about me before making assumptions; especially for a first date. Do you always leap to conclusions, or is this how you normally treat women?"

Manny hesitated to respond and pondered how to answer. *If I answer yes, then she'll say I'm a lame jerk. If I answer no, she'll say I missed the mark and should change. Either way I lose, so why not change the subject.*

Manny sighed. "I guess you would know what's best when it comes to how to treat a woman. How about I share my experiences dealing with women during my global travels, and you tell me what works? I'll listen."

"What does global travel have to do with me?"

"I'd guess you're sensitive to what men do to impress you. Let's just say we missed the mark on this one. Don't I get credit for trying? I thought my selection and planning was something nice." Manny sipped his wine.

"Well, you're wrong." Camille looked angry, raising the menu and hiding her face from Manny. "You don't get credit for being in control. How did you come to be the expert on women of the world?" Camille waited for an answer and when Manny didn't quickly respond, she continued. "I bet everything you've done has something to do with women you met near some seaport." Camille's tone had changed from the sweet voice she'd had when they arrived.

"What is so different between those women and you?"

"I'm not interested in finding a man who can take control of my life."

"You mean, your idea of people near a port - or should I say *women* near a port - is that they have an underlying objective to find a man who can give them a different life?"

"Yeah, that's right. I bet most of the women you've met laughed and pretended to enjoy anything you did." She frowned, lowered the menu, and stared at him with fire in her eyes. "And I bet your asshole friends married them and those women didn't care anything about those jerks. Those bitches left them after they got to the States. Am I wrong?"

Manny took in a breath and held it, fighting the anger, as he looked at Camille and shook his head in disgust at her insult. "You're dead wrong."

"I know what I'm talking about." Camille continued glaring at Manny. "My brother married a foreign woman, and she left him a few years after she had a child with him. Next thing you know, she's married to another guy, and her family is here. What kind of life did she give my brother? He can hardly see his kid, and the family never gets to see him." Camille looked at her wine glass. "Yeah, she accepted anything he did - just like the great idea you had for me tonight."

"You're saying all women from foreign countries near military towns have an underlying objective?"

"I said it and I mean it."

"I think you've just insulted 90% of military wives."

Camille sat in silence, looking around the room as if her comment was loud enough to bring unwanted attention. She glanced at the table, then held her head up.

"I didn't say all of them - but I bet a lot of them wanted a military man to take them away from their humdrum lives."

"Again, you just insulted a lot of military wives and my daughter's mother."

"At least she was smart enough to get out."

Manny held his tongue in response and signaled for the waiter. "Can you pack this to go and give me the check, please?"

The waiter nodded in response and picked up both plates from the table. Camille dropped the menu and scowled at Manny. "What about my dinner?"

Manny lifted his wine glass and gulped what was left. He sat the glass down and looked at Camille. "We can find a takeout place on the way home."

"I don't think so." She shook her head. "Asshole! I'll call a cab. You can go to hell on your way home."

"Are you sure? I don't leave women stranded. I bought you here and the least I can do is take you back."

"Oh, there you go again, assuming that I can't take care of myself. Look, asshole, I don't think you know crap about women. I can see why you're divorced. Your male chauvinist ego should go find a woman with low self-esteem! I'm not her."

Camille stood and walked to a different table, holding her purse and menu, and took a seat. Manny took the check from the waiter, gave him his credit card, and filled his wine glass. He watched Camille look through the menu. He knew Suzie would be upset at the outcome. *Oh well, she'll just have to get over it.*

On his drive home Manny remembered many successful couples who had it together and whose marriages had endured hard times and long deployments. He recalled young couples who had no idea about Navy life or the possible hardships ahead of them, and how they had pulled through.

As he turned left on the main drive, he stopped at a 7/11 convenience store and parked in front of the entrance. He got out of his truck and entered the business, walking directly to the beer and wine section. He picked up two beers and walked to the cashier. Manny nodded at the attendant, paid cash for his items, received the change, and took the bag with his beer. He walked to the truck and got inside, buckled his seatbelt, and put the key into the ignition. He then flashed to Camille's change of attitude during dinner and he shook his head in disbelief.

Manny arrived home, went inside, and booted up his computer, then sat at the desk. He removed his blazer and dropped it on the couch. His failed date consumed his thoughts. *Was Camille right?* "No, not at all," he reassured himself as he watched the desktop boot up. He sat down, logged in, took a beer from the bag and popped the top, and went straight to his email account.

A Cyber Affair

Tiffany,

You aren't going to believe my night. It was horrible, and I ended up coming home early from my date. Camille, the same woman you told me to take a gift to. She showed her true colors. It was surprising to hear how she feels about military people, especially men. Maybe I didn't notice her opinions during dinner with Suzie. But, man, were her opinions up-front tonight. I never knew a woman could be so judgmental.

You aren't going to believe what happened. Well, she insulted me, the Navy, men in the military and foreign women.

I tried to impress her with dinner and wine at a fancy restaurant. How was I to know she was lactose intolerant? She doesn't do milk products, including cheese, and I took her to an Italian restaurant. Who eats Italian without cheese? Now I know: obviously she does.

Oh, and she blasted women, too, saying how disappointing women are who don't seem independent to her. Like, wow: I suspect no one could get her into a state of dependency. No wonder she does everything for her business. She has serious control issues.

Okay, no more attempts to satisfy my daughter's dream. She'll have to accept who I like and stop trying to set me up with whomever she wants in her life. I'll have to have a chat with the young lady real soon.

Thanks for listening and reading this email and for letting me vent.

Take care,

Manny

Chapter 15

Tiffany stood in line at the post office, trying to read the delivery notice. She couldn't make out the zip code of the box's origin. She wondered if she had forgotten about an online order, or if today was a special occasion. She couldn't think of anyone who would send her a gift out of the blue. Twenty minutes later it was finally her turn at the counter and she handed the slip to the postal clerk.

"I'll be right back." He took the slip and walked towards the back of the warehouse. Tiffany's eyes followed the postal worker where she saw a multitude of boxes, packages, and bins through the double doors he left open. He returned with a 20 x 25-inch box.

"Nice-sized box for the lady," the postal worker smiled. "Sign here." He marked the spot on the form on the counter.

Tiffany grabbed the chained pen and signed the document. She took the box, smiled, and thanked him. Tiffany read the return address while in the building's foyer and sighed in relief that it wasn't from her parents. The last time they sent a box of this size, it had been a bundle of products Tiffany didn't use. She still had some in her cabinet, taking up space, just in case they visited.

Tiffany became agitated when she read the name on the return address. The box was from her ex-husband, Brad. She was angry that he'd contacted her because he broke the solemn promise to never communicate with her again. For Tiffany, it was over, and she feared this package was an effort to reopen the pain from where she had recovered. Tiffany knew their divorce had been eminent, but the emotion of failure always burned her ego. The appearance of the box puzzled her. They didn't have kids or any shared assets, so there was no reason to communicate.

Tiffany arrived home still puzzled over the box. Her excitement had drained into procrastination once she realized the box's origin. There was nothing she wanted from Brad, nor was there any reason to receive anything from him. Tiffany retrieved a knife from the kitchen, went to the box, cut the tape, and freed the top lid. She pulled the crumpled newspaper out of the box, placed it on the coffee table, and viewed the box's contents, then frowned in disgust.

The box was filled with torn pictures of her and Brad in happier times. What stared back at her were at least a hundred images of herself, minus Brad. Tiffany moved the picture remnants and spotted a large brown envelope. She opened it and saw four documents inside. Upon closer examination she saw they were an attorney's letter, a will, a bank letter with an attached check, and a letter in Brad's distinctive handwriting.

She put the other items aside and focused on the bank letter. The check was made out to her in the amount of twenty-five dollars. She then read the will and found that a substantial amount of money had been willed to her and Brad from his great-uncle Robert. She saw the amount and decided to read the attorney's letter. She then re-read a page of the will and, when finished, she went on to Brad's letter.

What you think should be yours really isn't. I've deducted what I thought this cost me my career, minus the time I invested in you and the agony of you forcing me to leave before my opportunity knocked while you supported us. Here is a check for $25.00. I suggest you spend it well. You can't fight for the rest, as *you're not entitled to the money because it came after our divorce. I suggest you buy yourself a couple of drinks and celebrate having nothing more to do with me.*

Tiffany continued reading the will and contemplated her next move. She went to her computer and researched California's probate laws.

"He was a sweet man, and I had no idea he had so much money. No wonder he didn't believe I'd marry Brad. Uncle Robert knew of his nephew's ways. He told me not to do it. I should have listened. Damn, he knew his nephew."

She remembered Brad's uncle and how kind he had been to her, but was surprised that he'd left her anything at all. She thought hard about communicating with the lawyer. Tiffany knew she could use the money. She sat back in her chair and looked at the blank laptop, focusing on the screen as if it could forecast the cost of a lawyer.

She leaned her head to one side, paused, and tipped her head to the other side. She stopped staring and the numbers in her head disappeared. Tiffany knew the legal cost of fighting Brad would be more than she made in a month. *Is it worth it? Is fighting Brad worth the headache?*

Her first instinct was to let the money go and be done with him. She thought about how peaceful her life had become since the divorce. *I don't think I want to get involved with Brad just because his uncle left me a few dollars.* She rose from her chair and walked into the kitchen, looked into the fridge, but didn't grab a thing. She closed the refrigerator's door and returned to the chair she had just left. *I could use the money.* She shook her head and placed her head onto her palms, resting her elbows on her thighs. *I'm not so sure what to do.*

A Cyber Affair

Tiffany booted up her laptop, went to her email, and wrote Manny for his opinion. When she logged into her email, she read Manny's note and was surprised at all he revealed, so she quickly replied:

Manny,

Oh my God, you crossed paths with the devil! She seems to have seriously overreacted. No woman should blast another female. What the hell? I can't believe she did that to you. Manny, you showed a lot of class on your part. She was ungrateful and not your type after all. I am so sorry.

No worries about Suzie, she'll be fine once you explain what happened. I'm sure she's mature enough to see that her father means well. Besides, Suzie probably doesn't know how Camille behaves outside the coffee shop.

Today wasn't good for me, either. I received a box from my ex-husband that contained information about an inheritance. His great-uncle included me in his will as Brad's spouse, so we both inherited the money. I don't want to fight him, and it was after the divorce, but I could use the cash. Should I get a lawyer or just let Brad slither back under his rock?

Let me know what you think I should do. I value your opinion. The question is: do I open a can of pain or do I keep him out of my life for good?

Tiffany

She returned to her research after she sent the email. Tiffany read about a person's rights and again pondered whether the fight was even worth it or if she had the will to battle, questioning if it was worth disrupting the harmony she had finally achieved. Tiffany wanted a better quality of life, and having half of the money would help her move along with her financial struggle - but peace was more her choice, and she enjoyed the calm.

Tiffany flipped flopped on the idea of fighting or not. She stood up from the desk, walked to the window, and looked down the street. The house she had dearly loved came to mind. It was the very home she and Brad had shared; the same house she was later forced to sell because she couldn't afford it on her salary. Anger and frustration emerged as Tiffany moved to the package, grabbed a hand full of torn pictures, ripped them into smaller pieces, and then tossed them back into the box.

I wish I'd known this came from Brad. I finally had him in my past, and out of nowhere he returns. Why did you send this, Brad? she pondered, repeating the question in her mind. *Why did you?* Tiffany called Valerie's cell phone. Without a greeting, Tiffany blurted out her anger.

"That bastard just won't go away!" She yelled in the phone.

"Brad?"

"Of course, Brad. Who else?"

"What now?" Valerie knew how Brad had tormented Tiffany throughout their divorce. She stood by Tiffany during her challenges with his infidelity and financial hardships. Valerie was there during Tiffany's breakup, stood by her side when she had angry moments that had caused havoc, and was there the time she decided to accept the death of her life as she had known it. Valerie was her rock.

"He sent me a twenty-five dollar check."

"Why on earth would he do such a thing?"

"His uncle left us a lot of money in his will. He didn't know Brad and I were divorced, so I'm still listed as an heir."

"So he's saying twenty-five dollars is your part of the money."

"I get that, but why not hide it from me?"

"He wants to bug you the best way he can. Why else would he do it, unless the inheritance was a substantial amount?"

"According to the lawyer's letter, there is enough for me to get out of debt."

"Then you better do something to get that money!"

"Valerie, you know what I went through with that jerk. I don't want to go through that again. Money isn't everything."

Valerie waited before responding. She knew Tiffany well enough to knew how relieved Tiffany felt, being away from Brad's drama. Tiffany and Valerie had analyzed Brad's misbehavior - his infidelities and his wild/reckless spending – and realized his childish drama would never end. Valerie remembered how happy Tiffany been the day her final divorce papers had arrived. "Well, at least he's not in your pocket anymore and whatever was between you two is over."

"Yeah, I guess you're right. I better let the dead dog lie in his own crap. I don't need the headaches."

"I think you better check your credit records, just to be on the safe side. And leave his ass alone. Let Brad have all the money and finally say good riddance."

"You know Valerie, that's good advice. Good riddance, Brad: you can't make me angry. I won't allow it. Thanks, Val. I'll talk with you later, okay?" Tiffany ended the call, ripped the check into small pieces, and threw it in the box. She tossed the box into the trash. *When I needed money, he was nowhere in sight. I am on my own, and even though it's a struggle, I have peace.* On that note, she turned in for the night.

The next morning Tiffany sat up in bed, looked at her alarm clock, then turned it off. She planted her feet on the floor, stood, and went into the bathroom, thinking of the day ahead. Showered and coiffed, Tiffany then chose her outfit. She was happy she only had one job and not three jobs, as she had had while supporting Brad.

"It would have been nice to stay in bed, and I could do it if I accepted my share of the money. But is it worth it? I did the right thing," she whispered aloud, convincing herself it was the right decision.

By the time she'd gotten dressed, had breakfast, and checked her email account, there were only moments left for her to catch the bus. She put on her jacket, picked up her purse, and left the apartment, headed for the bus stop. When she got close, she saw Tom and sighed.

Tom spoke loudly. "Good morning, world." Tiffany didn't respond and looked at the ground, hoping he would take the hint. He spoke again, this time directly to Tiffany: "So you're ignoring me this morning?"

She didn't respond because she knew her response would open the door to a conversation she didn't want to have. But, on second thought, she didn't wish to be rude. "No, not at all. But couldn't you have said 'good morning' like a normal person?"

"Looks like someone's in a bad mood," he frowned. "You aren't yourself today. I think I'll stay in my corner."

"Today, that would be a good thing."

"So you are in a bad mood. What happened?"

"It's nothing worth discussing. Have a good one." She moved away from the waiting crowd and avoided a conversation with anyone else. Tiffany felt that silence was more than a treasure. When the bus arrived, she boarded it and went to the back for a seat, as if to hide from the world. Her mood was somber and her frustration with men was running rampant. She recalled the pain from her past relationships, from her father to her divorce from Brad. Men were not in her favor. She looked at Tom, and her anxiety grew. She considered using him as a target to release her anger.

Tiffany changed her mind and decided to get off the bus at the next stop and walk the rest of the way. She allowed her mood to overtake her sensibility; she didn't care if she made it to Macy's on time. She needed to walk, and felt it important to avoid Tom. She realized that Tom hadn't done anything to deserve her anger.

Minutes into her walk, she contemplated her decision not to claim her share of the inheritance. Though she had her doubts, it seemed like the right thing to do: leave Brad and the money alone. Her mood improved with her final decision and although her current attitude towards men was still guarded, her dream of having a lifelong love still resonated. She couldn't help but wish for a strong man in her life: someone who was well on his way, emotionally and financially. She fantasized about the man she'd love to meet and the life she had always dreamed of having.

When Tiffany arrived at the store, she went into her work routine and kept small talk with co-workers to a minimum. It wasn't long before her day ended. Her route home would reestablish contact with her fellow bus patrons. She decided to detour to a coffee shop and look for solitude while still trying to embrace her decision about the inheritance and daydreaming about her ideal man.

She ventured into the same coffee shop where she'd met Steven - the site of her disappointing date. Fortunately, it didn't deter her from enjoying the moment. She reminded herself that the guy hadn't been so bad, except for the one-sided conversation. Tiffany sat at a table, coffee in hand, and chuckled at her own thoughts. Within minutes her mood changed as she watched some amusing patron traffic.

Person after person entered the coffee shop and purchased coffee or some sort of pastry. She watched the influx of customer movements: at slow times, she could count on one hand the number of patrons who sat in the shop until it was again engulfed in a crowd of folks. One young man asked to share her table, and Tiffany gladly obliged.

She scanned him from head to toe and noticed every obvious physical feature about him: his hair, nose, eyes, and of course, how his chest was in proportion with his body. She assessed his age and guessed at his marital status. Before she could start a conversation, a young woman arrived, and he asked if it was it okay for her to join them. Tiffany knew her opportunity had ended.

After two hours she left the coffee shop to go home. Her mood had improved and she found herself eager to get on line, hoping for a positive email or note from anyone. When she logged into her email account, she found a few in-box messages and quickly looked over the list of senders, deciding to open Manny's email first.

Tiffany,

A Cyber Affair

Are you kidding me? You and your ex inherited money? Don't give up your share. Who knows how much you'll receive, but at least you get something. I read where you asked for peace, but wouldn't you like to be better off than you are now? I think money brings improvement.

So I guess my vote would be to claim what's legally yours. I dislike people who play games. I understand that having less stress in your life is a good thing, especially with an ex - so maybe you're right about walking away. God knows I don't like the situation with my ex, but since we have a daughter, our paths still cross occasionally.

Okay, enough of that talk. How was your day? I hope it went better than the tone of your last email. I'm sure you've moved on to some other adventure. I'd love to hear about it. I don't have much to share right now. I'm more concerned with you and the decision you face. Let me know what you decide. Drop me a line and share. I'm all ears.

Manny

Tiffany responded to Manny's kindness: he didn't judge or push - he simply gave his opinion.

Manny,

I see your point about the money. Thanks so much for the advice. I didn't think you'd feel so strongly about it. It's good you have that spirit. I will consider your suggestion. As far as my day, it was better, and I got a chance to enjoy a couple of hours at a coffee shop. My day ended much better than how it started. I wasn't much on conversation today, but I enjoyed your email. You made my evening.

Lonz Cook

Tiffany

Tiffany clicked 'send' and closed her browser, shutting down the laptop. She got ready for bed and eventually fell asleep. The next morning her mood was even better and she was thankful she had decided on peace. She flashed to Manny's last email and remembered his support ...*having less stress in life is a good thing; especially with an ex. It's as if he read my mind. Well, back to the grind.* With that, she returned to her daily routine.

Chapter 16

After spending hours on the job, when Manny arrived home, he jumped into the shower. He always liked to clean up before cooking. After he started dinner he sat at his computer and logged in to his multiple dating sites and email accounts. He found Tiffany's email and clicked 'open.' Manny didn't find her email response soothing. He thought she had given up too quickly, but understood that fighting for her rights would be difficult.

He agreed with her about being free from drama. He didn't like drama from his previous marriage or relationships either. If it weren't for Suzie, he would never interact with his ex-wife, but he had to deal with Cheryl until Suzie's college graduation. Manny was not comfortable being in Cheryl's company because of hard feelings and a mutual dislike that never seemed to settle down. Any interaction with her reminded him of their failed relationship. He understood that not having conflict with an ex-spouse was a gift. Shortly after he read Tiffany's email, he responded.

Tiffany,

Let's Skype soon. This email exchange is fun, but I think we have much to share on this subject. What do you think? If you agree, look me up with my email address on Skype. Send me an invite and I'll connect. We can catch each other online and share much more.

I too have ex-spouse drama and maybe we can share our ideas on handling situations when they arise. I know I need help and it seems you could use a guy's perspective.

Looking forward to your invite,

Manny

Manny left his desktop and went into the kitchen for a beer. He returned to the computer and found he'd received new emails. He clicked on one, which read:

I'm looking for a serious relationship. I'm a great friend, a fine lover, and a contributor. If you're interested, contact me at missfixter@pikeluv.com.

He deleted the email. *Too forward,* he thought, and selected another message from a dating website.

You're a handsome man. I'm here to find a man who is ready to settle down, get married, and create a family. I'm God-fearing and love the Lord, so you'll have to be a Christian. I think within six months we could be walking down the aisle. What do you think? Are you up for a serious relationship with marriage as the objective?

Manny shook his head in disbelief, deleted the email, and decided to clear all messages in his inbox. He couldn't believe how some women were so forward and direct.

When he finally shut down his desktop, he reflected on his Navy days and hitting ports of call. He knew how wild many guys were when it came to addressing women, and compared those years to today. *Times sure have changed.* Manny decided to hit a local pub to escape his empty home. He knew Suzie was upset with the way he and Camille had not connected. For the first time, Suzie's selection was an unforeseen mismatch at an unprecedented level, compared to any of her other introductions.

He realized that Suzie had gone out on a limb when she had introduced him to her boss.

After dinner, Manny dressed in jeans and a nice polo shirt, got into his truck, and drove to City Place. He pulled into the parking garage and climbed level after level, making it to the rooftop before he found a parking spot. He caught the elevator to the ground floor and walked to BB King's Blues Club. He saw people he had met and waved at a couple he knew, who were sitting on a bench along the path.

The night was typical for summer: a cool breeze and a clear sky with bright stars. He entered BB King's Blues Club, found a spot at the bar, ordered a beer, and opened a tab, watching people enter and exit. He struck up a conversation with a gentleman who sat a couple of stools over and together they spoke to a few women who sat nearby. The guys found both ladies interesting, and Manny took to one in particular.

She was slender in build, with smooth legs and a bronze complexion. Her unique features - high cheekbones, sensual lips, and a small nose - hid her ethnicity. Her eyes looked perfect to him, and her smile was gravitational. She wore a flowered tank top and jean shorts. Manny, being observant, took a good look at her legs on his way to the seat next to her. It was his complimentary stare that grabbed her attention. He was not sure about her height, but he figured she had to be around five foot five.

Manny smiled as he sat in the chair next to her and the other guy took the seat across from him. Manny made conversation by adding his say-so to any subject the four discussed. During the band's break, he attempted to get her personal attention. "Okay, we've talked for a while and I still don't know your name. I'm

Manny, and you are?" He extended his hand in a typical greeting. She took it.

"I'm Frieda, and this is Heather," she said, pointing to her girlfriend. "I'm happy you took this seat."

"Me, too. I had to meet you."

"Who's your friend?" said Frieda.

Manny looked at the guy he had just met at the bar. "Hey, friend, what's your name?"

"Ladies, I'm Jim. And you are?"

"Manny. Good meeting you. This is Frieda and Heather," he said, and followed with an explanation of his and his new acquaintance's decision to join them. "Jim and I were chatting at the bar and we both wanted to talk to you ladies. I hope you don't mind."

"If we did, do you think you two would be here?"

"Good point," Manny said.

They conversed on multiple subjects, laughed, and even danced. They had a pleasant evening and the fun ran into the wee hours of the morning. It was coincidental that Jim and Heather hit it off. Manny watched Heather lean close and share something with Frieda and the next thing he knew, Jim was saying farewell and passed Manny his business card. Frieda looked at Manny. "I hope you don't mind hanging out with me alone," she teased.

"I prefer just the two of us. This gives us time to get better acquainted."

"I guess so. Where would you like to go?"

"I have someplace in mind."

"Is it someplace we can talk without interruption?" Frieda looked into Manny's eyes and winked.

"I can think of a place with just that in mind." Manny blushed with a big grin while making his suggestion.

"I'm game. We can take my car - or would you like me to follow you?"

"You can ride with me. I don't mind."

Frieda downed the last of her drink and stood up. "Are you ready?"

"I am."

"I've decided I'll follow you," Frieda insisted. "That way I can leave without you having to make an additional trip back to get my car."

"It's no problem. I can take you to it. I don't mind."

"What if we don't hit it off? Will you still want to drop me off?"

Manny looked at her from head to toe, reversed his stare, and stopped at her eyes. He grabbed her hand and led her towards the parking deck. "I don't think we're going to have a problem - at least, not from my perspective. Can I have your cell number in case I lose you?"

"No, but I'll take yours, if you don't mind."

Manny stopped. "Do you have a pen?"

Frieda grabbed a pen from her small purse and said, "I never leave home without one."

Manny smiled as he wrote his cell number on the back of the business card he had just gotten from Jim and handed it to her.

"Okay, got it, thanks." Frieda stopped at the parking deck entrance. "It's comforting to have your cell number. Let's go; time is precious. Where did you park?"

"I'm on the top floor of the parking lot. How about you?"

"I'm on the first floor. I'll wait for you. I'm in a white Toyota Corolla."

They walked hand in hand until they got to her car. Manny noticed she didn't stumble although she had been drinking most of the evening, and he was very impressed with her body. Earlier, he had dared to stare at her while she danced with her friend. It was his habit to notice a woman's body, especially when they were close. Unlike his forward behavior of the past, Manny didn't want to make a comment or seem like the aggressor looking for intimacy. Instead, he held on to his initial thoughts of her body and looked at her in a way that he thought would send an enticing signal.

While they had been talking and dancing, he thought of using her sexy body for his pleasure. With her hand in his while walking to the parking garage, he occasionally brushed closer to her, which let him feel her body. And at one point, on the main street, he placed his arm around her waist as if to publicly claim his prize. He admired her soft, smooth hands and appreciated her butt every time he let her to step in front of him for whatever reason. Manny was excited and thought about how he would enjoy a night of sexual indulgence.

"This is my car." Frieda stopped just short of the white Corolla and pulled out her keys.

"Okay, good, now I know what car to look for." Manny extended his hand for her keys and accepted them as she dropped the key ring. He unlocked the door and opened it for her.

"Thank you. I haven't seen that move in a long time."

"You're welcome."

Manny barely gave her room to enter the car and when she stepped towards the opened car door, he pulled her into his arms and kissed her deeply. She responded and held on for a second kiss. She threw her purse into the passenger's seat just as she broke the embrace, and before Manny could turn to leave, she clutched his ass and pulled him back to her. "Not so fast, we've just started."

Her lips explored his, which Manny took as an indicator of pleasurable confidence. She pulled him tighter and started to grind her hips against him. Manny loved it and happily reciprocated. They kissed for what seemed like ten minutes, longer than Manny usually spent making moves on new prey, and yet he enjoyed the display, which crossed the line of acceptable public affection.

They ignored people who passed by and behaved as if they were all alone. When Manny finally broke the embrace, he had gone beyond excitement. His erection throbbed in a battle to escape his jeans and his mind focused on ideas of how he would release his sexual tension. "We need to go to my place to continue." Manny jumped in her car. "Don't worry about my truck. I'll pick it up tomorrow."

"Are you sure?"

"I'm more than sure." Manny buckled in and gave instructions. "Turn left after you pass the cashier's booth."

"Okay, and then?"

"Once we get to Highway One, turn left again. I'll give you directions from there."

Frieda followed his instructions and drove to Manny's apartment. When they arrived, Manny jumped out of the car and hurried around to her door, opened it, and took her hand. She turned off the engine and stepped out of the car, with his assistance. Frieda looked over the apartment complex. "Nice-looking place."

"Yeah. I like it. I hope you enjoy it tonight."

"Something tells me it's not all I'll enjoy."

Manny led her to his apartment door, opened it, and they went inside. He brought her close, placed his lips on her neck, kicked the door closed, and moved his lips to hers, kissing her with interest and enticing her with a maneuver of military envelopment. She sighed, broke the embrace, dropped her purse, and pulled him close again. They kissed with increased intensity, removed their pants, then dropped his shirt (and her tank top) on the floor.

Manny lifted her into his arms and carried her to his bedroom. He laid her down, grabbed a condom from his nightstand drawer, and returned to Frieda without hesitation. He kissed her navel, moved his lips near her nipples, circled them with his tongue, and caressed her upper body with one hand while he balanced himself with the other. She grabbed his head and pulled him down so that their lips met for another sensual kiss.

Frieda took control. She peeled off her panties and bra, then mounted Manny, laying on top of him. She caressed and massaged him with her body and played with his erect, imprisoned penis. She grabbed his shorts, pulled them towards his ankles and released the towering statue of impression, then maneuvered her body into position, placing her vagina on his lips while her mouth watered excitement. She licked his erect penis.

Without hesitation, Manny obliged and explored her hardened clitoris with his tongue, took one hand and tapped her buttocks, and thrust his pelvis upward to get depth in her mouth. He felt invigorated, surprised, and accomplished. He helped her achieve an orgasm and allowed a spurt of cum to flow from himself - a trick he had learned from spending many nights in liberty ports. Manny embraced her body and brought her to her knees, rolled the condom on, and without a moment's hesitation, slammed his penis into her moist vagina. She yelped and he rode, thrusting fast, slow, hard, soft, deep and shallow; all mixed in without a specific rhythm. Just as he paused to change the rhythm again, she pushed back, as if taking over.

She clutched him strongly, wiggled him to her g-spot, and climaxed. As soon as she stopped clutching, he rolled her onto her back without pulling out completely, then pushed further into her again. This time he stroked hard and strong, as if he were dancing to the rhythm of a Latin beat. He pushed, moved side to side, and pushed more, kissing her roughly and caressing her right breast.

Manny felt Frieda change her composure and press back to him, meeting his rhythm and opening her body to his every thrust. He pushed, she bucked, and together they climaxed. She slowed her movements, but Manny continued to stroke in hopes of a second erection. He moved as he softened, and dared to stop. Frieda responded but when she saw he remained limp, she stopped moving and gently pushed him off of her.

"Lay on your back," she instructed. Manny followed her directions and watched Frieda position herself in front of his face again. This time she straddled his chest right below his chin, grasping the headboard. "Come on, big boy, you know what to do."

Manny grabbed her ass and pulled her to where his tongue waited, entering her as if he were a guided missile in enemy territory. She moaned while he tongued her. She moved and he explored. He felt her body shake and saw goose bumps on her skin. He didn't stop until she let go of the headboard and fell onto the bed, unmoving.

"That was intense," Frieda said, short of breath.

Manny lay there for a moment and didn't respond. He waited for silence and allowed her to slow her breathing before he said, "Yes, it was. Are you ready for round two?"

"No, I'm good."

"Can I get you something to drink?"

"I don't think so. What time is it?

Manny looked at his watch. "Nearly 3 am. What time do you normally wake up in the morning?"

"Around six, and that's why I've got to go."

"Go? You aren't anxious for round two at sunrise?"

"I'll take a rain check. Maybe next time."

"Next time? Sounds like a plan," he smiled.

Frieda pulled her tank top over her head, "Hey, I don't think there will be a next time."

Surprised at her comment, Manny responded, "Did I do something wrong?"

"No, but I have to be honest with you."

"Are you married?"

"No, not married. And I'm not looking for a commitment. I needed you, I needed to feel a man and release my built-up pressure. You did that for me."

"So, I'm your one-night stand? We can't plan something for next week, like maybe a walk in the park?" Frieda walked to the door and Manny followed as he slid his jeans on. "Can I call you sometime?" Manny asked, surprised that her motivation to leave came so abruptly.

"Man, are you that out of touch or what?"

"I was trying to be kind. I know most women want some way to keep in touch."

"Those women want something serious. I'm not interested. It's not that you're a bad guy or bad-looking, but I'm not ready for a relationship. I got what I needed, so it's time to go." Frieda kissed Manny once more and whispered, "You were perfect, and I have your number." She collected her bag and quickly walked out of the door without looking back.

Manny stood in amazement. For the first time in his life, he felt like those women he'd left in multiple seaports around the world. *Now I get it.* He locked the front door and went to his bathroom.

Chapter 17

On Monday morning, Tiffany rose from her bed for another work day. She had enjoyed the weekend with Valerie and they had had fun without focusing on men. She was happy the new week had arrived and her excitement came from a renewed attitude. Her walk to the bus stop was joyous as she realized that the past was just that: the past. During the journey she noticed those simple things that made her life great.

The location where she lived, its accessibility to public transportation, and the lovely people who owned those small mom-and-pop shops for quick goods and services - all these helped her embraces her move from suburbia. She was a few steps closer to the bus stop when she saw Tom, and before he could say anything, Tiffany greeted him. "Good morning, Tom. How are you?"

Tom was taken aback by Tiffany's greeting. He looked at her with raised eyebrows, remembering their last encounter and unsure if he should speak or move away. He stood firmly, positioning himself with a powerful response: "Good morning."

Tiffany approached Tom and looked at his face, hoping to connect to his eyes. "I'm sorry for the other day. I probably scared you when all you were trying to be was a friendly, positive person. I was having a bad day and I took it out on you. Please accept my apology. Sometimes we girls just don't know who to trust, and we retaliate on whoever is nearby. It wasn't fair to you at all."

"It wasn't, and I accept your apology." Tom halfheartedly smiled.

"Good. Are you ready for your day?"

Tom glanced at her, hesitating to respond. "I'm as ready as I'll ever be," he answered.

"Then it's going to be a good day."

"I'm sure it will."

Silence fell between Tom and Tiffany while they waited at the bus stop. When the bus arrived, they took seats at opposite ends with Tom in the back and Tiffany in a seat near the front. As the bus made its stops, she smiled at every patron who boarded it. Once her stop came, she disembarked and transferred to the cable car.

Tiffany smiled during the entire trip, recognizing the beauty of San Francisco. For being a typical morning, she felt an unusually positive vibe amongst the people in the street. It was a perfect day and Tiffany enjoyed feeling the purest emotions free from the fear of financial failure or the challenge of work. She brought that energy with her into the store.

Tiffany did her usual routine: clocked in, went to her locker, and read the assignment board. She noticed she had been reassigned. Instead of working in the perfume and makeup department, she would be working at the men's fragrance counter. Tiffany smiled, knowing that this improved the possibilities of interacting with gorgeous man. The best retail area to meet men in the store was men's clothing, but cologne was surely a close second.

Her assignment led to multiple interactions with customers of both genders. After lunch, a tall handsome gentleman walked into her section. Tiffany stopped what she was doing to gaze at him from behind a cabinet. Her mind went right into a fantasy of the two of them sharing simple words before his lips found hers in the store's dressing room. She watched him pace in her section as if he were on a mission to discover a new path to paradise.

His cologne danced among women he passed in the store. It beckoned the weak of heart and dangled in their nostrils as bait portending a fiery excursion. He walked in a strong, masculine, but graceful manner. He was dressed in a fine tailored shirt which perfectly fit his well-defined physique, his faultless butt invited views, and Tiffany could see that he attracted interest from the women who spied him from a distance. On the third pass he stopped in front of a new brand of cologne. When he looked up from the glass case in response to Tiffany's "May I help you?", he revealed brown piercing eyes as he spoke with a smooth, melodic voice: "I'm looking for *Dane* by that singer. I can't remember his name."

"I know which one you're talking about. I'll get it for you."

Tiffany nodded her head and left the counter to retrieve the item, and once her back was to the customer, she softly patted her chest as if catching her breath from a fast sprint. She returned with the cologne in a bag and placed it on the counter. After he purchased it, she handed him the receipt, and when he reached for the paper, she gently grabbed his hand and looked him in the eyes. "Could I interest you in anything else?"

"Not at the moment. Thank you."

Tiffany took an extra step to complete the transaction: she slipped a few samples of other colognes in his bag. "I added a few samples of our latest colognes. I hope you don't mind."

"Thank you." He smiled and gave Tiffany a wink before he left.

She couldn't believe how she'd damn near melted in his presence. Girls from the other counters came over and teased her enviously. "Did you get his card or number?"

Tiffany responded to their question by fanning herself, as if recouping from the heat of the moment. "No, but I have him in my memory." Her work day ended, she left the store for home.

During the ride home she daydreamed of the sexy gentleman customer. Once home, she changed clothes and sat on her bed with her laptop. Every time she came across a picture of a handsome man on the internet, her thoughts returned to her encounter with the handsome customer at work. He wouldn't leave her mind long enough for her to focus. Her body began to ache as she wondered what would have happened if he could have taken a moment to get close to her.

Tiffany closed her eyes and tried to shake the vision in order to concentrate on reading her emails. When she opened her eyes again, she came across one from Manny and clicked to open it. It was his invitation to Skype. Though she knew what Manny's looked like from his profile picture, it was her customer who held her mind's attention" her thoughts flared and her imagination and desire to interact with him roared.

Her memory swept over his face and body; his lips, eyes, chest, and his butt. She remembered his voice and movements. She imagined her head on his shoulder and her lips touching his neck. She thought of gentle kisses that led to greater things. Her imagination raced to where he grabbed her, lifted her in his strong arms, and carried her into a private chamber reserved for the passionate elite.

Tiffany fell back on her bed as if being positioned by her imaginary lover. Her mind dreamed about his touch and his lips, and she pictured him removing his shirt. She stripped off her clothes, reached into the nightstand drawer for her vibrator, and imagined his muscled body all over hers while she held his excitement in her hand, preparing her body for his hard penetrator of adulation. She licked her fingers before circling her breast, focused on the nipple, and with pleasure in mind, gently cupped her breast and squeezed it.

Tiffany moved the vibrator on a direct path and stopped short of her clitoris. She rotated her hips, tilting her pelvis toward the tip of the vibrator, and barely touched it to the top of her erogenous hot spot. Her heated blood roared in her ears, with the handsome man in her mind's eye moving his hands up and down her body.

Her imagination was so intense that she felt him explore her body with his tongue, kissing all the right spots. With a quick flick of her thumb, the vibrator came to life on medium speed. Tiffany gave it a push and explored the point of her enjoyment. Within minutes she felt a thrust of pleasure and then a hardening sensation that drove her to want more. Before she realized it, her finger had clicked the vibrator to its highest speed. She bucked from touching her key to excitement and the intensity drove her wild and into a powerful climax that shook her with a vengeance.

Tiffany then tossed the vibrator onto the bed, turned the vibrator off, and crossed her legs, soaking in the relaxed feeling to be had after an intense release. Her mind and body pleased, the fantasy of her customer faded and a deep slumber attacked her as though she had just received a full-body massage.

Tiffany awoke early enough the next morning to jump on her laptop before work. She viewed a few web pages, searched for the cologne her fantasy lover had purchased, and glanced at the models on the page. It pleased her to have had an imaginary lover who helped her achieve such a peaceful state of mind and body. With a click of the mouse, Tiffany entered her email account. This time she read Manny's note and paid attention. Skyping was new to her, since she didn't instant message much outside Yahoo or MSN. After she researched the program, it took her 10 minutes to download it, register, and create an account. She wrote Manny to let him know of her success.

Manny,

I opened a Skype account under my email address. Look for my invitation. I am anxious for our first visual chat and maybe a voice call.

Tiffany

A news popup from the local newspaper San Francisco Gate directed Tiffany to its website where a story grabbed Tiffany's interest. Titled "Mother Commits Suicide Over Fallen Soldier," she read the horrible mishap of a mother who took her life out of grief over her fallen son. After she finished the story, she ate breakfast and read the latest news, fashion, and sports. She closed the laptop and flashed back to the encounter with her sexy customer. Her thoughts of him improved her mood and motivated her to get herself together for work. Soon Tiffany found her mind and body back at Macy's on mid-shift, where she worked her usual location. Periodically she would tour through the perfume and cologne counters with the intent of meeting a magnificent specimen of a man.

Chapter 18

Manny clocked out, went to the gym for an hour and a half, and then headed home. When he arrived he saw a sticky note attached to his door and a box from UPS on his stoop. He picked up the box, took the note, and headed inside. There was coffee and a book in the box - the specialty coffee and unique book he had purchased for Camille. She had returned her gift with a note: *I don't accept shit from assholes.* The package surprised him, and without calling her every name under the sun, he calmly shrugged his shoulders and jumped to his laptop.

Minutes into the evening, he opened his email in hopes that Tiffany had replied. He quickly peered through his inbox and clicked on her response. *She said yes!* Manny smiled while he read Tiffany's email and clicked 'yes' in response to another Skype friend request. He stopped surfing and chanced contacting Tiffany by sending her a conversation box invitation. He knew for sure she wasn't home, but got a response: *Hey, I was just looking for you!*

Puzzled, he paused before he responded. *Are you there?* popped up in the box, indicating the other person's lack of patience. *Yes, I'm here. Is this Tiffany?* Manny typed, unsure with whom he was chatting. He remembered his 'yes' to a Skype invitation.

I can be anyone you like, the person answered.

I'm sorry, I must have made a mistake. I won't bother you. He became convinced that whoever was answering was not Tiffany.

No bother. I'm looking for a man. You're a sexy looking hunk. I want someone who will take good care of his woman. You know, the man who cherishes every moment, creates a love worth having, and wants to start a family. Is that you?

Manny couldn't believe his eyes. *What the hell? Sounds like a pick-up line used in some seaport.* He typed, *I bet you've been heartbroken many times and the men weren't worth your time. They don't understand you.*

Messenger: *How did you know?*

Manny: *'Cause I've heard the same pick-up line, lady. I'm not interested.*

The woman sent a downloadable picture file. *Open the picture and tell me, after you've seen it, that you're not interested.*

Curiosity overtook Manny's distrust. He opened the picture. He was startled at the woman's aggression, but not surprised at her second effort.

Manny: *I've heard of people like you, pretending to be someone they aren't. How do I even know you're a woman? Who sends a partially-naked picture? I bet this picture isn't you. The next thing you'll do is ask me to webcam with you.*

Messenger: *Actually, I want to know if you'd like me to dance or strip for you. It won't cost you, big daddy.* She added a smiley face.

Manny: *You are wasting my damn time and yours.* He closed the chat box, deleted the screen name from his contact list, and decided to find Tiffany using her email address. Unfortunately, he didn't find her. He thought she had set up her Skype account and sent a response, but he didn't see it. *Man, she's worth waiting for.* He sent her a note with the friend-invite in the Skype request, making it easy for her to respond. I hope she comes on tonight.

Chapter 19

Tiffany arrived home late that night. She had met Valerie after work and attended an art gallery show. Valerie admitted she wanted to introduce her to one of her new acquaintances.

"Again Valerie…really?" Tiffany said while they walked towards 49 Geary Art Galleries near Union Square.

"Don't do that, Tiffany. Don't get on me about my views about men. You'll see. Trust me."

"Okay, okay, I trust you," Tiffany sighed under her breath. "Is this the place?"

"Sometimes I wonder about you. I love you to death, but at times you burst my bubble and then start asking silly questions. Yes, that's the place, Tiffany."

"Bugger off, as my friends across the pond would say," Tiffany giggled. Valerie gave Tiffany a puzzled look. She knew her best friend could see their destination, since the gallery was well marked.

"Come on," Valerie directed, and stepped inside. The gallery's entrance was impressive. The Works on Paper was the first showcase (it involved the creative use of newspaper clippings contrasted to images and thought-provoking symbols). Valerie directed Tiffany's attention to that section because her new acquaintance had identified a piece of work that, he boasted, was excellent. They looked for her friend's show and since it was not on the first or second floors, they took the elevator to the third floor.

Tiffany and Valerie heard the sounds of faint music as the elevator rose towards their destination. When the doors opened, music from a three-piece jazz ensemble greeted their ears. A guy dressed up in black from head to toe stood in the middle of the crowd. He was in direct view of the elevator. Both Tiffany and Valerie looked at the statuesque picture he presented. His shirt was accented by elegant silver cufflinks and opened to the middle of his chest, where a silver dog tag necklace dangled to contrast against the shirt.

Tiffany knew that this man was Valerie's new friend. She was impressed with his slender build and exquisite demeanor. He commanded attention, and Valerie confirmed Tiffany's assumption. Valerie coaxed Tiffany to follow as she approached him with a huge smile.

"JT," Valerie called. He turned in their direction with a sparkling smile. His pristine veneers added to his perfection. As Tiffany got closer to JT, she noticed that his hair was immaculate, without a strand out of place. It was as if he had just left his barber. Every ounce of him exuded charm; down to the simple silver ring, large enough to share a unique English design of his initials, on his left pinky finger. He reached for Valerie with his open hand and took hers when she got within reach.

"Valerie, I'm glad you made it."

Valerie said, "I wouldn't have missed it for all of the money in the world." She smiled and kissed him on the cheek. JT responded and looked at the woman standing in front of him. He hadn't included her when he first greeted Valerie, but he nodded his head towards her now, acknowledging her presence. JT smiled and moved away from Valerie.

"And who is the lovely woman with you?" asked JT.

"Where are my manners? JT, this is my friend, Tiffany."

"Pleased to meet you." JT reached out with an open hand and attempted to make Tiffany feel at ease. When he touched her, he felt a spark of electrifying energy, and quickly pulled away. He said, "Do you always have this effect on people?"

"What do you mean?" Tiffany dropped her hand and looked surprised.

"I felt a shock, and it can't be static electricity. The floor doesn't have carpet."

"She shocked you?" inquired Valerie. "You aren't trying to come on to her, right?"

"No, Valerie, I'm not that type of man. I haven't gotten to know you yet." He looked at Valerie with seductive eyes hinting at the inevitable. "You and I have a lot of dancing ahead."

Tiffany glanced at Valerie with eyes that questioned the veiled comment. She gave a slight nod of approval and, without words, warned Valerie to be careful, but encouraged her to have fun.

"Aren't you going to show us your work?" Tiffany said.

"Of course, come with me." JT led them to the far wall. "This is my favorite. It's called 'Trouble in Paradise.' What do you think?"

Valerie saw a personal message in the picture and smiled.

"I'm your trouble, aren't I?" JT grinned, and without hesitation he approached Valerie, reached for her cheek with his hand, and gently kissed her lips.

"I can only imagine," he whispered.

His actions caused Tiffany to sigh and move towards the next painting as Valerie walked to the other side of the open room for a closer look at a painting that had attracted her attention. Tiffany stopped at a wall picture that appealed to her: an abstract of a field of flowers which reminded her of a place she had visited as a child. Tiffany looked at the painting's cost, and the sticker price shocked her. *If I fought Mr. Jerk for the money, I could buy this painting.* She stared at its brilliant colors and distinctive lines and revisited the idea of having enough money for a comfortable life. She focused on the myriad of colors and meditated on the painting's message while she stood in front of it. Those pictures spoke to her; a whisper to her spirit, as if guiding her to another place in time. For a moment she saw her body lying in the field of beautiful flowers.

"Excuse me." JT interrupted her subconscious journey.

"Yes?"

"I couldn't help myself when I saw this. I took the picture and then painted it. It's inspiring to the spirit."

"You know, I felt its influence." Tiffany paused, looked around, and said: "I'm surprised Valerie isn't with you. Where is she?"

"Walking around, I guess. I had hoped she would be near you. I came to find her."

"Last I saw of her, she was with you."

"Let me formally introduce myself." JT extended his right hand. "I'm Jorge Tanksley - that's Jorge with a J."

"Jorge Tanksley, it's nice to meet you again. I hope you don't mind me asking, but how do you get the 'J' from George?"

"Good question. It's from the Latin spelling of George, J-O-R-G-E and it's pronounced 'hor-hay' in Spanish."

"Family ties, I guess. Different." Tiffany took a step towards the next painting.

"Why are you alone this evening?"

"Who said I'm alone? I'm with Valerie." Surprised at his question, she looked for Valerie. "Hey, did Valerie send you over here to be a matchmaker?"

"No, not at all. I noticed you looking like you were missing someone; so much it's painful to watch."

"Oh, you have *got* to be kidding. That isn't a nice thing to say to a woman."

"Nice or not, is it true?" JT inquired with a solemn scowl, and waited for her response. Tiffany found his assumption to be pushy and said, "Don't you think it's a little too early in our conversation to reveal something so personal?"

"No, I don't think it's personal when you project a lonely persona in public. You see, some men can read your projection and tell if you're approachable. He'll know if you're open to his flirting, and even if he'll strike out. I know you're lonely because so many men have struck out."

"This isn't going well. You just told me I'm a cold bitch. Come on, JT, can't you find anything nice to say about me?"

"I thought I was. I'm not intentionally trying to offend you. I'm sharing what I see. You don't often find people who are honest and who would tell you their opinions."

"It's time we find Valerie - or, better yet, you find her and let her know I'm heading home. And the next time you feel free to share your opinions and call someone a cold bitch, let it be with a woman who asks for it, ASSHOLE!" Tiffany rushed through the gallery and out to the street.

Valerie caught up with JT after she got a glimpse of Tiffany's departure and asked, "What happened?"

"I guess Tiffany got a taste of reality, that's all."

After she entered her apartment, Tiffany logged onto her laptop, went to her bedroom, and changed into comfortable clothing. She returned to the laptop and sat on the couch, still huffing in anger, and surfed one web page after the other while fantasizing about finding JT on the street and pummeling him with her purse. Tiffany's sixth sense told her that Valerie had done it again: not only had she involved herself with a man she barely knew, but she had managed to drag Tiffany into it.

That damn Valerie, Tiffany thought as she reflected on Valerie's excitement. *She's at it again, dreaming of a new beginning with too much blind energy for JT. I'll have to pick up her pieces like I always do. JT is a disrespectful ass. How could he see me as a lonely spirit? No way; I'm not that damn desperate!* When Tiffany logged into her email account, she read Manny's message.

Tiffany,

Join me on Skype. I sent you a link, so it'll be easy. I'm excited to chat with you. I have lots to share and I hope we can reflect on the silly events of life. I'll be waiting.

Manny

Tiffany clicked on the link in Skype, unsure of what had happened to her invitation. A window appeared and she typed her initial message:

Hi, I'm finally here. She waited for a response.

Manny typed, *Hi.* He smiled, and his fingers kept moving.

I'm here, and it's nice seeing you on Skype.

Tiffany: *What a day I had. You won't believe the comment I received from this asshole I just met.*

Manny: *Really? I hope it wasn't that bad. I'm sure no one can say anything bad about you?*

Tiffany: *Men should feel ashamed of themselves, these days. They feel as if they can say anything to anyone. It's annoying.*

Manny: *I get the same feeling with some women, especially those who don't pay attention to the man who makes an extra effort.*

Tiffany: *It's not that they don't pay attention, it's that you're not giving them what they want.*

Manny: *So it's those guys who aren't getting what they want from you, who say dumb things?*

Tiffany paused and thought about how they were stereotyping men and women. She wrote: *No, that's not right; we shouldn't stereotype people. I'm just upset that an artist called me "lonely", and he'd just met me!*

Manny: *It was a pick-up line. I wouldn't worry about it unless you like him.*

Tiffany: *I didn't think of it that way. Maybe it's because he's supposed to be interested in my girlfriend.*

Manny: *Some men try for the prettier friend when he sees them for the first time - or something like that.*

Tiffany: *No way; men don't do that, do they?*

Manny: *And women don't? I've known a few who did, and who would still do it today. As a matter of fact, I married one. I was the better-looking guy in the bunch.*

Tiffany: *That's a conceited comment. I bet each member in your group thought he was the best-looking.*

Manny: *LOL. I thought you wouldn't catch that.*

Tiffany: *It's good to laugh, now. Life's been so hectic lately.*

Tiffany and Manny conversed for an hour, shared additional events from their day, shared family histories, and laughed about their horrible past dates.

Manny: *Hey, Tiffany, it's time I turn in. I have to work in the morning, and I'm not getting any younger.*

Tiffany: *It was nice chatting with you. I have to remember that you are three hours ahead. Talk to you again soon. Sleep well.*

Manny: *You too, and thanks again for accepting the Skype request.*

***

Days later, Tiffany rose from slumber at dawn. It was early for her, although she was not scheduled to work at Macy's until 10 a.m. She took advantage of her time, pulled out an exercise DVD, and gave it the old college try. As she finished her workout and prepared to get started with her day, she thought of her chats with Manny on Skype through the entire morning. Although she reflected on life, her mind stayed on Manny and compared his twenty years of traveling around the world to her dream of seeing Europe.

Tiffany always wanted to travel, and it was her dream to do it with her husband at her side. She remembered a statement Manny had written: *I married what I thought was a wonderful woman until she snatched my heart out from my chest.* Tiffany related to that very feeling. It was exactly how she felt when her husband had admitted that he had had an affair.

On her way to the bus stop, she concluded that she envied her new chat friend. He was the father of a daughter in college and he put a lot of effort into building their father/daughter relationship. His positive energy was also impressive. *How nice is that?* Tiffany analyzed how the chats with Manny intrigued her. She especially liked his cooking and dance club stories. Last night she had used a recipe he'd recommended, and put together a dinner she thoroughly enjoyed. Tiffany smiled, grabbed her things, and went to Macy's for her day of employment.

Tiffany was so into her work at the store, focusing on the new inventory, that she lost track of time and worked through lunch. She hadn't felt the urge for food, though her mind anticipated the conversation she and Manny would enjoy after she arrived home. When she finally clocked out, she rushed to her dwelling, jumped onto her laptop, and signed in on Skype.

Manny: *How was your day?*

Tiffany: *Fine, I was so busy! I tagged and hung new inventory. That shipment was huge because we're getting ready for the new season.*

Manny: *Cold weather has never been my friend.*

Tiffany: *It doesn't get that cold here, but its cold enough to start a fire in the fireplace and use an electric blanket.*

Manny: *Winters are warm here. I'm sure you know this. But in the fall, during hurricane season, we can get a lot of rain, sometimes, when a storm passes through.*

Tiffany: *I'd take a storm any day over freezing. I'm such a warm-blooded person these days.*

Manny: *I'm sure you'll find the right kind of warmth in the future. You are such a wonderful woman. I've never had so much fun chatting with anyone.*

Tiffany: *You know, I've really enjoyed our chats. I wish you weren't so far away.*

Manny: *Distance is always a battle.*

Tiffany: *Yes it is.*

Manny: *I know how we can get closer.*

Tiffany: *Are you planning to move?*

A Cyber Affair

Manny: *No, not at all. I'm thinking of finally making use of this Skype invitation. It's time we tried, don't you think?*

Tiffany had feared that their emotional connection would lead to that question. She liked his conversation and the way they shared history, family stories, and long discussions. He was so open with pictures; from which she knew that he was a handsome man. *What's the worry? He's three thousand miles away. What can it hurt?* she thought.

Manny hesitated as she pondered if she should agree to his invitation, and just when he started to recommend they do it another time, Tiffany responded: *Yes, let's video cam.*

Manny backspaced his text, and wrote *AWESOME!!!* and sent another invite. Tiffany clicked 'accept' and Manny's picture appeared on her screen.

"Can you hear me?" he asked as he waved, in the video.

"Sure I can," Tiffany responded. "I hear you just fine."

"How's the picture?"

"Fine. Can you see me?

"Yes, I can," Manny said, and smiled while he viewed Tiffany for the first time. "Pictures do you no justice."

"Thank you. I can say the same about you."

"You're kind. So, what were we typing about?"

Tiffany stared into the laptop screen. "We were saying how much we enjoyed our chats."

"Oh, yeah, that's right. I enjoy your conversation. I bet men compliment you on your voice."

"You don't remember that conversation? We talked about my men."

"I'm saying that those who listened to you had to enjoy it. I mean, a person's voice is unique and says a lot about them."

"What does my voice say to you?"

"You're lovely, exciting, admirable, witty, and strong."

"My voice says all that? Wow, I must be saying too much." Tiffany watched Manny's expression and waited for a response. "I got you on that one."

"No, you didn't. I'm sure you have ideas on what you should and shouldn't say to a person. Especially someone you meet online."

"You know, Manny, it's not like you're going to jump on a plane tonight and be here tomorrow." Tiffany covered her giggle with her hand. "I'm sharing just enough. Don't you think?"

"No doubt, just enough." Manny paused, shaking his head, looked at the desktop, and then raised his head, catching Tiffany's eyes. "What about me? Do you see as much in me?"

"I see a lot in you, Manny. It's because you've shared so much about your life. I was thinking about that today. If you weren't so far away, we'd probably have something together."

"Tiffany, we *do* have something. We're on Skype video camera together now. How many other men have you video called?"

"You're the first. I don't do long-distance."

"Oh, that's right," Manny paused. "Should we stop to keep your sanity?"

"It's too late for that. I could learn to enjoy this."

"Enjoyment. Good word," Manny smiled, showing Tiffany his best feature - his teeth. "Now, that's what you should do the next time we chat. Show me a huge smile."

"The next time?"

"Yes, the next time; because I have an early morning tomorrow. I'll call you when I get home."

"You don't have my phone number."

"No, silly; I'll video call you on Skype tomorrow."

"Oh, okay. Sleep well, Manny. Enjoy the night. Catch you later."

"You too, my friend; you too."

***

Tiffany watched Tom walk past her without saying a word. His silence surprised her and he didn't seem to be his usual smart, energetic self. She walked to Tom and stood next to him, comparing his countenance to other times at the bus top. She noticed his lower bearing - a shift in his posture. Tiffany looked at his face and said "I, ah…" stopping in mid-sentence because there was no response. She hesitated to say another word, frowned as she looked toward the ground, then raised her head to see if the bus was arriving yet. She looked at him a second time, crossed her arms, and held her tongue so as not to say what was on her mind. *Should I ask him how he's doing*?

The bus arrived and she boarded it, moving to the back, and sat in the center of the last row. She watched him find a seat and noticed that he hadn't said a word to anyone. His stony gaze reflected loneliness.

Something is really different about Tom, Tiffany noted, watching him until he left the bus. She walked behind him to the cable car stop and as they stood waiting for the next cable car arrival, she decided she had gone long enough without speaking. Tom looked her way, acknowledging her presence.

"Hi, Tiffany."

"Hello, Tom. Are you okay?"

"I'm fine."

"No. I'm asking: are you okay? Tom, what's wrong? Are you ill?" Tiffany looked concerned. "You aren't as playful or loud as usual."

"You think I'm loud?"

"'Loud' may have been harsh, but today you're different. You're not the same man I've come to know over the months we've taken this bus."

"I didn't think you'd notice."

"Really, Tom: how couldn't I notice? I think you nearly asked me out the first time we met. I only stopped you because you're married."

"Well, I'm not married anymore, but I'm still not asking you out."

Tiffany gave him a look of surprise and placed her free hand on her hip. "Did you get divorced?"

"Not at all. I loved my wife. I loved her with all my heart. I was only trying to get you to meet her."

"Loved your wife? Did she leave you?"

"You could say that."

"No wonder you've changed." Tiffany placed her hand on his back.

"It's nothing like that, Tiffany. It's not what you think."

"I'm here if you want to talk about it. I won't push you to share, but if you ever need an ear…"

"Thank you. I may take you up on it."

Tom stepped onto the cable car and took a seat in the middle. He didn't say good-bye to Tiffany - he just left. She was shocked at his behavior because he wasn't acting like the gentleman she had seen before. *Man, that woman took his soul.* She went to work with Tom on her mind, then called Valerie on her cell phone to share her morning experience.

"Valerie, remember I told you about this guy on the bus? There's something seriously wrong with that man."

"Yes, you mean the married guy?"

"That's the one: the nice guy who's always a gentleman. He had it all; good humor, great looks, and a decent conversation."

"Yes, did he finally ask you out?"

"Valerie, you forget I don't do married men."

"I know, but why are you talking about him, then? What was his name?"

"Tom, Valerie. Tom. His name is Tom."

"Why now? You aren't going to go out with him, so why bring him up?"

"Listen, and don't jump to conclusions. Something is wrong with him. I can't place it, but he said his wife left him."

"Well then, there you go. Opportunity knocks. You should pounce while you can."

"No, not at all. The wind has gone from his sail."

"Tiffany…why would you want a man in a bad frame of mind? Don't you know all you can offer is to be the transition woman?"

"You aren't listening again. Something is wrong, and I wouldn't date a broken man."

"Maybe he's the type for you after all. You don't like men who are energetic or well put-together. And you surely don't like creative types."

"Valerie, you're spinning my wheels. I'll talk to you later."

"Later, then." Tiffany returned her focus to work, finished her day, and hustled to the bus stop. She had high hopes of seeing

Tom again, and her nervous energy nearly drove her to find him. She looked in every direction. Tiffany thought about walking to his office, but she'd never asked where he worked or even inquired as to what he did for a living. When the cable car arrived, she stepped on and looked for Tom. He wasn't there. She watched for him at every stop until hers, exited the cable car, and waited for the last leg home on the bus. When the bus arrived, she searched for him amongst the passengers on the bus just like she had on the cable car. Once home, Tiffany poured a glass of wine, sat at her laptop, logged in on Skype, and immediately opened a video cam connection to Manny.

Tiffany asked, "Hey, are you around?"

Manny responded, "I am. How are you?"

"Remember Tom, the married guy I told you about who I nearly dated? He seemed so lost today."

"Nearly dated?"

"He's married and I don't do married."

"Oh, he was flirting. How do you know he was serious?"

"He was, I'm sure of it."

"Okay, so you didn't date him. Why are you telling me about him?"

"Because I saw him again today and he seemed so lost. Usually he's bubbly; a jokester who's always bringing attention to himself. Today, he hid in public."

"That's a big difference. Maybe he had a bad day."

"He said his wife left him."

"I know that feeling well. He's grieving and it shows. He didn't want her to go."

"I had no idea men grieved over failed marriages, too."

"Come on; we're human and we feel. Most of us don't show our pain. This guy is showing his. I should take his man card."

"Man card?"

"Yes, his man card - for showing pain in public over a woman."

"Are you that barbaric? I thought you were more sensitive than the average guy."

"I am, just not in public."

"See, now I've learned something else about you." She paused. "You have no feelings for your fellow man and then you seem to hit Tom hard when he's down. I'm shocked at you, Manny."

"You have to understand my life in the Navy. I've seen death and hardships and have experienced trouble most people never think about. I did what I had to do without letting my emotions get in the way." Manny waited for a response, hoping his explanation wasn't too harsh. When she didn't say anything, he uttered, "I guess it's still with me."

"So, in essence, you ignored what your heart told you."

"Let's say "rechanneled", because the pain is always there. It's like memories of the worst day of your life: those days can seem like yesterday."

"You don't forget?"

"I don't think it's possible to forget. But, back to your friend. Reach out to him. He may need a friend or a listening ear."

"That's a good suggestion. There is hope for you, Manny."

***

When Tom arrived at the bus stop, Tiffany was already there. She had fallen asleep with Tom on her mind. She had decided to follow Manny's advice to reach out to him. She stood at the side, away from the growing crowd of regular patrons, and approached him at a good spot just shy of an earshot to the others.

"Good morning, Tom," Tiffany smiled, eager to get a conversation going.

"Hi, Tiffany. How are you?"

"I'm glad to see you this morning. I noticed you came from a different direction. Did you take a morning stroll?"

"Not exactly. I went to breakfast."

"Alone?"

"Thanks for reminding me."

"I'm sorry. I meant no harm."

"None taken."

"I'll tell you what: if you ever need someone for a conversation or a companion to go with you to breakfast or lunch, just give me a call. I would love to join you."

"I'll remember that. It's kind of you to offer."

"I mean it." Tiffany pulled out a business card from her purse and wrote her cell phone number on the back. "Here, keep this and call whenever you like."

"Thanks," Tom replied, and placed the card in his pocket. Tiffany noticed that he didn't even look at it.

"Well, off to work we go. I'm supposed to do inventory when I get there. I hate inventory."

"I don't know what I'm doing today... if I do anything at all. I can't seem to get back into a groove, and my guys at the office are covering for me. I know I'm not pulling my weight. They're such an encouraging group."

"I think it's great that they're supporting you after your wife left. I never knew men could give that kind of support after a breakup." She turned to enter the arriving bus. Tiffany's face wrinkled in puzzlement as she took a seat near a window and invited Tom to sit with her.

"So tell me, how did it happen?"

"How did what happen?"

"Your wife leaving you."

"I'd rather not talk about it, Tiffany. Right now, I'm better off just focusing on going to work."

"I remember when my husband left. He was such an ass. I only wondered if what she did was extreme."

"I said...I'd rather not talk about it."

"Okay, let's talk about something else. I haven't seen you for a while. I thought you'd taken a different job."

"No, I went to Baltimore for a few weeks."

"Baltimore - a city I've always wanted to visit. Does it get cold there?"

"Winters can be harsh, some years. Others aren't so bad. It's colder than here, I'm sure."

"San Francisco gets cold. But you're right, it's not cold like the East Coast." Tom didn't respond and sat in silence for a good part of the ride. Tiffany couldn't bear the silence. She wanted Tom to share.

"Why are you so unhappy?" she asked.

Tom looked at her just as the bus stopped at the cable car connection point. "I guess I'm not supposed to be happy right now. How can you be happy when your whole life goes bad?" He stepped off the bus and onto the curb.

Tiffany followed. "Well, aren't you going to finish your thought?"

He looked back. "I just did." He turned towards the direction of his job. "I think we'll have to catch up another time."

Tiffany walked by his side, trying to keep up with him. "If you say so. Remember: I'm available to talk or have dinner. All you have to do is ask." She slowed to her normal pace and watched him create distance between them. Tiffany walked to work and looked at her surroundings, considering what she could do for Tom. His demeanor was eating at her soul: the friendly, outgoing man was merely a lifeless, functioning body now. Tiffany remembered what Manny had suggested and his words ate at her like a worm eating at her soul. It bothered her enough to push her mind into a frenzy of thought.

When she got off work, she couldn't wait to get back home. Inventory had been as frustrating as she imagined it would and she just wanted to get off her feet. She went to her favorite spot on the couch and booted up her laptop.

Tiffany heard her phone while she was checking her email and messages, but Before she could answer it, the ringing stopped. She looked at the caller ID on the screen and didn't recognize the number. Tiffany avoided answering the phone with numbers she didn't recognize, and therefore she thought nothing more of it. She returned to another Skype video conversation with Manny.

Manny: "I remember my tour of duty in Italy. What a place. Naples was a charming city and full of history."

Tiffany: "Italy? Sounds lovely. What did you do?"

"Believe it or not, I went to cooking class. Southern Italian cuisine. What an experience."

"I bet you can make one hell of a dish."

"Yes, I can. Maybe one day I'll get a chance to show you."

"I'd like that. What else did you see in Italy?"

"I visited Rome, Florence, and Milan on long weekends. It's a country you'll have to visit someday. The trains make it easy to get around and the people are very nice. I mean, *really* nice. Oh, and the gelato: wow!!!"

"I would love to travel there one day. I've always wanted to see the Vatican."

"It's breathtaking."

"The Navy had to have been a lot of fun for you. I can only imagine what else you experienced."

"It was a good life, but you sacrifice so much."

"Yeah, you told me. Family is a big sacrifice. I know you traveled a lot, but look where it got you." Tiffany hesitated before she put the words out there that could turn the conversation sour: "No wonder it's hard for military folks to have a family."

Manny wasn't surprised at her comment - instead, he agreed. "Yeah, it's hard on military families. Just like anything else, there are successes." Manny touched his chin. "For some, it's a mess from the start; but for others," he smiled, remembering a fellow Chief who had a very successful relationship with his wife and kids, "I'd say it's not so much of a challenge. I've seen both sides of the coin."

"And you were on the side that lost their family?"

"No. I mean yes, I lost my family, but I gained respect from meeting the perfect woman. You need her to have a great marriage and have a good family. I think a good marriage is a family's backbone."

"I see your point. Do you think you would ever marry again?"

"At this point in my life, I think I would. She'd have to get along with my daughter, though. I'm not sacrificing my kid anymore. I did that for way too long."

Chapter 20

Manny didn't expect Tiffany's response to his Skype invitation would lead to such intense conversations. His enthusiasm grew after he realized she was a genuine woman instead of just a pretty face and sexy voice. She was nothing like he had thought, from her pictures and emails. He admitted that her voice was unique, sensual, and soft, but also powerful and elegant at times, when she projected a sensitive moment. *Impressive. Too bad she has that "no long-distance relationships" rule,* Manny thought while he drove to his job. *I'm out before the race starts. Oh, well.*

By the afternoon, Manny had gotten three calls on his cell. Suzie's message was first, reminding him of their weekly dinner and that she was coming alone. The second call came from an old Navy pal with whom he had shared earlier days as sailors on board the aircraft carrier USS Eisenhower. The third call was from a woman; a familiar voice that he couldn't quite place. "Hi, I'm available for a drink tonight - are you interested?" Manny wanted to wait until he remembered the face that matched the voice before he returned the call. By the time he had narrowed his choices, it was quitting time. He went to the gym for a workout session, and his cell phone rang.

"Hello."

"Hi, Manny, how are you?"

"I'm doing okay. How about you?" Manny managed to connect the earlier phone message voice to the person on the phone. "I'm sorry I didn't get back to you sooner."

"I'm good. It's all right that you didn't. So, what's the verdict: are you free tonight?"

"I would say so. Refresh my memory. I recognize your voice, but I can't put a face or name to it." Manny admitted his lack of memory while he looked at his puzzled expression in the gym's mirror.

"It's been a while. I wouldn't expect you to remember me. Just know that we had a blast together."

"That doesn't really narrow it down, I still don't know who you are. Can you give me a better hint?"

"You'll find out if we're meeting. I'm sure you'll recall me, then."

"Okay, we can meet. Let's say at 9 tonight. That gives me time to finish my workout and get dressed. Are we having dinner?"

"We can. Actually, I'd love to."

"I know this great Italian place on US 1. We can meet there at 9 and enjoy a light dinner."

"I never heard of anyone referring to Italian as light." He heard her chuckle. Manny looked at his watch to confirm that he could make it on time. "*La Sirena* is the name of the place. I can text you the directions."

"I know the place. Good choice."

"Awesome, see you there." Manny drove home and after a quick shower, he changed into something presentable - a dark dress shirt and tan slacks, dashed cologne on his face and neck, and made it to *La Sirena* fifteen minutes early for his mystery date. He got a table and waited for her arrival. The table was perfect for observing whoever entered the restaurant. By 9:15 no one had showed and Manny got the waiter's attention. He ordered a glass of wine and asked if there were any specials on the menu. His date arrived at the door while his face was deep into the

menu. When the waiter asked him for his order, he dropped the
menu and looked to the front where a beautiful woman with
unforgettable features stood. He smiled and his heartbeat
increased with surprise. Manny excused the waiter, stood, and
waved, grabbing her attention.

She walked to the table with a seductive grace. "I told you
that you'd recognize me."

"You sure did. My goodness, you look great." Manny hugged
her.

"Thank you. You're not so bad yourself."

"Forgive me, but I can't recall your name." Manny pulled out
a chair for her. He remembered meeting her at BB King's Blues
Club over a month ago. She was the one who had wanted total
control.

"I think I told you to call me Frieda."

"You think? Isn't that your real name?"

"Of course not." Her smile broke the awkward moment. "I
don't give out my real name until I'm comfortable with the
person."

"No kidding? So you're finally admitting me into your inner
circle?"

"Yes I am, or I wouldn't have asked you to meet me."

"Okay, I get it, but it's not fair. I don't know who you really
are." Manny watched the waiter bring his wine order. "Can you
bring the lady a glass?"

"Yes sir, and will the lady be dining with you tonight?"

"Of course." Manny listened while the waiter gave Frieda the
menu specials, and then they both ordered. The waiter opened the
bottle of wine and gave Manny a taste before getting another

glass from the bar. He put the second glass down and Manny gave him a thumbs up.

"Thank you. It's delicious."

"Your dinner will be out shortly," the waiter confirmed before leaving. Frieda and Manny sat at the table in silence and then, in unison, they both spoke.

"What's happened since...?"

"I'm sorry; you first," Manny apologized.

"What's happened since we saw each other last?" asked Frieda.

"Before we go any further, I'd like to know your actual name."

"In time, Manny, you'll learn my name. Be patient and you'll discover my identity before you know it."

"Discover your identity? The mystery woman wants me to be patient, and she's in control. Do you know how difficult that is? That's like asking a pit bull not to eat a slab of steak sitting in front of him."

"I'm glad you consider me steak. Am I prime rib or roundhouse?"

"A smart-ass, too," Manny sighed. "This is going to be an interesting night."

"Yes, it is. I want to make it extremely interesting."

"You aren't thinking what I'm thinking, are you?" Manny asked.

"Well, I was thinking that after dinner, we can enjoy *us*."

"Not quite what I had in mind, mystery woman." He looked in her eyes, hoping to find truth. "Even though I like the way you think, I was going to suggest that we play a game. You could tell me if this is a setup to make your husband jealous. I wouldn't like getting shot for being with someone's wife."

"I'm not married, so you don't have to worry about that." Frieda took a sip of her wine. "Are you game?"

"I'm game to discover you. It's one thing to have a one-night stand and not know the person's identity, but to repeat it without knowing makes me uncomfortable."

"What if you discover it little by little? I'm not ready to disclose everything about me, yet."

The waiter returned with dinner and filled their wine glasses. "Can I get you anything else?"

"No, thanks," Manny said, and looked at Frieda, waiting for the waiter to leave the table before saying another word. "Now that we're alone again, what's your game?"

"Enjoy the moment, that's all I ask. I don't want anything: no relationship, no responsibilities, and no worries."

"I get it. No expectations - but it's too late. You've opened the door of curiosity."

"Let's say I cracked that door because I want consistency. All I ask is that when I call you, please try to be available."

"That leads to the responsibility of responding to your needs."

"And what's wrong with responding to my needs?" Frieda eased back in her chair and touched her mouth with the napkin. "Don't men do it all the time?"

"You're asking me to be like a mistress?"

"You have to be in a marriage to have a mistress, but I get the point. No, I was hoping to just keep it simple. If you aren't interested when I call, just say so. I won't bother you."

"Okay; so it's nearly friends with benefits without a friendship. We're just a couple of people who want to have sex."

"Sex is part of it. I want fun, too, and as I remember, we danced and enjoyed the time we spent together when we met. Going out with girls all the time is fun, but every once in a while it's nice having a man around."

"Especially when it's time to get that itch scratched."

"Who says that isn't an objective?" Frieda grinned and gazed into Manny's eyes.

"I see. Kind of works out for me. I'm in," Manny offered his hand and shook hers in agreement. When their hands touched, he pulled her closer and kissed her lips. "Now we agree."

"Thanks. That's what I like about you. You aren't afraid to show affection in public."

"I sure hope you aren't married," Manny reiterated. "I'm a stickler for feeling a sexy woman at every opportunity."

"This sexy woman loves being felt. I knew you'd be perfect."

Manny and Frieda went on with their little escapade. On their way to Manny's apartment, Frieda flashed her car lights, turned around, and drove to the Wal-Mart Shopping Center near the airport. He made a U-turn and followed. He found her Toyota parked amidst cars at the far, dark end of the lot. When he pulled in beside her, she motioned him to get in. To his surprise, she'd stripped from the waist down and instructed him to do the same.

"Here, use this." Frieda handed him a condom.

"I see you're an exhibitionist, too."

"Any arguments?"

"No; it just reminds me of being a teenager. The difference now is I don't get excited just from thinking about sex. I need encouragement."

"I can take care of that."

Frieda reached across his lap and pulled the lever to make the car seat lie flat. She quickly maneuvered her lips around the pleasure instrument she wanted to excite, slurping, bobbling, and licking him until it became erect.

"Slide on the condom," she ordered while getting into position to mount his stretched smile maker. She intended to ride him as if she were bareback on a pony. Manny added to the excitement and thrust as hard as he could once he entered. He knew that roving security could interrupt their session; he clutched her by the waist and tried to block her image in the car window to keep them from being obvious to an onlooker. The car bounced, its windows fogged, and in minutes Frieda was screaming at the top of her lungs.

"Yes! Yes! Yes! God, yes!" When it ended, she collapsed into his arms. They lay silent, heavily breathing, sounding like they had completed a hundred-yard dash at full speed. Frieda got up and reached into her glove compartment. "Use this handy-wipe to clean up."

"Talk about chance. Don't you know we're pressing our luck at getting caught?"

"I need the thrill and love spontaneity. I knew I could convince you to go along."

***

Manny arrived home and immediately went online. He invited Tiffany to a Skype video call.

Manny: Hey, call me when you get home.

He reduced the chat window and sent Suzie an email with plans for a father-daughter weekend getaway. Since he had retired from the Navy, he and Suzie often spent quality moments together and shared events to catch up on what he considered to be lost time.

When they had visited during her childhood, there was a limit to their time together because Cheryl had her daughter transitioning to a new dad. If Manny had an opportunity to travel with Suzie, her mom would shorten their visiting time. So they spent extended weekends doing fun things like amusement parks, seasonal professional sporting events, and shopping, which enraged Cheryl because it made Manny seem like a typical fun father while George, her current husband, took the role of the mean disciplinarian. When Manny tried to discipline Suzie, Cheryl would defend their daughter and scold him about his views on training and child development. Manny couldn't win at any cost.

He had found a great travel package for Spring break and wanted Suzie to take one week of her break to head for Cancun, Mexico. Manny felt they should go together, and during their travels he, too, could have some fun, enjoy the scenery, and explore the Caribbean Riviera. As he inserted website links and finished the email, Tiffany came online and the Skype indicator flashed an acknowledged message.

Tiffany: *I'm here Manny. Are you still available?*

Manny: *Let's video call.* He invited her via the video connect button. Manny waved when Tiffany's face appeared on the screen. "Hi."

"Hi, what's up?"

"The strangest thing happened to me tonight."

"Really?" Tiffany placed her hand on her face. "What happened?"

162

"I went out with this woman once, but never got her contact information. She... well, you know, got busy with me one night. I hadn't run into her again. So, out of the blue, she calls and wants to meet. After dinner she took me to a parking lot for some wild passion. You know, it was weird because it took me back to being a teenager. We're too old to get caught for indecent exposure."

"It sounds like she's looking for a friend for fun. I don't think she would risk it unless she trusted you."

"Interest and trust are the least of it. And I've never had anyone treat me like that." Manny grimaced at his last comment. He realized he might have shared too much.

"A man of your experience finds himself in a new, mind-blowing situation. Swimming in uncharted waters?"

"I am, and I don't know how to take it . On one hand, it's like a compliment; but on the other hand, it's dangerous because of the unknown."

"What is she doing that makes it dangerous?"

"She won't tell me her name and wants me at her beck and call. I have the alternative not to take part, of course, but it's the hiding I don't feel comfortable with."

"Manny, you shouldn't fear the unknown. Obviously, it's excitement for her. She's doing whatever makes her feel wanted and empowered."

"You may have a point. I don't know how to handle not being in control or not being able to call when I feel like calling."

"You have control, Manny. Didn't she say you don't have to participate if you weren't interested? She doesn't want a commitment; she just needs you just be there when she wants you."

"You make another good point. I don't have to play whenever I feel it's not worth it. The control is different, in this case."

"She's out for a good time; that's all. I don't know why she's hiding so much, but it reminds me of a married woman having fun."

"She said she wasn't married," Manny replied.

"Did you notice her hand? Was there a ring, or some sort of a ring mark?"

"People wear jewelry. I did see rings, but not a diamond or wedding band."

"Okay, then you're safe; but keep in mind that some women do those things and never let the man in on the secret."

"Yeah, I'll keep my eyes open for signs. That is, if and when she calls and I get a chance to rendezvous with her again. Let's change the subject. How are you, these days?"

"Oh, I'm not bad. Working and living. Nothing out of the ordinary is happening. I took your advice and talked to Tom. He hasn't opened up enough for me to know what happened between him and his wife, but I'm going to find out. There's got to be some way I can brighten his mood and change him back to the Tom I met instead of the way he is today."

"Be careful with that, because some men don't like women to pry. Let him come to you and don't be pushy. He's probably needs closure before getting on the bike again."

Tiffany noticed that Manny touched the tip of his nose. "Did something bite you?" she asked.

"What do you mean?" said Manny.

"You messed with your nose."

"Oh, I think it's a pimple."

"You're still a teenager," Tiffany chuckled.

Manny and Tiffany talked for another hour, bringing up living habits, jobs, and ideas. They agreed on some cities in the United States that each would like to visit one day. They both agreed that Las Vegas was the number one city they wanted to experience.

Tiffany waited for Manny to disappear from Skype before logging off. It was her habit to be the last one online, just to make sure she got the view she could remember. Manny was becoming her norm and she enjoyed looking at his handsome features.

Chapter 21

After Tiffany snapped her last memorable view of Manny, her cell phone rang. She looked at her caller ID and didn't recognize the number. Again, it was similar to the one she hadn't answered earlier. She decided to answer this time.

"Hello."

"Tiffany? Hi, how are you?"

"I'm good." Tiffany slowly responded. "How are you?"

"I'm good, except that I can't seem to get you off my mind."

"Who is this?"

"I'm a guy you met weeks ago, and I hoped it would be okay to call."

"If I met you just weeks ago, I would recognize your voice."

"I was with your friend, Valerie."

"You were with Valerie when I met you." Baffled, Tiffany tried to place their meeting.

"Yes, you were with Valerie when I met you, but I seem to have said something that rubbed you the wrong way."

"Damn, JT."

"You got it. Why the damn? We can't be cordial before you get angry?"

"Why are you calling me?"

"Hold on, Tiffany. I called because I wanted to surprise Valerie at an event and thought you'd give me some insight, or help me with guests."

"You intend to surprise Valerie. Hmm, that would be nice. How did you get my number? Why didn't you leave a message the first time you called?"

"I got it from Valerie's cell phone, and I usually don't leave messages. It's just a bad habit of mine."

"Okay, what do you want to know? I may be able to help."

"I was thinking about surprising her at my appreciation party, for no other reason than to get her friends together with mine."

"JT, are you serious about Valerie? Is that what I'm getting from you?"

"Yes, she's my golden woman and has the best spirit I've experienced in my life. She's the star of my night, the joy in my song, and a vision of beauty I see even when she's not in front of me."

"I know: sweet words can get you everywhere with her."

"Can you help me?" JT waited for a response and when Tiffany didn't answer, he asked again. "Will you help me?"

"Sure, let me think about what Valerie would like. Is it a surprise party?"

"Yes, it's a surprise for her, but not a surprise party." JT paused waited for a smart remark and then asked, "When do you think you can share those names and addresses?"

"Give me a week. I'll call you and then you can text me your email address."

"That's fair," JT responded, and then explained why he wanted to surprise Valerie. "I have to create something unique for Valerie." JT found his new interest adorable, vivacious, and energetic beyond the usual women he dated. He went on without Tiffany saying a word. "It was our trip to Napa Valley that got me. She undoubtedly connected to my spirit; a special energy that I never felt from any other woman. We hiked on a hillside in the vineyard and had a breakfast picnic where we watched the morning change from cool to the heat of noon. Another time, we went to Angel Island, walked along a path until we got tired, and then sat on a park bench and talked until the last ferry. Valerie is awesome: she posed for pictures and I'm enjoying making an oil painting of her. She impressed me by embracing my lifestyle and considers me a true artist."

"JT, I'll help you. I've never heard anyone explain deep feelings in reference to Valerie." Tiffany fell silent and waited for a response. "Are you there?"

She heard a muffled sound like he was holding his hand over the phone mic. Tiffany thought she heard another voice right before JT spoke. "I have to run. Thanks for your help." He ended the call.

Tiffany couldn't believe what JT had told her. She had known when Valerie met JT that their girl time would abruptly end, but they still occasionally talked on the phone. It's what usually happened when one of them became involved with a man. Valerie hadn't mentioned JT much during their last conversation, which ideally meant something more was happening. Tiffany called Valerie on her cell.

"Hi," Valerie answered.

"Hi, what are you up to?" Tiffany said.

"Not much today. Hadn't heard from you lately, is everything fine?"

"Valerie, I think we should have lunch tomorrow."

"I don't know. Let me see what JT is up to. Hold on." Valerie clicked over and called JT just to make sure they had nothing planned. She clicked back to Tiffany. "What time?"

***

A Cyber Affair

Tiffany arrived at the coffee shop ten minutes earlier than Valerie. It was the same coffee shop where Tiffany had had her date with Steven, the narcissist from hell. Today the crowd seemed warmer and friendlier than before. People shared tables and entertained each other with small talk. When Valerie arrived, Tiffany stood and greeted her with a hug as though she were a long lost friend.

"What gives?" Valerie said.

"Nothing. I'm happy to see you. It's been a while since we've had a chance to share." Tiffany smiled. "So start sharing."

"Share what?" Valerie smirked with her response. "You know me so well." She giggled like she was hiding a happy secret in her purse.

"Come on, we've been best friends for years. I know that when we don't talk for an extended time, it's because one of us is dating. But when we talk, it's like we've never stopped. So spill the beans."

"He's awesome, kind, sweet, and a gentleman. The only thing is he doesn't have is a lot of money."

"Valerie, you know we've gone through the money phase. Isn't there more than money to worry over?"

"Not with him. I mean, we've found a simple connection and lifestyle. We don't overextend ourselves and we don't risk going too far into the fancy life San Francisco offers. You know, we don't club too much, or dine at five-star restaurants, but I have to confess that I've enjoyed every moment with him. I'll sacrifice those finer things for a great time with him."

"Wait, my Valerie makes sacrifices?"

"Come on, Tiffany, this guy is different. I wouldn't dare hang out in every park around the city, listen to street entertainers for hours, or go vegan for just anybody."

"You're not eating meat? Are you serious?"

"Right now, I'd love a hamburger." Valerie laughed. "I'm serious. I was hoping you'd say a restaurant on the wharf instead of here."

"I'm sure you'll get a hamburger soon. So tell me, who is this man of influence?"

"JT, You remember. You screamed at him when you met him. I never understood why."

Tiffany didn't want to discourage Valerie, and loved how happy she seemed. "He made a smart-ass comment about me being lonely that didn't sit well with me."

"You want to share?"

"No, not really. It's all good. You look so happy."

"Yes, I am…somewhat."

"Somewhat happy … why would you say that?"

"Well, he always has other women around. One day I walked in on a naked woman in his studio. What I didn't get is why she was the one who got angry when I arrived. Suddenly she went on the offensive. She gave me a scornful look and asked me why I was there. Another time, he disappeared for a couple days - no call, no text, nothing. He came back and said he had gone to the mountains to find inspiration. The third crazy thing he did was invite a third person to our private party."

"You mean a sexual encounter private party?"

"No, Tiffany, it was a fancy dinner - which we rarely do."

"That upset you? You had a chance for meat and it didn't go as you liked?" Tiffany laughed.

"It's not funny," Valerie giggled. "And to make matters worse, she was vegan, too."

"Okay; outside of being a vegan, what don't you like about JT?"

"He's perfect for me. Though I like everything other than his eating habits, he's got to let me be me when it comes to food."

"I didn't know being a vegan was one of his requirements. Didn't you tell him you enjoyed a good steak in the beginning of your relationship?"

"I certainly did not."

"Which means you haven't come clean, yet."

"Okay, you should know that I did claim to enjoy the vegan lifestyle, but I would go home and indulge every so often. I've given it a serious try, but I'm craving a hamburger."

"Okay, we'll get you a hamburger - but if you like JT so much, you will have to come clean with him soon."

"After my burger, I'll spill the beans. I promise.

***

Tiffany returned to her apartment, got online, and wrote Manny an email after her attempt to catch him on Skype.

Manny,

It's wonderful when people find love. It's like there is a fire burning inside and a vibrant aura circles them. It is mind-blowing, especially when one of your closest friends finds love - you always wish them the best. My best friend found love and I'm so happy for her. I had to share.

Hope to catch you on Skype soon.

Tiffany

Chapter 22

During work hours Manny had a strict "no-calls" policy (except for Suzie), so he hadn't answered Frieda's call. When he got to the gym, he listened to his voicemail before changing. "Hey, meet me at Calder Race Course around 7 and text me when you arrive."

After a fast workout session, Manny drove to Calder, sent Frieda a text to let her know he had arrived, and waited for a response. What he couldn't believe was how quickly she showed up, riding a horse, with one in tow. Manny jumped out of his truck and looked at Frieda, who was dressed in a riding outfit complete with jodhpurs, boots, hat, and a button-down blouse.

"Look at you…and you can ride, too. Very impressive."

She dismounted and approached him. "You know how to ride?"

"It's been years, but I catch on fast."

"Here." She handed him the reins. "She's a good horse and very gentle, so don't be rough with her."

"Sounds just like a woman." He raised his left eyebrow and laughed.

"*Some* women." Frieda frowned, mounted her horse, and waited for him to do the same.

Once he was in the saddle, she kicked her horse into a trot, and when he followed her close enough, she and her horse moved into a full gallop. Manny tried to keep up as best he could, but he rocked from side to side and held the stirrups with his legs, like pressing lunges in the gym. *Man, this is going to hurt,* Manny admitted to himself. Two minutes into the ride, he noticed Frieda was slowing. Manny took advantage of this and caught up to her.

"I like a man of many talents," Frieda shared. "I can only imagine what other talent you have in that body."

"I get the funny feeling you have something in mind, and you're about to find out."

"Yes, I think your funny feeling is right." Frieda smiled and pointed to the stable. "Follow me over there."

"You're the boss," he said, and did exactly as she told him. The night was falling and Frieda had plans. She stabled Manny's horse, took off its saddle and bridle, and then closed the stable door. Manny held the reins for Frieda's horse and observed her changing her clothing.

"You know how to take off a saddle?" she asked.

"I think so. I remember doing it some years ago."

"Gently remove the saddle and set it on the wall over there," Frieda instructed.

Like a good sailor, Manny followed instructions. By the time he hung up the saddle, Frieda had gotten into a sun dress, placed a condom in the hat that she used for keeping her hair in place, and mounted the horse bareback.

"Jump on."

"What?" He couldn't hide the surprise in his voice.

"Come on, it's going to be fun."

She helped him mount the horse and sit behind her. "Now, hold on." Frieda kicked the horse into action and together they exited the stable area. She guided the horse down a riding path into Calder's wooded area and stopped, giving Manny the reins while she turned around to face him and then leaned forward, placing her arms around him and positioning her legs over his.

"Don't kick her, and feel me close," she whispered.

Manny kept the horse moving and felt the move that Frieda made on him, which was the opposite of what he had expected. She rubbed against him, and it worked wonders on his manhood. Next, he felt her lips on his, her thighs rubbing majestically in rhythm with the horse's stride, her hips pressing forward.

"Let's go over to the bush so you can you put that thing of yours someplace that makes me happy," she instructed.

Manny smiled, tugged the reins, and stopped the horse when they arrived at a secluded spot in the woods. *She's one amazing woman*, he thought.

Frieda pulled a condom from her hat. "It's time we put this on," she said, giving Manny a smile of excitement.

Manny moved lightning quick, lay flat on the weeds, and stripped his jeans in time for Frieda to roll the protection onto his protruding sperm shooter. "Let me straddle you," Frieda said. She wiggled to angle herself on Manny for a direct entry and kissed him, pulling him up so she could sit in his lap and straddling him while she nibbled on his ear lobe. Frieda felt a warm sensation, raised her legs, and placed them around his neck.

"Rock me," she insisted. "Lift me up and down."

Manny increased the rhythm with his thrust, just like Frieda wanted, and lifted her slightly without exiting her. She squirmed to hold on so as not to lose the feeling. Manny felt incredible, but when his concentration dwindled, he climaxed right after she found her pleasure point.

"Stop," she commanded, and repositioned herself when she turned around with her legs parallel to Manny's. "Can you get that up again?"

"I can try."

"Please do."

The two maneuvered rear entry, and Frieda got him to help her movement.

Manny released a second time and Frieda stopped moving when she felt her second orgasm.

"I don't know where you get your ideas, but I love the experience," said Manny.

***

Manny returned after his evening excursion. He jumped in the shower and heated up some leftovers for dinner from the refrigerator. After he had surfed the net, he saw Tiffany's email, and without losing a moment, he read it. Happy that she had written, he responded:

Tiffany,

One day we'll find that feeling; the feeling of sharing, and the excitement of giving and receiving. You know: the deep emotion where you whisper I love you while your partner's sleeping. I want this bad enough to create a life of tomorrow that follows me to the grave. When the right woman comes along, it's going to be remarkable. Hats off to your best friend; she found it.

Manny

Manny didn't try to Skype - he was tired and felt compelled to relax. He turned in earlier than usual. His legs were throbbing and pain shot from hip to ankle. *I knew riding horseback was going to hurt.*

Chapter 23

Tiffany was successful in her efforts to get closer to Tom as she pestered him to get over his situation. Tom had still not explained why his wife had disappeared, even though Tiffany felt that he wanted to. She knew it was difficult for him to share information. Tiffany tried to show him a great time in multiple environments: though Tom fell short of her shared excitement, by the fourth outing he and Tiffany broke through his wall of despair and made progress. For the first time, Tom allowed himself to feel happy. It wasn't a huge milestone, but it *was* an accomplishment.

Tiffany called him one afternoon, and he invited her out to an evening of music. She accepted his offer and accompanied him to an after-hours event which was being held by the symphony. The size of the crowd and the age of its attendees stunned her: she had always thought the symphony was for senior citizen types. When the quartet took a break between sets, a couple who were acquaintances of Tom's greeted him.

"Hi, Tom," the man said, holding a drink in his hand.

"Hi John…Emily." Tom returned courtesies.

"How's the music tonight?" Emily raised her glass. "We've been here just long enough to order a drink."

"It's fantastic," Tom said, and followed with an introduction. "Let me introduce my friend. This is Tiffany," he nodded towards her.

"Tiffany." Tom touched John on the shoulder before he said, "Meet John and his wife, Emily."

"Nice meeting you," Tiffany said, and shook their hands. "How long have you known this guy?"

"Tom? Maybe a few weeks at the most," replied Emily.

"We met at a function like this and had a great time," John added.

"I'm glad I left my townhouse that night. The walls were closing in and I had to get out." Tom admitted. "Those nights seemed to happen more and more, back then."'

"It's good to hear that you took my advice," Tiffany said, and smiled. "It speaks volumes about our friendship."

"*You* got this mug out here?" John said jokingly.

"I got him somewhere," Tiffany bragged. "He was a hard case after he broke up with his wife."

John and Emily gave Tiffany an incredulous look and then they turned to Tom with a surprised stare.

"She doesn't know," Tom commented.

"Doesn't' know what?" Tiffany said, puzzled. She looked from Tom to John and Emily and back at Tom.

The quartet started another set and the roar of voices dwindled while music took over the room. The group played for twenty minutes, and at the end of the event, Tom placed his empty glass on the tray near the exit door. Tiffany followed, and couldn't wait to hear Tom's explanation about why John and Emily had looked so surprised.

"Are you going to tell me?"

Tom moved to the side, pushed the door open, and allowed Tiffany to walk through. He quickly followed. "I was going to explain it to you at a different time."

"Explain what to me? Is it about your breakup?"

"I didn't have a breakup."

"You're still married. Damn you, Tom." Tiffany frowned.

"No, Tiffany, I'm not married - well, technically I'm not." Tom sighed and walked towards the bus stop. "The fact is...I'm a widower."

Tiffany stopped, grabbed his arm, and pulled him around to face her. "Did I hear you right? Are you saying she's *dead?*"

Tom closed his eyes before he answered. "You heard correctly. She died nearly two months ago, now."

"You mean to tell me, you led me to believe she left you and in reality, she died?"

Tiffany couldn't understand why Tom had chosen to maintain silence about his relationship and had allowed her to assume that his wife had left him for other reasons. "I thought maybe she caught you fooling around, or finally decided against staying with a man who flirted."

"No, Tiffany, it's nothing of the sort. I loved my wife so much. I didn't mean to mislead you. You assumed I was after you. When we met, I was trying to find women who would meet her, since we were new in San Francisco and she didn't get out much. She fought depression over being alone without friends or relatives outside of me. I thought that introducing her to other women would be good for her. Everyone needs friends."

"Tom, that was sweet of you to do for your wife. And all along I thought you were after me."

"If things were different, I would have been. But I am, um..." Tom paused to correct his thoughts "...or, I should say, *was* married."

Tiffany moved closer, placed her arms around Tom, and hugged him with concern. "I'm so sorry for your loss," she whispered.

"Thanks; you've been a good friend. I appreciate you getting me out of the house and making me live again. And the reason I didn't tell you is because I didn't want to depress you and have you feeling sorry for me. I get enough of that at the office."

"You know, somehow I understand." Tiffany released her hug and grabbed his hand and they walked to the bus stop, sitting on its bench.

"It's going to be fine. One day, you'll share the story with me."

"Well, I have to get accustomed to telling folks. Bottom line is, she overdosed."

"Overdosed? Was it suicide?"

"Not exactly. I think she made a mistake with her meds. The autopsy said the mixture included OxyContin. The drug mixture stopped her breathing and she was already gone when I got home."

Tiffany remembered reading about a death in the neighborhood. "Did you have a son in the Army?"

"How did you know?" Tom asked, surprised. "I don't remember telling anyone about my kid."

"You didn't. I read it in the paper. I didn't know she was your wife. I didn't know your last name until recently. I'm so sorry. I should have been more encouraging. If you need anything - a good meal, or maybe someone to run an errand - just let me know."

"Since I haven't asked you for anything before now, I don't think I will. I recognize everything you've done for me." Tiffany didn't respond, figuring his situation was difficult because of he had lost someone he'd loved.

"The offer still stands." When the bus arrived, Tiffany stood, entered first, and took a seat. Tom followed and sat next to her.

"Did you understand what I meant back there?" asked Tom.

"I think so, but do know that my offer stands. You're a nice guy and I don't mind hanging out with you. I'll get beyond why you had to keep your wife's death a secret, but I'm still here for you."

"I appreciate you; I do. Thank you for showing me so much these past weeks."

"You're welcome. "

"Tiffany." Tom took her hand and held it, grateful that she was a part of his transition. "I can tell you're an incredible woman who loves deeply. And I'm lucky you're in my life."

"Tom, I'm your friend; nothing more." Tiffany pulled her hand back to make her point.

"I understand, and I want you to know that I respect your decision. I guess I should have opened up to you earlier."

"Yes, you should have. Getting to know you could have been much easier for me, and made more sense, if I'd known the truth."

"Are you angry with me?"

"Not at all." Tiffany paused before adding, "Especially now that I know. I thought you were hurt and angry, and was hiding your emotions. I'm glad you came clean. At first I thought my efforts were useless, but something happened, and you're returning to being the Tom that I met originally."

"I honestly couldn't have done it without you."

The bus arrived at their usual stop. After they exited, both Tom and Tiffany walked towards their homes.

"Would you like a nightcap?" asked Tom.

"No, I need to get home. Tonight was a little too much for me. The truth shocked me, and I need to think about how I feel. Can I ask you something?"

"Sure, go ahead."

Tiffany waited a few seconds to gather her thoughts. "So you were never into me as a potential date? It was all really for your wife?"

"Tiffany, you're a very special woman, with looks to die for, but in this case I was hoping you'd become my wife's friend."

"No interest at all?"

"Not then, but now it could be different."

***

Tiffany returned home and immediately went to her laptop and logged in. She clicked into her email account and, without reading her inbox, started a new email for Manny.

Manny,

You are not going to believe this, but I feel like such a fool. Remember the guy I wrote about, when I told you that his wife left him? Well, I guess I shouldn't have made that assumption. His wife didn't leave him, she committed suicide. She died!!!

I don't understand. Tom could have been a man in my life, but now there's no way. Do you think I should continue this friendship?

Tiffany

Tiffany decided to call Tom not long after she wrote the email.

"Hi," Tom responded.

"I know it's late, but I wanted to talk to you. I don't know how to ask this, but I think I should be straightforward…"

"…You don't have to ask anything if you're skeptical. I enjoy our friendship and that's why I didn't tell you how Mary died." Tom interrupted before she got a chance to form her question.

His answer surprised her. She took a breath and held it a moment before exhaling. "I don't understand how you could withhold something so important."

Tom had expected her frustration and had rehearsed his response in his mind. "Because sympathy is something I don't need or want. If I had told you, your entire outlook would have been different. You see, I enjoyed your energy and the way you encouraged me and pushed me back into being alive. Had I told you, it would have been different. Instead of your encouragement, you would have probably kept your distance until you felt I had finished grieving."

Tiffany pondered his answer and said, "You're right. I would have encouraged you to take time to grieve. I think it's tough for a person to be active so quickly, yet I realize you have been very active. That says a lot about you."

"Like what?"

"Well, it says you're not grieving anymore and that you are ready for life."

"I was ready because I realized I began grieving during Mary's fight with her depression."

"That doesn't make sense. She didn't leave you. She was there for you and spent her life with you."

A Cyber Affair

"Physically, yes, I agree; but emotionally, it's different. She left me emotionally and I had to continue to fight to keep us going. I tried everything from relocating to trying to help her find new friends, group counseling, social outings - anything to get her back. I've had her see a psychologist and a psychiatrist. And for what? She left me holding the bag, all alone. On one hand I can't blame her, because she fought hard to come back; but on the other hand, I feel that she just gave up." Tom fell silent. This was the first time he had shared his true feelings with anyone.

"I understand it's been a long process for you. I admire your persistence in trying to make it work."

"She was my best friend, my companion, and my wife. I *had* to make it work. I took our vows seriously."

"You're a sweet man, Tom. I know you'll bounce back soon. I think I understand why you didn't tell me and I feel better about it. It's time I say goodnight, Tom. We'll catch up tomorrow."

"Bye, Tiffany, and thanks for another great night."

***

Lunch at Macy's was the highlight of Tiffany's day. She had time to focus on two invitations without interruption; the first when Tom texted her with ideas on how to spend the evening, and the second when Valerie called and invited her to a girls' night out. What she had discovered about Tom had decreased her desire to spend time with him, even though she enjoyed his company. Valerie needed advice; she heard it in her voice during their conversation. Tiffany responded to both invitations and decided to focus on Valerie for the evening. She told Tom she had a friend in need, which he could surely understand. At the end of Tiffany's shift, she walked to Valerie's area.

183

"Are you ready?"

"I'll be just a minute." Valerie cleaned her area while Tiffany waited, and within minutes they both headed for the door.

"Are we going closer to home or staying downtown?" Tiffany asked.

"Let's do the wharf."

"We haven't been down there in a long time."

"It's because it's so touristy, but tonight I want to feel like I'm from a different city."

"Okay, Valerie; I hear it in your voice. What's going on?" Tiffany gave Valerie a concerned look. "I haven't seen you so serious in years. What gives?"

Valerie didn't respond right away, and walked in silence until they approached Tiernan's Irish Pub. "Let's go in here," she said. Tiffany followed without question.

"Will you tell me what's going on?" she asked. They took seats at the bar and ordered drinks. "Come on, the suspense is killing me."

"You know I love life, and going the extra mile to have fun keeps me in tune. Well, I'm lost this time, Tiffany. I'm, like, really confused about JT."

"JT, the artist who confessed he loves you? The man who wants to give you the world?"

"Okay, I get the point - but he's such a womanizer."

"Womanizer? Honestly, I can see why. He's not a bad-looking man, and he's a photographer as well as a painter. He's had a lot of women come on to him. I have no doubt he's been a player for a long time. But you knew this from the beginning - right?"

"That's just it. I knew, and I came on board for fun. Now he's in love with me and I don't know if I can love him in return."

"Valerie, you've had worse men in your life, including some who've treated you like a sponge, giving you things you could soak up and then squeezing the life out of you. I don't think JT is going to do that to you."

"I knew what to expect with those men. I was out for fun and knew that nothing serious could ever come develop with them. Now JT seems so serious. He's always trying to prove that I should trust him."

The bartender placed their drinks in front of them, put their receipt upside down between their two glasses, and returned to the other side of the bar. Valerie waited to continue her thoughts. "Just the other morning I saw him behave in ways that would make any woman cringe. I mean, he had this nude woman posing in front of him in such an inviting way."

"You were there the entire time?"

"Yes, I was his helper."

"Did he make a move on the woman?"

"No, not in front of me. That isn't the problem. I know he'll respect me when I'm around, but what about when I'm not? That's my concern - what he does when he's alone with those beautiful women. I'm not sure I can trust him."

"I see. It's a trust issue. I know how trust is a huge factor for you." Tiffany looked down at the bar, then raised her eyes to Valerie. "If you can't trust him, then why do you want him?"

"Because I love the way he makes me feel. I haven't had a man show me so much or share so openly before. It's like he knows what I'm thinking, and for the first time in my life, someone can finish my sentences before I do. Do you know that feeling?"

"It must be a great feeling. You're blushing, and I haven't seen you blush without a man in your presence before. I mean, you're really feeling JT."

"One day he took me to Napa Valley and we had breakfast in a vineyard on a ridge overlooking the valley. It was amazing and simple, but so different. On our second date, we went to Angel Island. He took so many pictures. I never knew how lovely the park was from a photographer's viewpoint. He gave me a new appreciation of nature."

"I don't understand. You love being with JT, but you can't trust him when he's around other women. Has he done anything suggesting he's even thought about being unfaithful to you?"

"Tiffany, I don't think he is. Even when I visit unannounced, he's doing exactly what he said he would, and is always excited to see me."

"JT is in love with you."

"I know, but what should I do? Ignore my gut instinct?"

"That's a tough question that only you can answer."

Valerie took another sip of her drink and held her head in her hand with her elbow resting on the bar. "You know, it's a simple thing to deal with as long as I don't find out something that will hurt me."

"Valerie, you're making this worse. I know you're afraid of being hurt. But this guy is showing you so much. I can't remember a man who's shared more with you. It's like he breathes to be with you. Are you afraid?"

"No, I'm not afraid. But you're right: no man has ever openly shared so much with me."

"It's different. I remember my ex-husband used to do that, and it made me happy."

"I should be happy with JT being an open book."

"Yes, you should. If I were you, I'd put my fear aside and enjoy the relationship. Don't look for reasons to stop. Open your heart for a change. You're crazy about JT, so make it work."

"Make it work."

Tiffany decided to let Valerie in on Tom's information. "I found out Tom is a widower."

"What? Are you kidding?"

"No, I'm not. All this time I thought he was getting divorced."

"What game was he playing?"

"He had his reasons, but it's all about his perception. You know, he thought that I would be overly sympathetic."

"You weren't sympathetic at all. I bet you nearly pounced on him. I knew you liked him."

"No, not now, because I don't want to be that transition woman; it would be like walking into a wasps' nest of emotions. Either I'd feel left out because I'd be compared to his dead wife or, if he's divorced, it'd be like walking into an angry storm. He would treat me like I'm the one causing him pain."

"I heard of women waiting it out. Either they're friends until his wall falls, or they wait in the wings until he's forgotten his lost wife. Some women will do what it takes. I am so glad you aren't one of them." Valerie raised her glass for a toast. Tiffany obliged, and they heard the soft clink of their glasses touching.

"You're right. I'm glad I'm not one of those women."

Chapter 24

Manny waited for Frieda at the corner store, just like she had instructed. He got there just before sunset. *I know she'll be here,* he thought, and looked at his watch. It wasn't long after he'd scanned his wrist for the third time when she arrived, waving to him from a blue convertible 2010 Mercedes SLK55 AMG with its top down. He couldn't believe his eyes. This wasn't the older Toyota she normally drove.

"Hi, nice car," Manny complimented her. "You look great driving it."

"It's a friend's," Frieda informed him.

"Really? Some friend. I'm impressed."

"Get in and let's go. I have some place special to take you."

"You didn't tell me to dress up."

"You look good enough. You'll fit right in."

Manny sat in the passenger's seat and buckled in. She took off, heading south on US 1. She turned right at a crossroad and entered 1-95 South towards Fort Lauderdale. They drove in silence and watched the sun disappear as day became night. Frieda exited the Interstate on Boulevard Gardens and drove into Fort Lauderdale until she reached Broward Street, entering the parking lot to Johnny's Club-Bar-Lounge, an all-male review of strippers. Surprised, Manny looked at Frieda and shook his head.

"I don't think you want me to go in there," he said.

"I can't believe you. You're a world traveler, a man who lives for excitement and thrills, and a retired sailor who's seen it all. Are you telling me you're afraid to be here?"

"It's not fear. It just doesn't interest me."

"You can do it for me, just this once. Who knows, you might enjoy watching women react to male strippers."

Manny got out of the car and followed Frieda. *She makes a good point, but I'm not here on the prowl. I thought she had another sexual excursion planned.* Five feet away from the entrance, Frieda was swept into a dancer's arms. He was youthful, built with a physique most women drooled over, and did not have one hair out of place. He wore tights that showcased his manhood, which had a vile look, like it intended to be used. He walked Frieda to a booth near the stage. She pushed him back and dropped into a seat, looking for Manny and waving for him to join her.

"Are you sure you want me here?" Manny asked.

"He's harmless. Of course I want you here." Frieda pulled him closer to sit next to her. As the music played, she watched the dancer on stage and pointed to one of the women to the left of her.

"See her? She'd pay anything for a night with him."

"Is this your idea of seduction?"

"Not at all. Just watch for a few minutes." When Frieda finished her comment, a tall, dark and physically impressive man walked in front of her - stopped, winked, and then flexed his butt cheek.

"Whenever you're ready, call me," the dancer suggested.

"No way. I'm not watching you get a lap dance." Manny said.

"I don't let them dance in my lap, but I love the entertainment."

"Girl, you're a wild one."

Frieda moved to the next table, where four women sat. She whispered to one lady and pointed at Manny. One woman smiled as she looked at him, and before he could wink an eye in the smoke-filled room, there she stood in front of him.

"I hear you're a dancer, too. You give private dances during your off time?"

"What? Ah, no - you can't believe what that wild woman told you."

"You're a nice -looking man and there isn't anything I can do to get you in tights?"

"Not my cup of tea, but I appreciate the interest."

"One hundred dollars for a ten-minute dance."

Manny looked at the woman with a raised eyebrow. "What? Are you serious?"

"Sure I'm serious. I want a ten-minute private dance from you, for a Benjamin."

Manny shook his head in disbelief. "I appreciate the offer, but I'll have to pass."

"Are you sure you won't do it? How about two hundred?"

"I'm not for sale, and besides, I don't work here."

"I know you don't, and that's why I want you to give me a private dance."

Manny stood and looked towards Frieda before responding to the woman. "I appreciate the offer, I really do; but I can't do it for a thousand dollars. I'm not that kind of guy." He stopped one of the dancers. "Hey buddy, this woman wants a private dance. How much do you charge?"

"Two hundred for fifteen minutes," the dancer said.

"You have a customer," Manny took the woman's hand and placed it into the dancer's. "Enjoy!" Manny gave the woman a smile. He walked to Frieda and reached for her to take his hand. "Okay, I guess you've made your point. Why don't we leave?"

"I'm not ready. You have to come with me."

"I think it's time we talked."

"Come with me first and we'll talk afterwards." Frieda took him by the hand and led him to a back room. "Drop your pants," she instructed once they were behind closed doors.

"No, I'm not doing it," Manny angrily replied.

"You're cramping my style. What's wrong with you?"

"I don't think being at a male strip club works for me."

"You aren't with men. I didn't think you would have a problem with it."

"I don't exactly, but I have a greater problem with you trying to pimp me out."

"It would have been fun. She's harmless," Frieda giggled.

"That's not the point. I'm still not interested. I'm beginning to wonder what gives with you."

"You're not dropping your pants," Frieda scolded him while she reached for his belt and zipper. "You aren't helping."

"Let's go, I thought we were going to talk tonight."

"Talk?"

"Yes, talk."

"Now, you sound like my husband."

Manny fell silent. This was the first time she had mentioned being married. "Damn it."

"Damn what, Manny?"

"You're married. I knew it."

"Damn it, yes, I am, but don't get angry. I can explain."

"Explain?"

"Yes, I can explain."

Manny left the room and headed for the front entrance. He left the strip club and went to the side of the road opening his cell calling for a taxi.

Frieda scurried after him and grabbed his arm. "Where do you think you're going?"

"Home."

"Why?"

"I don't do married women. I asked you that and you lied to me from the very beginning. Although I've been asked by other women, it's not what I'm into. I don't get involved with another man's woman."

"I'm married, yes! And you're right, I wasn't honest with you. If I had been, you wouldn't have done what I wanted."

"No shit."

"Don't get angry; hear me out."

"You enjoy yourself and go back to those strippers. I'm heading home."

"You *have* to hear me out," Frieda insisted. "Then I'll take you home so you don't waste money on cab fare."

"Frieda, or whoever you are, I don't like the fact that you put me in a defensive position. I don't like the fact you could have gotten me shot over stupidity. I'm not a fan of married women who try to make their husbands jealous."

"It's nothing like that. I don't make him jealous. I make him quite happy."

His face wrinkled. "He's happy you're out with me. Yeah, right. I'm supposed to believe you."

"Drive back with me and we'll talk on the way. I won't try anything; you'll see. I just hope you'll understand."

A Cyber Affair

Manny turned back and followed Frieda to her car. He admired the sexy, smooth way she walked, but became more angry with each step she took. His number one rule was not to get involved with a married woman. He watched her, remembering their sex-capades, and became disgusted with himself and disappointed in her when he thought of what he'd become.

Manny remembered the time when he had returned from a deployment and no one was waiting at the pier for him. It had been his fourth tour on a West Pacific cruise. Suzie had been an infant when he left. He was excited over his reunion with his wife and child. When Cheryl and Suzie weren't on the pier, he pushed back the inner doubts he'd felt because he hadn't received any letters from Cheryl during the last month of his deployment. He remembered calling his house, only to discover their phone had been disconnected. Manny had to contact his neighbor in base housing to find out if his wife was okay. Frieda reignited those bad feelings of how he had dealt with his wife leaving him for another man.

He watched Frieda get into the Mercedes and stood at the passenger's door for a moment, flashing back to a conversation he'd had with Cheryl years ago.

"What happened to the phone?" he'd asked.

"Nothing. I changed the number. You shouldn't call here anymore."

"What do you mean, I shouldn't call my wife and kid anymore?"

"'Wife' is a technical term."

"Wait - so now you're not my wife? Are you saying you don't love me?"

"I'm not the same little girl you met years ago. I'm a woman now, and you being at sea so much was not what I signed up for."

"You knew I was in the Navy when we met. I told you about my travels and that there would be times you could meet me in liberty ports. I can't believe you're changing on me."

"I'm tired of being alone," Cheryl countered.

"Being alone? Damn, Cheryl, I thought we had a great marriage."

"If you were here, it could be; but you're never here," Cheryl sighed. "I want a family, and I don't want to be responsible for raising our daughter alone."

"Are you leaving me?"

"I'm moving soon. I'll be out of this house on Friday, and don't try to stop me. I suggest you find a barracks."

"But what about Suzie? Will I get to see her?"

"You're her father. We'll work something out. We have to."

Frieda broke into his reverie when she shouted at him: "GET IN, MANNY!" Manny snapped his focus to Frieda and sat in the car. He was about to click his seat belt when Frieda left the parking lot on screeching tires.

"So now you're angry?" Manny asked.

"Not at all. I love driving. Look, Manny, you have to understand: this is my life, and I need to enjoy it."

"You don't have to enjoy it with me."

"And why not?"

"Do I have to remind you that you're married?"

"I know who I am and what I'm doing."

"Okay, Missus Frieda - if that's your real name. I'm curious; so what's your story?"

A Cyber Affair

Frieda turned onto the Interstate, heading towards West Palm Beach. "Before I tell you, promise me you're open to continuing our relationship."

"Oh hell no, Frieda: we don't have a relationship, and there's no way this will continue."

"Why?

"You already know why."

"You're telling me you didn't enjoy our sexual excursions?"

"That isn't up for discussion." He frowned at Frieda. "I need to know your story."

"As if knowing will help you sleep better with a clear conscience?"

"Maybe it will. But right now, I'm more curious than needy. Why don't you start with telling me your real name?"

"I think that's fair. I'm Pamela Friedman. I married a lovely man fifteen years ago. What happened was youthful misconception."

"Youthful misconception? Meaning you married young. We all do that."

"Young, not really; but younger by far - yes."

"You married 'younger by far', meaning he's much older?"

"He was nearly twenty years my senior."

"Your husband is twenty years older than you?"

"Yes, and we got married when I was twenty-two years old, fresh out of college."

"You graduated from college and married a forty-two year old man. Didn't you feel like you were out of your element?"

"No. I had everything I wanted, including good sex with my husband."

"Okay, it's fifteen years later and here we are. What happened, and why?"

"What do you say we find a coffee shop and talk?"

"I don't know. I feel like I'm under surveillance now."

"No way. I wouldn't put you in jeopardy. I know what I'm doing."

"So, you do this all of the time?"

"No, but I have fun when I can," Pamela admitted with a sly smile.

"What made you want to get out and mess around on your husband?" Manny needed to know. He wanted to get the whole scoop.

"You don't beat around the bush, do you?"

He looked beyond the car into the night sky and remembered the time Cheryl had answered that same question for him.

"No, I usually don't."

"I guess you could say that time happened. He got older, and I got wiser and found less satisfaction in our marriage. I wanted more without losing everything that I gained in the marriage. Don't get me wrong. I love my husband; but I'm not satisfied with our sexual intimacy anymore. We've tried everything and the problem is that he's not interested in sex like he was before."

"He's older."

"When I met you, I'd finally realized that was the case. I'm lucky if we get together twice a year."

"Twice a year?"

"Twice a year. And it doesn't matter what I do to him, he's just not that interested."

"Why don't you leave him?"

A Cyber Affair

"And go where, to start over? I love my life, my freedom, and my commitment. I love my kids."

"I didn't know you had kids."

"Yes, and I love them to death. They're home now. They're beautiful."

"If he's not that into you, when did you get pregnant?"

"Obviously before he lost interest, Manny. That was a dumb question."

"Okay, I get it. It's nearly perfect except for the sex; and sex is important."

"Sex makes me feel alive. Doesn't it do the same for you?"

Manny thought about how excited Pamela had seemed at every sexual excursion. He couldn't believe a woman so alive and so gorgeous was on the prowl with so much to lose.

"Does your husband approve of your excursions with men?"

"He doesn't know."

"So you're taking a hell of a chance. Is this one of your cars, too? The one he knows and can spot at any corner?"

"Yes, of course. I usually use my friend's Toyota, but she was using it tonight. She doesn't mind when we exchange cars."

"I see. I understand how you creep now. Hmmm, smart move."

"I don't let things get between my husband and me. This way, I can enjoy life."

"And I guess, for you, that's a great accomplishment."

"Are you still with me?"

"No, I'm not. I won't be involved anymore."

"We were doing so well. I wanted you to know, so that we could continue. I need you, Manny. I want you and I like being with you," Pamela insisted. "We can finish our night at your place, like the first time we slept together."

"We shouldn't have then, and we're not going to now. I don't want anything to do with this."

"Why?"

"You're married, and I respect marriage. If you want another man, leave your husband or get his permission. And even with his permission, I'm still not the man for you."

"Manny, you're the one I want."

Manny noticed he was within walking distance of his apartment. "Stop the car. Stop the damn car."

"I'll take you home."

"No, you won't. This is good enough. Just stop the car." Manny pulled the door handle and released his seat belt. Pamela quickly stopped the car and he jumped out.

"Look, Frieda, Pamela, whoever you are. It was an experience and I enjoyed the ride. Now lose my number."

Manny arrived home and grabbed a beer from his refrigerator for a nightcap. He sat next to his desktop and within minutes, he was in his email account.

Tiffany,

When you think you have something special, strange things can happen to change your thoughts. I may have had a blast with this woman, but she turned out to be a liar who totally deceived me. Why can't a woman be honest? I'm sure you're asking the same about men. One day we'll find the reason for both.

Can't wait to chat with you,

Manny

Chapter 25

Tiffany's cell phone rang. When she answered, JT got down to business. "Do you have the list?"

"I have it, but I'm not so sure I should give it to you," Tiffany said. "She's not feeling you like she used to."

"You'll have to trust me on this one, Tiffany. I'll show everyone that she's the woman of my life. I really mean it. You have to give me those names and addresses."

"I'll do it under one condition. Don't tell her I gave you this tip. She loves it when a man takes her shopping for shoes."

JT laughed at Tiffany's response. "Okay, I'll remember to take her shoe shopping. I don't know how that helps build trust, but we'll catch several shoe sales. Should I be afraid, now?"

"Afraid of what?"

"Have you seen her closet? She's got hundreds of shoes. I didn't know she has a shoe fetish. It's like she wants several pairs to match every outfit. Perhaps I should be afraid of shopping all day for shoes; If I make an insensitive comment, my efforts will be lost." JT shook his head in disbelief.

"No, JT, I'm telling you: she'll fall for you deeper than she already has. Her philosophy is if a man has good taste in shoes, he's a man after her heart. Once you advise her to buy an awesome pair of shoes, you're in for life."

"Picking out a pair of shoes she'd love will make her trust me?"

"I know it's hard to believe, but it's Valerie we're talking about. You love her, right? Then try to understand some of her logic."

"I have to pay more attention to her ideas. I can't let her get away. She's the first one I can't live without."

"Ah, that's sweet, JT; really sweet. I'll send you the list."

"Thank you so much. Here's my email address: JTart1@JTsart.com."

Tiffany emailed JT the list she had created. After an hour of reading the local newspaper, she went on with her day. It was the weekend, and she hadn't thought about contacting Tom. It was the third Saturday since he had told her the truth about his wife. Until recently, Tom had been her focus, and she had created an active schedule to get him out of his mood. Today, having been educated about the truth, she felt used by him, feeling that her efforts had not been for her benefit but for his change.

Tiffany fiddled with the idea of helping Tom find a new woman, but her heart wasn't in it. For a few moments during this effort, Tiffany had found Tom attractive and thought about becoming the next woman in his life, but after he had finally told her the truth, she decided it would not be in her best interest. Tom was worth it, but his dishonesty was a deal-breaker. Tiffany had the urge to fulfill her empty void. She checked Tom's address on her cell phone. That afternoon Tom answered a knock at his door, and there she stood.

"Hi, I wasn't expecting you."

"I don't know why I came," she said as she stood at his front door.

"Are you coming in?"

"I'm not so sure I should."

"What's bothering you?" Puzzled, Tom stepped outside and closed the townhouse door behind him. He walked around Tiffany and sat on the stoop.

"Sit with me."

Tiffany did, and although she was unsure of where to start, she forged ahead. "I want to share something with you."

"I figured as much. I know you well enough to know that something is bothering you."

"I like you, and what you withheld had an impact on me. I think I wanted more from you; maybe for us. Now it's like I want you, but I'm not sure how to go about it."

"Let me save you some time and effort. Please stop thinking about us as an opportunity. I like you, enjoy your company, and love your spirit, but I'm not ready for a relationship."

"I figured that, but I had to ask."

"You have to follow your instincts. You know I'm not quite right yet. I haven't let go of Mary long enough to start another relationship. Hell, I haven't even thought about having sex, yet. I wouldn't know where to start. All I know is that I'm not ready."

Tiffany gave him a halfhearted smile. "I'm so glad you're being honest with me. Here I am not sure why I'm visiting, and you're telling me you won't give me a chance."

"Is this your way of saying you're vulnerable and I can take advantage?"

"I have to admit that yes, I am. With a little effort, you could have your way with me."

Tom placed his arm around Tiffany, pulled her close, and moved in for a kiss. She responded, only to find Tom's lips on her cheek. "You are a wonderful friend and I'd rather keep it that way. I'm not ready for anything more right now." Tom kept his arm around her and gave Tiffany this advice: "One day you'll find a man you can love. Just make sure he's your friend first, and let it thrive. Remember me telling you this once before?"

"I remember. I've thought about it. But which friend are you referring to? I have a lot of acquaintances, but very few friends. I wondered if you were talking about yourself. I mean, I knew you were pushing me away. Now I understand why, but I had a feeling you were the one, and we were starting as friends."

"I am your friend, but not the one I'm referring to. He's the guy to whom you can say anything and everything to without worrying about any backlash. He's the guy whom you know is exciting in one way or another because there's a little chemistry between you two, and he provides you with a comfortable connection. The man who shares with you and isn't afraid to give you his honest opinion, even if it hurts sometimes. He's the one you need to think about."

Tiffany sat and thought about who in her life might fit what Tom was describing. She considered her recent dates and her past relationships, and since Tom wasn't a possibility, Manny rose to the top of the list.

"Thanks. I think I know what to do," she said, giving Tom a goodbye hug. Tiffany left him on the stoop and headed back to her apartment.

Chapter 26

The Florida sunset caught Manny sitting on his deck, enjoying a beer and surfing the Internet with his newly-purchased laptop. His cell phone rang and he checked the flashing ID. *No way! Pamela doesn't give up*, he said to himself, and ignored the call. He dialed Suzie instead.

"What's up, kiddo?"

"Hi, Dad; glad you called. Are we still on for tonight? You didn't confirm and I really need to get away."

"Get away? Is it Camille? Is she giving you a hard time? Did something change?"

"No, Dad: nothing changed with Camille. She's great, but between work and school, I'm burned out."

"We'll talk about it over dinner. I'm cooking. What time are you arriving?"

"I'll be there by 8." He heard Suzie sigh and assumed it was from exhaustion. Manny searched the web for a chicken recipe and found one he thought Suzie would enjoy. He knew his kid well. Whenever Suzie felt tired or irritable, he would create a masterpiece dinner, giving her what he called a "slice of comfort and love". Usually the result would be her spilling every thought that was affecting her attitude. Once Manny got dinner started, he sat at his laptop and read the latest email from Tiffany.

Manny,

I know your feelings all too well. Deceit is evil. I am still in shock over Tom's situation, too. I am so mad at myself for playing around at the mercy of a man who was hiding the fact that he's widowed when I thought he was a divorcee in the making. I could have done something really stupid. He isn't fun anymore, and my efforts to bring him into my world turned out to be a big NO-NO.

One day, I hope you and I will meet a pair of honest people who will embrace having a down-to-earth companion. I know that you're a down-to-earth person, too, since we complain about and experience the same things in life.

Keep your head up. I know the best candidates are about to present themselves to us. I can feel it.

Talk to you soon,

Tiffany

Before Manny responded to her email, his cell phone chimed. He reached for it, scanned the caller ID, and pressed 'ignore'. *Pamela keeps trying.* He shook his head in disgust when he realized the sexual escapades may have added spice to his life, but they hadn't happened under the conditions he'd wanted. He felt the need for more.

Suzie entered the apartment with her book bag, laptop, and a large soda. She walked into the kitchen and greeted Manny. "Hi, Dad," she said, and kissed him on the cheek.

"Glad to see you, Baby Girl. How was your drive?"

"Not bad; just long. Today it seemed longer than usual, probably because I'm so tired."

"You aren't sleeping well these days?"

"No, I'm not. Midterms and projects, then work at the coffee shop. It keeps me running every hour of the day."

"No worries, kid, you'll get through it. You've been a serious trooper all your life and I know that whenever life gets tough, you somehow pull through."

"You should tell Mom that." Suzie opened the soda bottle, poured a glass, and got a bottle of wine from the counter rack. She opened the bottle with the corkscrew she pulled from the drawer and poured a glass for Manny. "She's on my last nerves, Dad."

"I can't think of a day when your mom hasn't gotten on your bad side."

"Good point. Why do I keep forgetting that this is the norm?"

"Imagine her not saying anything," Manny said while draining the water from his pot of noodles in preparation for the chicken pasta dish he was creating. "We would think something was wrong."

"When does it change, Dad? When will she realize that I'm not a kid anymore?"

"You'll always be her kid, but you have to tell her how you feel. Tell her and be honest. That's the best advice I can give you."

Suzie set the table. It was her routine, every time Manny cooked. She took a seat and waited for him to place dinner in front of her. When Manny put dinner on the hot plate holders, she served herself and waited for Manny to do the same.

"So, what makes life so unbearable these days?" Manny said.

"Like I said before, Dad, it's exams, work, and the pressure to do well. My brain is fried. I can't find time to relax and close my eyes."

"Do you have to work tomorrow?"

"Fortunately, I don't. I don't have anything scheduled for tomorrow, except for studying and completing a project."

"Good. So you can crash here and take your time doing your schoolwork. I'll help if you need me. I'm not planning anything either, so it's a quiet day, tomorrow."

"Quiet for you? That's unusual, Dad. Most of the time you're busy on your off days. I thought you were dating a woman. What happened?"

"It's really something, talking about my love life with my daughter."

"Never stopped you before," Suzie said. "You don't have to spill every last detail; but at least tell me something."

"I'm not dating right now. I've run into a few roadblocks and I'm getting tired of the games women play."

"You mean, at your age, women still play games? I thought they would subside by then."

"*My* age?"

"You know - *mature*, Dad - you're *mature*."

Manny put down his fork and looked at his daughter, tempted to talk about the excitement Pamela bought him. He knew it would be inappropriate to tell her details of his sexual excursions. What he chose to tell Suzie caused him heartfelt pain. "I'm afraid of meeting someone you won't get along with. I've got you in my life, and I'm not willing to give you up for anyone."

"I'll always been in your life."

"You know what I mean. It's better than just a weekend here or there and being separated for months in between. Right now, it's like we're beginning a new phase."

"As long as we're together, I'm okay. I love being with you."

"That's why I asked about spring break. Do you have plans?"

"Well, to be honest," Suzie sighed, "I don't think we should go."

"You don't want to go?"

"I'm saying that we - as in you and I - should not go."

"Oh, so this year it's going to be your week of independence?"

"I'd like to at least try. I think you should find someone to hang out with during that week."

"I thought I was going to hang with you, but don't worry about me. I'll find someone; but like I promised you long ago, it's got to be someone you can relate to."

"For a week's vacation?"

"Well, I'm thinking that it's time I got serious with someone, but I have stipulations."

"I've always wanted you to be happy. I didn't want to be your reason for not having a wife."

"You aren't my excuse, but you *are* a reason, and I'm extremely picky."

Suzie sat forward with her elbows on the table, holding a soda pop in her hands. She took a sip, then looked at her dad. "You know, Dad, it's your happiness that's important. You shouldn't wait for my approval. I'm sure you'll choose the right woman. Wait; let me think about that before I put my foot in my mouth." Suzie giggled. "I mean, outside of those crazy dates and the women you've been running into, you usually don't get serious with a woman unless you think I can deal with her." She sipped her soda, placed the can on the table, and sighed. "I honestly thought that Camille was perfect, but I didn't know she had had a controlling boyfriend about six months ago. She didn't mean to be hard on you, and I'm so sorry, Dad: I had no idea. She said you were sweet, but she wasn't over her last dramatic experience like she had thought. I guess she started dating too soon."

"No wonder that was a date from hell." Manny sighed with relief. "I would have never known."

"Yes, she told me about that guy after she returned your coffee gift."

"Now it totally makes sense. Thank goodness she said no, or it would have been hell trying to prove to her I'm not like that guy."

"As for other women, Dad, you'll have to live with the one you select, not me. I'm only a visitor in your home."

"But a very important visitor."

"I understand that; but again, I can deal with whomever you get involved with as long as I know you're happy."

Manny paused before he responded. He looked at Suzie, gave her a warm smile, and touched her arm. "You've grown into a wise woman. I'm sure you'll love whoever I select."

"That's it, Dad. So when are you going to introduce me to her, so I know you're okay?"

"I don't know."

"Are you interested in someone who talks with you about anything and everything? I've read that's the type of person you need in your life."

"Where did you read that?"

"Some women's magazine."

Chapter 27

Valerie went to Tiffany's apartment and entered with the key Tiffany had given her, opening the door and walking in. "Yo, Tiff, where are you?"

"I'm in the bedroom. I'll be right out."

Valerie sat on the couch to wait, picked up a magazine, and was surprised when Tom walked out first.

"Pardon me, I was just leaving." Tom said.

"Hope you have a nice day."

"I plan to," replied Tom. He exited through the front door. Tiffany came out and laughed at the expression on Valerie's face. "Surprising, isn't it?"

"No kidding. How the hell did you get him in your bedroom?"

"It's not what you think. I was just helping him get out a deep splinter. Instead of going to the emergency room, he came to me for help. He lives close enough to make it convenient."

"Sure, tell me anything, Tiffany," Valerie chuckled. "You're a slut."

"Not even close. It isn't what you think." Tiffany went into the kitchen and poured a glass of orange juice. "Would you like some?" she asked.

"No, but I do want to know more about this relationship with Tom."

"Friends; we're strictly friends and nothing more. How are you and JT?"

"Don't change the subject. What's going on with you and Tom?" Valerie persisted.

Tiffany went to the couch and sat next to Valerie. "Girl, you know I don't mind sharing something worth boasting about. Truthfully, there is nothing going on between us. I wanted to, but he's not interested. Well - not interested in being lovers. He's a friend whom I can help or who can help me occasionally. That's all there is to it."

"Are you serious? After everything you've done to chase that man, you're willing to accept him as a friend - not even a friend with bennies?"

"Strictly friends, and that's it. I can't change what happened, but what I've learned from the widower is that he'll be a great catch whenever he gets over his grief."

"I hear widowers can sometimes be great, but they can also be horrible. I guess you know your limits. Are you sure there's nothing more?"

"Not with Tom; but with Manny, maybe."

"Manny? You mean the guy online?"

"One and the same."

"Are you're going to tell me or make me beg?" Valerie glanced at her watch.

"Do you have to go? I don't want you to be late," Tiffany said. "I can share my wonderful online experience later."

"I was just thinking about checking on JT."

"How's that going?"

"Awesome, but let me hear what happened with Manny."

Tiffany smiled in excitement. "Now you know I'm not one to get crazy on the internet, especially since it's not likely we'll ever cross paths. I mean, it's hard to meet with a guy who lives near Miami; but this guy is special. We've talked for months at levels I wished I'd had with the men here in San Francisco. He's charming, smart, and aggressive; yet he's sensitive, because he listens. These last two weeks we've Skyped for hours, and I'm sure this guy is the one. Out of all the fears and considerations we've discussed about us finally meeting, the greatest concern for him is that his future partner embraces his daughter from a previous marriage."

"How old is she?"

"She's about nineteen or so: a college sophomore."

"That shouldn't be too difficult. So what was the most profound conversation you've had with him?"

"We got to a point where I wanted to strip off my clothes in front of him, and if I could've climbed through the computer screen, I would have jumped his bones. I wanted to be close to him and feel him inside of me."

Valerie couldn't believe her ears. The toughest woman she knew when it came to men was falling for a man across the country. "Are you telling me the truth?"

"About what?" Tiffany asked, and looked confused.

"You're excited over a man who is three thousand miles away. What happened?"

"Manny happened. He seems to say all the right things and his comments have substance. He didn't just say things, he *says* things, if you know what I mean."

Valerie shrugged her shoulders. "I guess it's like JT knowing how to get my blood going. He pushes all the right buttons and I can't say no. Even if I wanted to, I couldn't."

"You're in love and you should just admit it," Tiffany suggested.

"Okay, I admit it, but still he's not what I expected. At the same time, he's funny and caring; and girl, he's just what the doctor ordered."

Tiffany agreed with Valerie's enthusiasm and identified with her attitude.

"Now you know how I feel about Manny. He has those same qualities. I mean, those deep conversations we shared gave us a stronger connection. It wasn't that way until Tom gave me a little insight. He told me to go after the guy I could share anything with. I realized that's Manny. And I took a chance. Once we got there…wow! Manny blew me away, and if he'd been here, I don't think you would have gotten into the apartment with your key. I would have used the chain bolt for good measure."

"You mean to tell me, with all the men you've gone out with, Manny - the man who's over three thousand miles away - has you melting from a video call? *A video call?*"

"Our conversations go on for hours. Like I said before, I'm damn near naked when I'm talking to him. I thought about doing it, but caught myself. You know, we have that weak-in-the-knees type of connection."

"I know that feeling. Last night, I experienced it firsthand. JT had me screaming. I swear one day his neighbors are going to complain about my visits." Valerie dramatically touched her hand to her forehead, pantomiming an actress feeling faint. She flopped back on the couch and then bounced back. "I get weak just thinking about it."

Tiffany laughed at Valerie's antics and shook her head. "You're still my girl: crazy as hell, but my girl. Tell me, what are you going to do about JT? I mean, he's showing you so much."

"He is, he is. I guess I'll let him continue to do what he wants. I get the best feeling about this. Well…I think I do."

"JT is crazy about you. I know it, for sure."

Valerie left Tiffany's apartment without inviting Tiffany out for a night of fun.

Tiffany thought it was great that her friend approved of her enthusiasm, and this motivated her to write an email.

Manny,

We had another night of great conversation. Who knew we had so much in common, and would feel like we lived around the corner from each other? I love how we connect. You say one thing and even though I've heard it from other men, it's not a deal-breaker with you. I see it as honesty because I feel you're being open with your thoughts.

I'm not sure I'm giving you everything you need from a woman. But right now, I feel I am. I'm giving you the power and ability to create an immediate impact on my life. I'm not trying to rush you or make it easier for you (actually, we're too far apart for that), but I am opening up more to the idea of one day seeing you. The reason I feel so compelled is because you're a unique man. We've connected and you know how to entertain my mind, and to me that's dangerous. Maybe we should talk by cell: my number is 415-990-0010.

I look forward to your response (and I'm sure it's going to be something worth reading) - or just surprise me with a call.

Tiffany

Chapter 28

Manny ran on the treadmill at the gym and allowed his thoughts to roam. It had been a week since Manny and Suzie had met for dinner. He had shared his dating ideas with Suzie and how his goal was to select a woman to be his wife. His thoughts drifted to his first true love. His dating experience with Cheryl, his ex-wife, had been a dream romance. Manny recalled their first date; how nervous and awkward it was, and how he was embarrassed when she'd refused to ride on his motorcycle.

Cheryl gave him a run for his money, determined to make him earn her heart, and kept just enough distance to reel him in with her seductive antics. She enjoyed their nights together, but would run back to her dorm for protection, and she toyed with Manny's emotions when he had to deploy. Manny remembered his first homecoming from their official separation as newlyweds. That was the night they had conceived Suzie.

A runner moved next to Manny, and it startled him. He looked at his watch and realized that he'd run an extra ten minutes. He stopped the treadmill and walked to the weights to begin his next routine. Before his first lift, he replayed his daughter's comment during their last conversation: "...you'll have to live with her, not me...someone who talks to you about anything and everything..." He pushed on the weight and pondered Tiffany's responses on Skype. *She can hang with the best, she's a heavyweight contender*, he smiled. *I can't believe I can talk to her about anything and she either has an opinion or a sharp, funny comeback.* He finished one set in his routine and worked on another, which made his body ache. *No pain, no gain!*

He thought while he pushed and pulled through various machines. He finished his workout and relived his many discussions with Tiffany.

On the drive home, he stopped at the light and fantasized about feeling Tiffany in his arms. He drove into a strip-mall parking lot and retrieved his phone. With multiple taps on his cell phone keyboard, he wrote:

Tiffany, I want to know you like a lover knows his woman. I want to spend my Saturdays learning everything about you. Will you teach me?

He hesitated before pushing 'send', realizing that he didn't have her number. *Of all the Skype video conversations we've had, I never once shared my cell phone number, and she didn't give me hers.* Manny looked up from his cell phone and gazed into the parking lot. *Maybe it's good, because I'm being too forward?* He stared into space as if trying to connect with his ego while battling his desire for a serious relationship. *No, I'm not. I wish I had her number I'd send my text right now.... dammit.* Manny saved the message on his notepad.

Manny returned to his drive, thinking about how a person's appearance can be deceiving. He hoped his intuition, trust, and feelings were in line with his perception of Tiffany. When he arrived at his place, he booted up the laptop and clicked through Tiffany's profile, looking for every picture that she had shared. He shook his head for doubting that Tiffany looked exactly as he'd seen her on the Skype video calls.

His stern Naval validation training kicked in, and he looked for the details of anything that seemed out of place. He reviewed her image on his Skype account and searched for anything that looked false or any hint of a Photoshop adjustment. Manny then took the time to review the videos he had captured in his subconscious.

His desire to see Tiffany grew, and he wondered if their chemistry would complement their mental attraction. He remembered that meeting up could be difficult because she wasn't interested in cultivating a long-distance relationship, and it was a fact that he didn't want to move away from his daughter now that their relationship had finally come together. He knew that Tiffany didn't like the idea of moving to Florida. They had discussed why they liked living where they did, but Manny had the urge to revisit that subject to see if there was a chance that she wanted to meet him.

He wrote:

Tiffany,

I know we chat nearly every night, but I wanted to write you about my thoughts. Maybe we should discuss meeting. I'm on the verge of flying to San Francisco, out of curiosity, just to connect with you and confirm my assumptions. You see, we're (well, I am, for sure) enjoying our evenings on the video calls. Our time spent together keeps me going all day until we talk again. I can't call you on my cell because I don't have your number, even though I think we could talk for hours. Don't get me wrong - I love that about us.

You have impressed me and I want to see if we have the total package. I know you aren't serious about long-distance relationships, but can we just meet and enjoy being true companions for a few days? We may find a different path to travel in the future.

A Cyber Affair

Let's talk about it and, of course, other subjects too, as we continue to enjoy sharing our lives. I can't wait to discuss the possibilities with you. Here's my cell: 561-045-9771.

Manny

He sent the email before he checked his inbox. When he scanned the list of messages, he found a notification from Tiffany. He read it and smiled, since it answered his question. In an instant he recorded her cell phone number, sent a text message from his notepad, and Skyped her in hopes she would respond. Unfortunately, there was no answer. He surfed the web and periodically looked at his cell phone, anticipating her response.

Chapter 29

Tiffany heard a car horn in front of her apartment. She looked out of the front window at the curbside and saw Tom dialing his cell phone. When she answered, he said, "I'm here."

Tiffany walked towards the car after locking the door to her apartment. When Tom saw her approach, he jumped out from the driver's seat, ran to the passenger side, and opened her door.

"Always the gentleman," Tiffany said.

"Thanks for inviting me," Tom said. He closed her door, returned to the driver's seat, and they took off for JT's appreciation party. Tiffany ensured that he followed the specific directions JT had provided because she wanted to be one of the first to arrive.

"Turn left at the next road," she directed him. "Turn right at the light ahead."

"Is there a problem? I've been there before," Tom said, after he made the turn.

"I didn't know, but I'm making sure you take the shortest route. It's important I get there before everyone else so I can see who arrives."

"Expecting someone important?" Tom asked.

"Everyone - and besides, I don't want any drama with this one guy named Bobby, who used to date Valerie."

"Are you kidding me? Who'd invite an old boyfriend to a party she's attending? Talk about unpleasant surprises."

"I know, right! I gave JT his contact information and since he's not aware of their background, I'm sure he probably invited him."

"Didn't you try to warn him?" Tom paused, then shook his head in disapproval. "It would have been nice if you had."

"I didn't because at the time, I didn't realize how important JT is to Valerie. But now I'm afraid I've made a mistake."

"Do you think he'll show?"

"Of course he will. Bobby loved Valerie, but the feeling wasn't mutual."

"Ah: one of those relationships where the guy gets taken for granted."

"You know of those, or are you assuming? It's the type of deal where she controlled the situation."

"I wasn't always a married man. Of course, I experienced the worst before finding my Mary."

"Tom, you amaze me. You really loved Mary."

"I did." Tom looked at Tiffany. "I still do. Thanks for noticing."

"Aww, you're welcome." Tiffany pointed. "Turn left at the next road."

"Really?" Tom looked at Tiffany again, before turning at the road that would place them in front of the building. He parked near the front door to avoid valet parking. Tiffany didn't wait for Tom to open her door: she jumped out of the car, closing the door quickly, and led Tom to the building's entryway. They entered the art gallery and observed the band setting up. As they turned to walk into the larger space, Tiffany's phone alerted her to a new text. She looked at her phone and read Manny's message, smiled, and looked at Tom before putting her phone back into her purse.

"What is it?" asked Tom.

"It's nothing." Tiffany said as she moved into the room.

"That's a good "nothing", to get a smile like that," Tom commented as he followed Tiffany. They ran into Valerie as they walked further into the large room.

"Hi, so glad you two made it," she said, greeting Tiffany and Tom.

"I wouldn't miss this even if it took place in Egypt. And I had to drag the cat from the house."

"Oh, stop it. I'm not a hermit, I do get out. Can I help with anything?" Tom said.

"No, I don't think so, I'm sure JT has everything under control. Find yourself a drink and take a look around."

"I can do that, and maybe we can find something to snack on," Tom said, and took Tiffany by the hand to direct her away from Valerie. "We'll let you get back to greeting other guests."

"Right, I should. See you two later." Valerie smiled and turned to greet some new arrivals.

The venue was roomy, with an empty middle floor and six bars strategically set up around the room. JT's paintings, photos, and campaign posters were displayed on the walls around the main floor. He had his model portfolio streaming on the overhead screen which was centered on the back wall above the band. Servers walked the floor with trays of wine, champagne, and hors d'oeuvres. Around the room were random tables with chairs, situated so they wouldn't interfere with the traffic flow of those who wanted to look at the art work, or people who wanted to dance.

Tom stopped near a painting and took Tiffany's arm. "I know the answer, but I have to ask again. Why on earth would you invite an old boyfriend of hers?"

"Well," Tiffany sighed. "Like I said earlier, I didn't know how serious she was about JT at the time. At first I thought Valerie was just another notch on his belt. After I got a chance to talk to her, I realized I was so wrong. Those two are really in love." Tiffany paused before finishing her response. "Or, at least, I think they are."

"What are you going to do when he shows up?"

"I don't know, and I hope he doesn't. But from the way this guy treated Valerie, and the way she played him, I know he'll be here."

"Then you better screen the door for every man that walks through it."

She nodded at Tom, said "Good idea," and then maneuvered herself towards the front entryway, drink in hand. After twenty minutes of screening, she'd only met a couple of old friends and a few of Valerie's relatives. With most of the RSVPs already there, Bobby was nowhere in sight. Tiffany recognized a woman who was an old acquaintance. They had a quick conversation, which helped her realize that the attendees were composed of a crowd of techies and some standout models.

She did not see Bobby nor get an answer from the text she'd sent him. His not responding made her nervous. She feared that shame over her action would rear its evil head, embarrass her, and make her friend very angry. Another ten minutes into the party and JT had the band kick up a song that made most of the people dance. The party was in full swing and there was still no sign of Bobby. Tiffany felt relieved that he hadn't shown up. She mingled with the crowd and danced with some old friends that she and Valerie shared.

Tiffany stopped dancing long enough to watch JT positioning himself in front of the band, picking up the microphone. He welcomed everyone to his appreciation party and encouraged the crowd to eat, drink, dance, and enjoy the occasion. Tiffany moved from the open floor behind a few couples, following JT and hoping he hadn't seen Bobby. Instead, she observed JT greeting someone who probably had done business with him. The person must have said something funny, because JT laughed as he looked in Valerie's direction. Valerie's curiosity was piqued and she walked over and took hold of his arm. Tiffany didn't mean to be nosy, but she walked within an earshot of their conversation.

"So this is the lucky woman who's got your focus," the businessman said.

"Yes, she certainly does. Makes it hard to get things going the way I want," JT replied.

"You have a good man." The businessman looked at Valerie. "But you'd have a better man if you talked him into joining my company as a partner. He's got the right drive and vision to help us. I love his eye and would love having him full-time."

"Really, now?" Valerie looked at JT for confirmation.

"Yes, Babe. I do more than art you know."

"I'm learning." Valerie smiled at JT, who turned his attention back to the guest.

"Enjoy yourself, and please excuse us. I have to dance with this lovely woman."

"Sure." The businessman raised his glass and gave them an affirmative nod.

JT and Valerie walked passed Tiffany to the dance floor and she watched them dance, moving fluidly to music while focused on each other. To onlookers, it seemed as though their dance was choreographed to show how connected they were. At the end of the third song they left the floor and JT excused himself to mingle with his guests. Tiffany tried to catch Valerie, but she had managed to maneuver into a position where she was chatting with old friends. While the band took a break, JT went to the center of the venue and spoke to the crowd. Tiffany connected with Tom and waved him over to stand next to her. They listened to JT giving several gifts to his patrons and supporters. He gave out gag gifts, where everyone laughed, and handed out strategic gifts with impact on future engagements and business deals. At the end of his gift distribution, JT made an announcement.

"There is a special presentation ahead where I will unveil my latest masterpiece. It's a work of love, and hopefully it's accepted with the compassion I share. Oh, and no peeking behind the veil."

The party grew in size as everyone seemed to enjoy the outing. Tiffany and Tom were talking with others when she spotted Valerie's old boyfriend. *Damn, he showed!* She bit her lip in angst and tapped Tom on the shoulder before walking over to Bobby.

"Hi, Bobby, it's been a while."

"Hi, Tiffany, I haven't seen you in a long time. How are things?" His smile seemed genuine to Tiffany.

"Good, good." Tiffany pointed to Tom. "This is Tom. Tom, this is …"

"Bobby?" Tom smirked, offering his hand as a greeting.

"Nice meeting you, Tom." Bobby shook his hand. "Tiffany and I go back a few years."

"Yes." Tiffany moved to Bobby's side. "Excuse us, Tom." She took Bobby's arm and guided him to a corner near a bar setup. "I wanted to talk to you before Valerie sees you."

"Oh, really? You have something in mind?"

"Well…not exactly." Tiffany looked around before she continued her comment. She had devised a plan to get Bobby's support and have him approach Valerie without any lustful intentions. "I sent you the invitation because I know you'll always be in love with Valerie, but in this case, I hope you don't do anything to get her attention. I mean, it's not like you have to do something to get her away from her current guy. This isn't sounding right, is it?"

"Actually, I think I understand what you're trying to say. Believe me, I'm over Valerie and I came here only as a friend."

"Really?"

"Yes, really." Bobby pointed to a tall, red-headed woman in a coral chiffon dress. "That's my date."

Tiffany's facial expression could have woken the dead. She was surprised to see that the woman bore no physical resemblance to Valerie, and she said, "I'm happy for you."

"Thanks. Don't worry about me and Valerie. I only wish her the best." Bobby left Tiffany and strolled over to his date. *I sure called that wrong*, thought Tiffany as she watched Bobby greet his date with a kiss on her cheek. There was something about Bobby's act that made her feel jealous. Valerie saw Tiffany from a distance and walked over to her. "Why are you frowning?"

"Am I?"

"I saw you." Valerie touched Tiffany's shoulder, "Hey, there are too many men in here for you to stand alone in a corner. Why aren't you out there dancing or flirting with one of JT's single friends?" Valerie looked around. "Where's Tom?"

"He's around." Tiffany looked at Valerie with raised eyebrows. "I was just talking to Bobby." Tiffany pointed to Bobby and his date.

"Wow, she's very pretty. I'm glad he's here with a date. I'm surprised he showed up, considering how badly I treated him."

"I guess he got over it."

"I'll go talk to him." Valerie started in his direction, and Tiffany grabbed her arm.

"Wait, are you sure you want to do that?"

"Why not? There is nothing between us, and he's here supporting JT, right? I want everyone to have fun, and there's no bitterness between Bobby and me. We talked long ago and even got together once. I didn't tell you, but we came to a friendly agreement. He won't stalk me, and I don't need to get a restraining order."

"And it worked?"

"Funny thing, he was already breaking up with me right after we met. I didn't think anything of it because he had met the woman he's with now."

"Guess I worried over nothing."

"So you're the reason all my friends are here." Valerie pulled Tiffany into a hug.

"Thank you so much. You're the best." She let go, and Tiffany watched her head directly for Bobby and his date.

JT took the microphone from the band and walked towards his veiled painting. He motioned to the band to lower the music and spoke loudly to get everyone's attention.

"Folks, it's time for the main event." He looked around, but couldn't find Valerie. "Valerie, please join me?" JT waited a few moments before he spoke again.

"He's at the mic. You'd better go!" Tiffany shouted and waived towards JT.

"As I said earlier tonight, there are a few things you are fortunate to be able to do in life. One is to enjoy the work you do so much, that it isn't work at all. I am fortunate to do just that: play at my job." Some in the crowd laughed and others nodded in agreement.

Someone from the group shouted, "You play a lot, JT," and laughter filled the room.

JT waited for the chuckles to die down before he continued. "In this case, I followed my passion, which resulted in this inspired painting." Valerie made it to the front and stood by JT's side. Tiffany positioned herself for a perfect view and Tom moseyed up beside her.

"I met Valerie months ago, and we've become inseparable. I admire the way she supports me, picks up after me, and then encourages me to make life fun. She became my inspiration for this painting and I'm fortunate enough to have fallen in love with such a woman." JT waved his hand and the band played a new song. It had become their song: the classic by Barry White called "My First, My Last, My Everything." JT spoke again.

"It's not every day that you find someone who makes your heart flutter. You usually only dream of meeting that special person who takes your breath away and simultaneously makes you want to live. I am fortunate to have met that special woman." JT turned towards the painting and asked Valerie to center herself in front of it. "Stand right here, Sweetie," he directed her, and gave her the string attached to the veil covering his masterpiece. He moved to her right side and placed one hand in his pocket. "I dedicate this picture to you, my Valerie." JT knelt on one knee to the right of Valerie. "Pull the string," he coaxed, and retrieved a ring box from his pocket. He opened it and waited for the veil to fall to the floor. When it did and the picture was displayed, a whispered "Ah" went through the crowd. It was an abstract painting of a diamond ring. Valerie's eyes widened in surprise. Tiffany covered her mouth, in awe of his work.

"It's beautiful." That was all she managed to say.

JT continued. "I want this life we've recently created to last forever. I need you to be my inspiration, my joy, my sun and moon. I want us to bring new life into this world, created by our love. I want us to endure everything together and most of all, I want you to be my partner, my best friend, and my wife."

Valerie looked at the painting while she listened to JT describe what he wanted for them. A little confused, she wondered how she was supposed to wear a picture of a ring. Tiffany, Tom, and Bobby shouted in unison from various positions in the crowd, "Look at JT."

Valerie didn't understand, and kept facing the picture.

More people from the room shouted. "Look at JT."

Valerie finally looked and saw JT on one knee, holding the exact ring from the picture in his hand.

"Will you?" he asked. Valerie covered her mouth with both hands and started shaking.

"Well?" members of the crowd asked.

"I, I ..." Valerie held her right hand over her mouth, extended her left hand towards JT, and nodded her head in agreement. With tears in her eyes, she watched JT place the ring on her finger and stand up. She threw herself into his arms. "Yes, yes, yes," she said.

The crowd clapped, and Tiffany ran to her. JT released Valerie, giving her the opportunity to hug Tiffany.

"It's been a long time coming. Congrats, girl, he's a good man!"

Valerie nodded. "Thanks - and you're going to be my maid of honor."

The crowd surrounded JT and Valerie and gave them congratulations. The band roared into a festive song and one of JT's friends took the microphone and shouted a toast: "To JT and Valerie! We hope your marriage will be as stellar as his proposal!"

***

When Tiffany arrived home, she went straight to her bedroom, changed into her pink nightgown, and prepared for bed. She selected a magazine from her nightstand and found an interesting article, "Why Don't You Find Love?" Points made by the author touched Tiffany on many levels, and one in particular hit closer to home, more so than the others. The advice to "Remove those obstacles to finding love" bought her to tears. She mustered the strength to avoid falling into depression. Her mind reviewed numerous conversations with friends about finding love, taking a chance, and reducing her strict standards of quality.

She lay in bed, looking at the circle of light on the ceiling from the night stand lamp. *If Valerie can find love with all of her flaws and weird habits, then I can, too. What am I not doing? What am I not doing?* Tiffany pondered while she reached for the lamp and turned it off. The room went dark. "What am I not doing?" she repeated aloud before falling asleep.

Chapter 30

The weekend found Manny and Suzie excited over their spontaneous drive to Key West. In the past, from time to time, Manny would get up early, call Suzie, and invite her out for a drive. They hadn't done it since Suzie started college, and Manny felt it was time for an excursion. He capitalized on the fact that he lived in close proximity to Suzie. He rose before sunrise, drove to her college dorm, and picked up Suzie for a ride down Highway 1 towards the Florida Keys.

"Dad, can you stop for coffee?"

"We'll stop at the next gas station", responded Manny.

"Good: it's early, and I can use a cup." Suzie yawned and reclined the seat to get as horizontal as possible. "I stayed out too late and didn't sleep."

"We haven't done this in a while. I'm surprised you didn't want to bring a friend."

"We haven't done much together outside of having dinner, lately. I think we'll have fun together. I want to visit the fort this time."

"I haven't been there in a while. We can catch the late morning ferry. Are we snorkeling or not?"

"I'm more excited about snorkeling around there. We've only been to the fort once, and once you see it, you want to go back and explore it again."

"So we're water folks for this weekend. What are we doing tomorrow?"

"Let's play it by ear. We should relax and have fun, do a little sunbathing, drink a few margaritas, and just chill."

Manny couldn't believe his daughter's comment. "You want to drink margaritas with your ol' man? I don't know about that, but since you're a young adult, I guess you can have one. Guess I have to let you grow up. Okay, so it's one night in Key West and we'll drive back tomorrow. Sounds like something a doctor would order."

Manny stopped at the next Quick Stop near Homestead. They got out of the car and went straight for coffee. He poured a cup while Suzie selected a doughnut. "Get me one too," Manny suggested. He gave the cashier an extra twenty dollars for gasoline. "Anything else you want?"

"No, not really."

It was twenty minutes into the drive, and neither had spoken a word. Suzie broke the ice. "Well, , did you decide to go see that lady you've been Skyping with?"

"I did. I sent her an email for that reason. What's funny is, I hadn't read her email, which suggested the same thing. I tried to Skype with her and talk about it," Manny chuckled.

"Dad, you're lame."

"Why lame? That's no way to talk to your dear old dad."

"Because you're not making more effort. Why haven't you called her outside of Skype?"

"You know, that's a great question. We should try calling one day. We talk so often on Skype, we didn't think about it."

"And why haven't you used her cell number?"

"Honestly, I didn't think I'd need to. But this past week, after I sent her my note, I'm not sure. I mean, it isn't like it's so hot that I want to throw myself into long-distance dating. How often would I see her?"

"You've met women from all over the place and now you're worried about distance? I can't believe you."

"I have a good reason not to move."

Suzie glanced at Manny, shaking her head. "Come on, Dad, it's not like you and I are living together. We can see each other just like we've done for years. So what's really holding you back from dating her?"

Manny didn't immediately respond to Suzie's question. He had no real explanation. Being near Suzie was his excuse. "Look, if you're not afraid of my being far away again, I could date a woman who lives across the country."

"Across the country? You never said where. Or did you?"

"You weren't paying attention. I told you San Francisco."

"Oh yeah, I remember. So why haven't you gone to visit?"

"Because we're just warming up to the idea," said Manny. "We both wrote about it in our emails and I'm waiting for a response."

"I'm sure she's leaning towards visiting you, or she wouldn't have written you encouraging you to think about it."

"Actually, you had me thinking about it before I read her email."

"I know my dad." She chuckled. "And I know how to influence your decisions. I've known how to get you to do things since I was a kid."

"Manipulative kid."

"Proud sales professional. It's what I do at the coffee shop."

"My damn kid, the most influential person in my life."

They laughed and recalled their first excursion to Key West, when Suzie was a child. She had cried over everything Manny encouraged her to do. He remembered she told him that her mother had warned her that everything he would try to get her to do would be a disaster, and she had believed it. It had taken him years to earn her trust.

Manny kept talking while he parked in the Holiday Inn parking lot. They were too early for check in, so he checked on their reservations and they changed in the lobby's bathrooms. They went downtown to the far end of the island and boarded the ferry to Fort Jefferson.

They snorkeled for hours and returned in time to check into the hotel. Next, they rented bicycles and rode around the island, just like they had done years ago. They stopped at their favorite Cuban restaurant for an early dinner, enjoyed people-watching on the pier, and watched the sunset. Being in her life since he retired from the Navy opened doors for them to become closer. Manny realized that one day soon he would have to let his daughter become a woman. While they sat on a bench and watched the crowd and entertainment, he put his arm around Suzie.

"You know, I've been thinking. You're right. We're pretty solid; better than we have ever been. I don't think adding a woman to my life will impact our relationship."

"Dad, I told you that earlier."

"Well, now I'm admitting it. I want to spend days with a wife the way I've spent   quality time with you. You know, having fun doing things…. always laughing."

"You can never replace me, Dad, but I understand what you're saying. It's been awesome and I'm always up to doing stuff like this with you anytime. Today was just like when I was a kid, but better this time; because I'm old enough to let you go and remember how we always loved being together."

Manny hugged Suzie closer. "You're a hard act for any woman to follow, kid," he said before he kissed her forehead.

***

Monday morning came too quickly for Manny. He and Suzie had returned Sunday evening. No matter how often he worked out, swimming always took a toll on his body. Muscles hurt that he knew hadn't been trained. He made coffee for his morning drive.

It wasn't long after Tiffany arrived home from work that she read Manny's email. She smiled at his message, picked up the cell phone, and dialed his number.

"Hello, Manny, it's Tiffany," she said.

"Wow, I'm happy you called." The sound of her voice brought a smile to his face. "I have lots to share. Let me start by saying thanks for calling."

"You're welcome. It's good to hear you're excited that I'm on the phone with you. I love a man with enthusiasm."

"I don't know if its enthusiasm or nervousness. Let me tell you, it's been a long time since I've courted a woman on the phone."

"Really? Why are you nervous? We've talked for months on Skype. I don't see the difference." Manny didn't want to sound overly anxious and thought about his next words before speaking.

"I, ah, think a phone call is more intimate than Skype. Even though we can see each other on video, it's nothing like a phone call. You know, now we get to talk on the run. I like being able to talk with you at a moment's notice."

"I see your point. I don't mind you calling. This way I can share what's on my mind without having to wait until I get home since I don't have the latest iPhone."

"Exactly, see: we're on the same path. I'm convinced it's more important that we talk. It's as if we're thinking alike." Manny chuckled. "I think we can talk our way into a good position. Wait, that didn't come out right." Manny laughed and then said, "I mean that we can keep our connection going."

"I hear you," Tiffany agreed. "So what's next?"

"I believe we should be spontaneous. Whenever the urge hits, we'll make a call."

"You wouldn't mind a call at any time day or night? Don't forget: we're three hours apart."

Manny didn't wait to answer. "Anytime. If I don't answer, I'll get back to you right away."

"That's fair. The same goes for me." Their conversation went on for an hour. They talked about how they connected and specifically discussed how they had arrived at their current conclusion.

"I'm happy we finally got here." Manny paused before asking, "Have we reconsidered meeting in person? Do you think you're still up for it?"

Tiffany had her reservations. Her goals didn't include an involvement with someone far away. After a moment of silence, all she said was, "Well…" and Manny felt he had pushed her too soon in their first conversation.

"Well? You think I'm overstepping my boundaries?"

"I was going to say, I was thinking about it."

"Is that a positive? Are you finally coming to grips with our reality?"

"Grips with our reality? Are you planning to move if things work out between us?"

A Cyber Affair

"You know, I haven't thought that far ahead, but I've been told I'll never lose my daughter if I did. What about you?"

"I've never been to Florida. I hear it's a nice place to visit."

"I've been to San Francisco, and its one place I wouldn't mind seeing again."

"I'm up to meeting you, but let's hold off on moving."

"Who's moving? We have to see if there's a physical attraction first."

"I agree. We've been so focused on Skype, and from what I see we shouldn't have a chemistry problem, but you know physical chemistry is very important."

"Extremely important! I'm willing to find out. Thinking about it has me excited. When are you flying to Florida?" asked Manny.

"As soon as you get to San Francisco," Tiffany said. "I can show you a great time. Why don't you think about coming here?"

"I have, and I'm eager to travel, under one condition."

"I'm not promising anything sexual." Tiffany made sure she put that out there so there was no misinterpretation. "I'm no floozy, and unless we're serious, it's not going to happen."

"I respect you for that. I believe if it's meant to happen, it will. Look, if we're together day in and day out, I'll get to know you better and I hope you would get to know me as well. By then we'll know whether or not we'll look forward to getting back with one another or whether we'll be anxious to get away."

"I have an idea, and I want you to really think about it," said Tiffany. "If we visit each other in our hometowns, we can't let other people get involved. I want your total focus, and no one else's opinion means a thing."

"There is only one person's opinion I'll seek if there is a need for approval. We've talked about it and she's the person who matters most in my life. My daughter, Suzie."

"Well, of course I'd love to meet your daughter, but that can come later. I don't expect to see her during our first meeting."

"What if I know you're the one?"

"Don't you think I need to know you're the one, too, before we start planning a family?"

"Good point and I agree. We'll meet others only after we're sure."

"If that's the case, we should meet someplace neutral," said Tiffany.

"Yes, someplace where neither of us has friends. I'm limited because I've been in the Navy and tend to run into so many people I've served with."

"I understand, and that's fine as long as no one influences or interferes with us."

"Not one, not one sailor at all." Manny considered a location.

"Hey how about San Diego?" Tiffany suggested.

"No, I have too many friends there and that's a big Navy town. I'm sure I'd run into someone. Tell me three places you'd like to visit. Don't tell me now; let's wait until we talk again. We've already been on the phone for over an hour."

"Time flies when you get lost in the conversation. I can tell you tomorrow."

"Good, let's share then. Thanks for letting me call you."

"Good night, Manny, I enjoyed talking to you. Let's put a rush on our meeting. I know we'll have a great time."

"I know, right. I can feel it too. Take care, Tiffany. You'll hear from me later tomorrow." Manny ended the call and reviewed a few travel websites before he crawled into bed.

***

Tiffany surfed a few websites to research Florida. She explored cities like Miami, Tampa, and Orlando. She read about the Florida Keys and especially the island near Fort Myers. Tiffany became excited about meeting Manny and ecstatic over their future travels - she scanned many reviews on each location, and investigated cities between Florida and California. She focused on tourist towns in Colorado, Missouri, Arizona, and Texas. When she saw pictures of San Antonio, she smiled, because it was a place she'd always wanted to visit. She imagined what they would do during their time at each location

A beach picture on the Gulf Coast caught her eye next, while San Padre Island brought her into a daydream of her and Manny walking hand-in-hand on the beach. An advertisement banner for New Orleans appeared on the web page, and she clicked on the link. It was the jazz and the food that made her want to explore the city of music.

Before Tiffany knew it, the time had crept into the wee hours of morning. Tiffany crashed as soon as her head hit the pillow. She dreamed of places to explore and felt excitement about enjoying them with someone. Her heart felt complete and was filled with hope. She couldn't wait to meet the man she had talked with for so long.

***

The next day, Manny didn't waste any time exploring travel opportunities. He remembered when travel was part of his job, yet since retiring from the Navy, his focus had been on Suzie. Their father-daughter relationship had kept him grounded. Manny reveled in his excitement over meeting Tiffany and he concentrated on various locations for the visit. He needed an impressive city for their adventure because he didn't want to end up in some town with little or no entertainment lest they run out of things to do.

Manny couldn't allow boredom to set in. He didn't want empty moments between them where they looked at each other with blank stares or forced conversations that included small talk. Manny didn't like limitations. If conversation was going to happen, he wanted a location that offered a lot to talk about. He surfed the web for cities between San Francisco and West Palm Beach. After reviewing Cancun, he stumbled on a page where he read about a city of serenity and a plethora of activities, easy travel, and entertainment. What he didn't know was whether Tiffany would be up to the challenge.

Manny researched his perfect location and began pricing his ticket. He ventured onto the city's webpage and discovered opportunities for fun under the sun and in the cool shade of night. In page after page he found facts of interest - and something that supported his idea that it would be a perfect setting to get Tiffany into his arms.

Chapter 31

Tiffany left her job and met Valerie for an evening drink at a local pub. They sat at the bar receiving their beers. "How's it going?" Tiffany asked.

"It's going good, but nothing's changed much. The only difference is that I'm wearing an engagement ring."

"And a beautiful ring, too." Tiffany stared at Valerie's hand, holding it for a better view. "He did a good job."

"You didn't have anything to do with it, did you?"

"No, not at all. The only thing I did was give JT a list of our friends."

"He did everything," Valerie smiled and then added, "I'm so proud he's my fiancé."

Tiffany looked at Valerie's engagement ring a second time and smiled. "He did great, and seeing you in love, after all those years of ups and downs, is definitely worth the wait. I mean, it's fortunate you found JT when you did."

"What do you mean?"

"Weren't you on one of your usual manhunts when you met JT? I don't remember you telling me how you two met."

"I didn't?" Valerie looked surprise. "I thought I did."

"No, you didn't. It's no big deal. You found the man of your dreams and that's all that matters."

"I did, and yes, it is, but I don't mind telling you." Valerie sipped her beer and told Tiffany of her journey into the art store where she first bumped into JT. "He was handsome, and the only reason I went there was to attend a wine and art class. I guess you were probably online, because we didn't go together. Anyway, he attended the class and I mistakenly thought he was a student and a wine connoisseur like me. We chatted for a few minutes, and when people began filling the room, he excused himself and headed to the front of the class. It surprised me that he hadn't mentioned he was teaching the class. After class, we talked, and it went on for hours. He's one of the few men I've met who didn't talk about sex that first night. I knew then he was different."

"Wow, you met at a wine and art class. Is that why we went to the art gallery that night?"

"Partially. But actually, that wasn't the first night that JT and I spent time together. It happened a couple of weeks after we saw each other for at least five of those fourteen nights."

"Where was I during your dates?"

"I think you were focused on surfing, or maybe on chasing Tom."

"We both know online didn't work. Well, not yet. But I didn't think Tom and I were supposed to work I don't think."

"And I thought you were busy with Tom."

Tiffany placed her empty mug on the edge of the table to signal the waiter for a refill. "At least I had some activity - not like yours, but I had some fun with Tom."

"No one is saying you didn't, but I'm glad you aren't upset with me."

"Upset?"

"Yes." Valerie looked into Tiffany's eyes. "Jealousy is hard, but when one has something the other wants badly, resentment can make a person ill. I feared you would envy JT and me."

"I'm happy for you! I'm not jealous." Tiffany looked at her beer. "You know I've had my share of men."

"But not the type of men that sweeps you off your feet at any given moment. JT does that to me."

"So, you're in love." Tiffany smiled.

"Shouldn't I finally be in love? I mean, like you said, it's been a well-traveled road to find a love worth having. You can find it too, Tiffany. I have faith in you. You have to be careful with the men you choose." Valerie paused for a moment and looked at Tiffany for a reaction. She searched for a response or at least an attentive facial expression. When she saw it she said: "How's that online thing going?"

"It's going great. As a matter of fact, I'm thinking about meeting him."

"Meeting who?" Valerie shook her head in disbelief. "What part of the city does he live in?"

"He doesn't live near San Francisco at all. He's across the country."

"You've lost your mind. I mean, what happened to your 'locals only' rule?"

"Things change. I see something different in him and I think it's worth giving him a chance."

"Are you that crazy or deranged? What are you going to do, travel across the country to meet a man you only chatted with online? He may be a rapist; or worse, he could be a serial killer! I mean, come on, Tiffany don't be silly - it's dangerous."

Tiffany disagreed with Valerie's comments that Manny was a maniac or something. "Valerie, don't go there. Manny and I have talked for months. I can't imagine not talking to him every day. He's sharp, funny, looks good, and has values I like."

"You can't be serious? I mean, he's across the country. Why can't he find a woman where he lives?"

"Now, that's a double standard. You would go to a club, meet a guy on the street or in a store, and eventually sleep with him in the first week, and you're worried about a man across country? Remember, I know your past."

"Okay, you made a valid point. Can you check his police record or get a private investigator or something so you have an idea of his background?"

"I would, but I think I know him well enough from all of our conversations. I mean, he hasn't revealed anything out of the norm or said he had any specific challenges. I have a great feeling about him. I can call him at any time, discuss anything, and he's straight forward about himself. But I guess it wouldn't hurt to do a little investigating."

"You should have done that long ago, or at the first thought of meeting him." Valerie said, and gave her a look of deep concern.

"I don't do that for local men. Why would I do that for someone across the country?"

"Because you can have someone come and get you in minutes when you are local, whereas if you're lost in the middle of nowhere across the country..." Valerie advised.

"Miami isn't in the middle of nowhere, you know."

"You're flying to Miami?"

"I don't know for sure. We haven't decided where we should meet. I think we'll talk about it the next time we're online."

"Do you have a place in mind? Maybe a city where you have friends or relatives?" Valerie asked with concern when she saw Tiffany's sincerity about meeting her online interest. "Do you have people you can trust outside of San Francisco?"

"I do, but I don't think I want them around. I'm feeling positive about Manny. We have a connection I haven't felt in years. I mean, it's better than any I've had since my marriage."

"I remember how that turned out," Valerie smirked. "I'm concerned for your safety."

"Thanks. You're a great friend, but I feel I have to meet Manny, and I have to trust my intuition on this."

"Will you at least take every precaution? I mean, let the world know where you are and who you're with. We should have a picture of Manny, a number to contact him, a number for the hotel you're staying in, and your travel arrangements. And, of course, take mace."

"That's damn good advice, Valerie," Tiffany admitted while she reflected on Valerie's request. It was something she needed to consider. Trust or not, those stories of hope she had heard about didn't always lead to happy endings. "You're a great friend."

Tiffany and Valerie waved farewell and blew each other a kiss. They went their separate ways when they left the bar. On the way home, Tiffany pulled her cell from her purse, looked at the time, and calculated what time it was in Florida. She dialed Manny, because Valerie's issue was relevant to her future travel. Manny answered, as her call woke him.

"Hey, Tiffany, what's up?"

"Something important; can you talk?"

Manny fought his sleep-weary body "Yeah, sure" and changed his position from lying to sitting. "What's on your mind?"

"I want to make sure we're doing this. I mean, meeting. I don't want to go through all the scenarios in my mind if we're not going to do it."

"We're doing it. As a matter of fact, I was thinking of making it really easy and just coming to you."

"No, I don't want it here. Like we said, it has to be a neutral location with no friends trying to influence us."

"I agree. Okay, so what can I do to help you understand that I'm serious?" Manny questioned.

"You can send me a picture of you, the latest picture, and your social security number."

"Hey, wait. I'm not sure about the social security number, but a picture I can do. Why do you want my social security number?"

"So if anything happens to me, someone can track your whereabouts."

"Oh, so now fear and caution are coming along on our trip? I get it. Let me say this: I'll share what you share."

"What?"

"I'll share what you share. A picture, phone number, friends' contact info, social security numbers, the works."

Tiffany didn't expect his response, but was happy that he wanted to give her everything she was willing to share. "We're going to share all of our information so if something happens to either of us, we're confident that we can be found."

"Agreed. So it's a deal. I'll send my list tomorrow."

"I'll send mine, too. I feel better, don't you?"

"I trusted you from the start, but if this makes it easier for us to relax and enjoy, I'm all for it." Manny yawned. "I have to get up in a few. Good night, Tiffany."

"Good night, Manny."

Chapter 32

Manny finished his work day, worked out, and then went to B.B.King's Blues Club, the place where he had met Frieda. He watched others having fun and started a conversation with a guy at the bar. "I'm trying to select a city that's fun and offers nightlife, entertainment, and sightseeing for a weekend."

"You mean a place you can be safe, have the time of your life, and make some memories?"

"That sounds exactly like what I want, but I can't think of any location that's the total package. You know, I need a place where there is balance. Somewhere where, night after night, there's never a boring moment but if you need to escape to somewhere quiet, that's available, too."

"Dude, that sounds like Vegas."

"Las Vegas. I didn't think of that. I was all over the place. I bet she'll like the idea." Manny gave the guy's shoulder a friendly tap. "Thanks, man."

"No problem, bro. You'll have a blast."

"I'm sure we will." Manny finished his drink and sent Tiffany a text: Vegas? He went home and researched the city for its dynamic entertainment and activities.

***

The next morning Tiffany awoke to a text alert and picked up her cell phone to see a text from Manny, which she quickly opened. All it read was: *Vegas?* She texted back:

That sounds wonderful. I didn't think of Vegas. We'll talk about it later. Will you be online, or should I call you?

Manny received the response when he went to his locker. He answered. *Call me when you're free.*

It was almost 9:00 pm when Manny's cell phone rang.

"Hey, Tiffany, glad you called."

"I think Vegas is a great idea. It sounds awesome and I've never been there."

"So it's a first for you. It's been years since I've been there. What shall we do?" Manny asked, and then recanted. "Here's what I think we should do. Let's meet there on a Friday evening and, for safety, we can get separate rooms at the same hotel."

"I think separate rooms is a good idea. We can manage that."

"Great. I've researched events and shows we can attend - or maybe we should play it by ear? There are so many shows to choose from that I think being spontaneous could be better." Manny looked at his phone calendar. "How about the Wednesday after next?" He paused. "Will that do?"

Tiffany got up from her couch and walked to the kitchen wall near the fridge where she kept her hanging calendar. "I think that's a little soon. I need to let my job know that I'm taking off that weekend, so it's all about scheduling." She counted the number of days for the lead she needed. "I think three weeks will do. Let's do the following Wednesday. I am sure I'll be ready then."

"Okay, three weeks away. We can save a few bucks on the flight. I'm okay with that." Manny nodded his head in agreement. "Good timing."

"I'm so looking forward to our first weekend. I know we'll enjoy it. When should we start scheduling our flights?"

"How 'bout now? I'll call you when I have everything up online."

"Sounds like a plan. I'll search for my flight and hotel." Tiffany disconnected the line and got busy pricing flights and hotels. *This is exciting,* she thought. *I haven't been this excited since I went on my honeymoon.*

***

Manny found great airline and hotel prices for his trip. He Skyped Tiffany and sent his plans for her to review. When Tiffany logged onto Skype, she reviewed his message, looked for flights, and responded with her own possible travel itinerary. The closest they could coordinate would have her arriving either an hour early or three hours later than Manny. She started a video chat.

"Hey, are we doing the right thing?" she asked.

"We are - I, at least, feel that we are. I'm excited; aren't you?" She saw him smile. "After everything I've read about Vegas, we're in for a great time. It's changed since I was there years ago."

"I love the idea of meeting in Vegas. I've heard so much about it."

"Yes, this should be great for us. No friends, no influences - just me and you and whatever we can get into."

"I like that idea. So you're flying in at three that afternoon?" Tiffany asked for confirmation.

"For me, that's leaving at a great time. What about your flight? You didn't give me the details of which flight you chose."

"Either I get there before you and wait an hour, or arrive after three hours after you. I was thinking I'd take the first option, get there early, and maybe we can share a cab to our hotel."

"Yes, that sounds awesome. Did you choose a hotel?"

"I like Treasure Island. Do you think its okay?"

"Sure, I'll make my reservation and see if I can get a room close to yours. I'm glad you selected Treasure Island. I remember it being an awesome hotel and casino."

Tiffany and Manny set up their travel plans and communicated over the next two weeks. They explored Las Vegas websites and agreed to attend Cirque du Soleil shows and a music concert, visit dance clubs, and even identified which restaurants they might enjoy together. There was such a buildup of excitement that they forgot to share their safety information from their earlier conversation.

Chapter 33

On the travel day Manny woke earlier than usual. Anxiety got the best of him. *By the end of today I will finally see the woman who has held my attention all these months,* he thought while checking his luggage for the third time to ensure he had packed all the proper attire. He went through his home, secured everything, and left instructions for Suzie to follow while she stayed in his apartment. He went to his desktop and read a few of Tiffany's emails before driving towards the Fort Lauderdale Airport.

Manny turned off of the expressway to Fort Lauderdale and made a quick stop at a coffee shop. He purchased a Danish and coffee, and then drove to the airport's extended parking lot where he sat in his truck eating breakfast, imagining Tiffany's touch, remembering her voice, and reflecting on her mannerisms which he'd observed via Skype.

Manny left his truck, took the shuttle to the terminal, and checked in for his flight. When he got on the plane, he had magazines, a DVD movie, and his laptop to entertain him during the five-hour flight. His nerves filled him with mixed feelings and he couldn't seem to relax. Within the first hour, he pulled out the DVD and watched "Sleepless in Seattle" with Tom Hanks and Meg Ryan. He compared his new adventure to that of the movie characters. At the end of the movie, he thought, *How things have changed, yet remain the same.*

***

Tiffany finalized her checklist. *Let's see: toiletries, dresses, shoes, nightie – just in case, shower cap, shorts, a couple of tops and my bikini. I think it's all here.* Her doorbell rang while she was securing her carry-on luggage.

"Who is it?" she yelled as she approached the door, rolling her small suitcase behind her.

"Trevor and Trevor, Attorneys at Law. I'm here for Tiffany Miles," the voice behind the door answered.

Tiffany looked through the peephole and saw a gentleman holding a briefcase. She recognized the name from the television commercials about finding a lawyer after a car accident. She cracked the door with the chain lock securely in place.

"I haven't been in an auto accident."

"No, ma'am, you haven't. Are you Tiffany Miles?" Mr. Trevor said.

"Yes, I am. How can I help you?"

"I'm here to deliver a letter. Can I come in?"

Tiffany hesitated and looked at the gentleman once more before opening the door.

"Sure, come in. Please have a seat," she said, and pointed at the sofa. "What brings you here again?" The lawyer opened his briefcase, reached inside, and pulled out a document. "This is the will from your deceased uncle."

"Wait, you mean *my* uncle? Oh my God!!! My uncle Teddy died?" Tiffany burst into tears and covered her mouth with both hands.

The attorney stood. "I'm afraid there's been a misunderstanding. I'm actually referring to Mister Robert Henry Miles, your ex-husband's uncle."

"You scared me. Why didn't you say that in the first place? Okay, I heard he'd died. He was a very nice man. Too bad my ex-husband inherited whatever from him. I hope he loses every dime."

"I can't disclose what your husband inherited, but I'm here to give you this check. It's the last thing I have to do to complete his request." The lawyer pulled another envelope from his briefcase with the name Tiffany Miles handwritten on the front. "According to the will, he left you a considerable sum of money." Tiffany opened the envelope, unfolded its enclosed letter, and read the handwritten note.

Tiffany,

My nephew may be a lot of fun, but I know that sometimes he can be bothersome. I guess you could consider him a work in progress. Hang in there with him because he's not always the sharpest knife in the drawer. The one good thing he did in his life was marry you. I appreciate how you look after him. Please make use of this gift to make life enjoyable, and hopefully you can increase it for your future.

Love Always,
Robert

Tiffany retrieved the check, looked at the sum, and fell into her chair with her eyes wide. The amount of $250,000.00 overwhelmed her. She jumped to her feet and grabbed the lawyer, yanking him from his seat like a child grabbing a rag doll, gave him a hug, cried out "Thank you!!" and tried to escort Mr. Trevor to the door.

"Wait, you have to sign here before I leave. It's to confirm delivery." Mr. Trevor pulled out the document and placed it on the coffee table. He grabbed a pen from his briefcase and pointed to the highlighted area requiring her signature. Tiffany followed instructions and signed where he directed.

"Now I can leave. Enjoy your money," Mr. Trevor instructed.

"Just in time for Vegas," Tiffany laughed.

"Gambling isn't a very wise way to invest your money. If you'd like I could recommend…."

"Not to gamble. It's to meet Mr. Right." Tiffany smiled and opened the door for Mr. Trevor to exit.

"Have fun in Vegas. Here's my card, if you need any legal services."

"Thank you," Tiffany said as she closed the door and jumped for joy. She thought about her ex-husband's note and the twenty-five-dollar check. "Look who's laughing now," she said aloud.

***

Tiffany rushed to Valerie's car for her ride to the airport. "Hey, Valerie, thanks for taking me."

"You're welcome. I can't let you go without you giving me some info about the guy you're meeting. Remember, women have been murdered by men they met online."

"Okay, okay, okay. I'll give you his cell number, and we'll be staying at Treasure Island. I have my own room. You can catch me there if you need to, but something tells me I'll be fine."

"I hope so, but there are crazy people online. Murder is no joking matter."

"Valerie, we've had this conversation before. Think positive for me, will you? I like this guy. He seems very nice and I need to take this chance. Can't you be supportive?"

"Yes, I can support you. But if anything happens, just know I'm on my way."

"You're the best. Oh, and by the way, remember that box I got from Mr. Asshole?"

"The torn pictures and the twenty-five dollar check?"

"I got more than he could imagine. A lawyer came by and settled the last part of my ex-husband's uncle's will. Let's just say that I will have a quarter of a million in the bank soon."

"What? Are you serious?!" Valerie screamed.

"I am, and I'm happy for two reasons, now. Meeting Manny and finally being financially secure."

"Don't get any crazy ideas in Vegas, my friend. No gambling."

"I don't take unnecessary chances with money, remember? That's something you do."

"You're right."

They arrived at the airport's passenger drop-off. Before leaving the car, Tiffany wrote down Manny's cell number and gave Valerie the hotel reservations and also a list of places they planned to visit and shows they wanted to attend. Tiffany kissed Valerie on the cheek.

"Thanks again, and don't worry."

Tiffany left the car with her carry-on and walked into the airport. She found her terminal gate and paced back and forth, frowning. She looked at the gate and then at her cell phone and contemplated *What the hell am I doing? Once I'm on the plane, it's almost a two-hour flight. I can't get off in mid-flight and I sure can't make the plane turn around. What if he's a serial killer like Valerie suggested? What if he isn't anything like he appeared online?* Tiffany heard the gate attendant announce the flight and boarding instructions.

Chapter 34

Tiffany viewed cloud formations through the plane's porthole and thought about how had Manny influenced her to go against her own rule of local men only. Earlier in the year, she had stood firm and had no intention of meeting a man who lived on the other side of the country. She shook her head in disbelief that she was actually on a flight to meet Manny.

I hope I'm doing the right thing. Tiffany did a mental check of her expectations and reflected how Manny met all of them except distance. She weighed pros and cons and agonized over success and failure. When the flight attendant inquired if she wanted a drink, Tiffany retrieved her purse and ordered: "Red wine - no, white wine … no, neither one."

Tiffany sat there fighting skepticism and confusion. She was happy that she was following Tom's advice about connecting with the man she admired, but feared doom as she envisioned scenarios of death or dismay in Las Vegas.

He could kill me, chop my body into small pieces, bag me and throw me in the nearby dam, or bury me in the desert. Tiffany shook her head in disbelief again. *He could rape me and hold me hostage. I could become his sex slave.* That made her smile as she thought, *I need a man with a strong sex drive. I know he has one* She giggled.

She made an effort to relax while she repeated conversations with Manny in her mind. She recalled Tom's advice, Valerie's surprise engagement, and the 'kiss-my-ass-you-deserve-less' letter from her ex-husband. All these things had led her down this path of chance. *But what if this visit went wrong?* Her tapping foot and slight rocking, nervous energy distracted the stranger next to her. He asked, "Is this your first flight? You seem nervous."

"No, it isn't. I'm on an adventure," Tiffany grinned.

"Adventures are good, regardless of the result," he nodded, and then added, "I mean, you had to have something exciting happen to get you on the plane."

"I did, but I am not sure how it's going to turn out."

"Are you afraid of gambling?"

"I took a gamble getting this far, so I guess I'm not."

"You know, the stakes are higher when you face something outside of your comfort zone. Don't worry. Vegas has a way of making things right."

"You really mean the cliché about whatever happens in Vegas?"

"No, I mean there is so much to do that if something bad happens, there is always an opportunity to turn it around. No matter what happens, you can bounce back."

"I bet you're right."

"Trust me. I've been to Vegas a few times. Each trip, I got to do something special. It doesn't matter why you're going. You'll be fine, so relax and enjoy the ride."

Tiffany's flight arrived on time. She deplaned and followed the signs that read Baggage Claim - Ground Transportation. She felt good about being able to physically view Manny first, but her nervous excitement gave her butterflies. *Will he impress me as I think, or will I regret traveling here?* Those insecure thoughts - *kidnap, rape, murder* - traveled around her mind like the luggage on the baggage claim carousel. Tiffany sat in front of several slot machines which gave her a direct view of the escalator to baggage claim. She was glad they had decided to meet at the airport. Tiffany thought it was better than meeting at the hotel because she worried that if Manny didn't meet her expectations, at least being at the airport would give her some sense of security. She was confident the airport offered a way of retreat if her gut told her to escape. *If Manny doesn't resemble his pictures or the person on Skype, I can leave on a return flight. Or, if I don't feel thrilled or connected, then fun in Las Vegas is my alternative or I can go home.*

She kept cool and searched for Manny's features on every man who descended on the escalator. She touched her brow, pushed her hair back with her hand, and again tapped the floor with her right heel in a nervous twitch. She knew her confidence would not have been a concern if they were going on a date in San Francisco, but a rendezvous at McCarran International Airport was an extreme step outside of her comfort zone.

Tiffany and Manny had agreed that Vegas lessened the risk of being influenced by any of their friends, and Las Vegas offered all types of venues which they felt reduced the pressure on them to amuse each other, more so than if had they stayed in a secluded location, if either ended up alone.

Not long after she arrived and while she was waiting for Manny's arrival, Tiffany bought coffee from the Starbucks, joined the crowd gathered around the baggage claim, and blended in. She stood near the slot machines and peeked through slits for her match, positioning herself in case she had to move. Tiffany knew Manny was the same person she'd gotten to know, and knew her worry was likely unnecessary. *After all, we agreed to meet for a great reason.* That thought squelched her uneasy feeling and settled into an internal smile.

She again recalled multiple conversations leading up to this day, and recognized that his presence gave her a chance to satisfy her curiosity. Even with reservations and insecurities, it was apprehension that kept her alert. She stood and stared at the escalator with coffee in hand, ready to grab her bag and either sprint to the exit or move towards him. She remembered their last Skype video conversation.

"Hi," Manny answered as he responded to Tiffany's call from the Skype window he had left open on his laptop.

"I'm glad you're home. How was your day?" Tiffany inquired.

"Pretty good, but now it's exciting."

"Oh, really?" Tiffany smiled because she knew exactly what was coming next. It was a dream, having a guy who considered her to be promising.

"You know why. It's because I'm finally getting to see you."

"Yeah, I'm feeling the same way. Glad I caught you online. It's been a long day; even longer since we haven't talked to each other. I'm so glad we're meeting soon. One day and counting. I can't wait. I mean, seeing you online is one thing, but the thought of finally being in your arms excites me. I'm arriving early at the San Francisco airport to make sure I don't miss the flight. We'll have a great time."

"I'll be there with a huge smile." Manny paused before adding, "I can't wait to see you, Sweetie."

The memory made Tiffany smile.

Chapter 35

Manny's flight arrived at the terminal as scheduled. It took an additional five minutes for him to deplane because of terminal traffic: his airplane had to wait for another to move from the terminal door. It felt like an hour to Manny, because of his anxiety. Every second delayed his mission. He looked at his watch, grabbed his cell phone, and announced his arrival to Tiffany via text. She responded, *Waiting in baggage claim.*

He deplaned, maneuvering around the crowd as he walked into the terminal, went down a flight of stairs, caught a tram, and headed for the escalators to baggage claim. Manny saw a bathroom and decided to freshen up for his first impression. He brushed his teeth, ran his fingers through his hair, and tightened his shirt. Manny flashed to his past routines in preparation for a Navy inspection and chuckled. He felt compelled to impress her with their first physical encounter. Not only did he want to make an impact on their first sighting, but he wanted Tiffany to be sexually aroused. .

He left the bathroom with his carry-on luggage and waited in line at the downward escalator. When he got to the bottom of the moving stairs, he looked for any sign of her. He'd hoped she'd stand out in the crowd. To his disappointment, she was nowhere in sight. His cell phone rang and he answered "Hello?"

Before revealing her presence, Tiffany confirmed it was Manny on the escalator. She scanned pictures they had shared through their cell phones. She compared those scattered pixels to his actual image - the fine man she saw online. Tiffany didn't jump to meet him right away, but instead called his cellular phone, watching him respond as he rode the escalator. By the time he answered, Tiffany had tossed her coffee into the trash can, put her phone into her purse, and was walking towards him with a huge smile. "I wanted to make sure I wasn't dreaming," she confessed.

He dropped his bag, turned his phone off, and hugged her tightly, feeling her soft body. He pressed his lips to her cheek right at the corner of her mouth and held them there for an extended moment before pulling away. To Manny, Tiffany was not a figment of his imagination; instead, she was everything he'd hoped for, confirmed. This realization marked the moment as the highlight of his journey.

"You know how to make a woman weak," Tiffany said. She wanted to jump on him and settle the heated sensation her body felt, but managed to restrain herself and keep her composure.

"When opportunity knocks, a good sailor shows up." Manny smiled.

Tiffany wasn't surprised at the kiss. It was exactly as she had imagined. Although they had communicated for months, she'd fantasized that the first time they kissed would provide the proof that he was "the one".

"Come on, let's go. We have things to do." Tiffany smiled ear to ear.

"I thought maybe you'd like another kiss."

"I would, but I'm not sure I could stop, if we start," Tiffany winked.

Manny smiled in agreement and pointed to the exit. "Let's go."

He walked next to her and placed his arm around her waist while he pulled his baggage along on its rollers. Once outside,

Manny hailed a taxi and held her hand while they waited for the cab to stop in front of them. She slipped her arm through his and placed her head on his shoulder. "I knew you'd feel like this," she whispered.

"Yeah, I thought the same thing."

Tiffany entered the cab first and took the seat behind the driver. When Manny followed, she pulled him close and whispered, "We're doing the right thing, Manny." Her mind reiterated *It IS the right thing*.

Manny said, "Yes, we are." He looked at her with his piercing eyes, driving his passionate message to her soul, and leaned slowly towards her, closing his eyes, and pressed his lips upon hers. Tiffany's heart raced and her breathing raised her bust against his arm. His touch increased the burning flame of her desire, melting her will to stand strong against the odds of doing something raw and in the moment. She was surprised he didn't press forward, and his gentle kiss made her want more. He kissed her again, increasing her desire.

"Which hotel?" The cabdriver looked in the rear view mirror, waiting for a response. Manny turned towards the driver, removing his lips from Tiffany. "Oh, yeah: Treasure Island, right, Tiffany?"

"Yes, Treasure Island," she sighed. Manny and Tiffany sat in silence, looking out the window as the cab moved through the city.

Tiffany looked at Manny while the driver maneuvered through traffic. "I'm happy we made it." Tiffany stared at him, looking at his inviting eyes and hoping he'd caught a glimpse of her heart.

"So am I, Tiffany; so am I." Manny positioned his arm around Tiffany's shoulder, "What's on your mind?"

"Can I be honest?" Tiffany paused. "I was nervous for a moment, before you arrived. Now I'm not nervous at all."

Manny winked at her with a smile. "I'm glad you aren't nervous."

They arrived at Treasure Island, exited the cab, and followed the bellhop to the check-in counter. Manny looked at Tiffany and pressed her to check in first. He stood aside, sizing up Tiffany from head to toe, observing her full figure, and taking in her features.

Tiffany stepped to the counter and reached for her cell phone, retrieving the reservation number and giving the clerk the needed information.

Manny stood patiently, allowing Tiffany enough room for privacy. He smiled whenever she turned to glance at him. She raised her key and stepped aside. "I'll wait for you."

Manny checked in, got his room key, and walked to her. "Are you ready?"

"Sure," Tiffany wasn't hesitant. "Which room is yours?"

"Should I tell a complete stranger my room number?" Manny laughed.

Tiffany looked at him, surprised. "I..."

"...I'm only kidding. I'm in room 1622."

"How'd you get lucky and snag that kind of view?"

"I don't know." Manny glanced at the flowers displayed in the center of the casino. "Which floor are you?"

"I'm on the 9th floor."

"Okay. Which room?"

"909 is the number."

"Got it."

They walked to the elevators, unaware of their surroundings. Smiling, he followed her into the elevator and pressed her floor number, and stood next to her, avoiding contact with anyone else. "Hey, are you hungry?"

"Not at the moment, but I'm sure I will be before long." Tiffany looked at the floor. *That was a dumb response - everyone gets hungry sooner or later*, she thought before responding, "I think we could do something if you'd like."

"I would like to see some of the sights. I haven't been here in years. Maybe we can catch a show tonight. Are you up to it?"

"Of course. That's why we're here, right?"

"I'll call you after I freshen up a bit."

"Sounds good." Tiffany stepped off of the elevator and Manny followed closely. He grabbed her luggage. "I'll take this while you get your key,"

"Okay." Tiffany let go of her carry-on and opened her purse for the card key, turning left instead of right from the elevator doors. They walked down the hall in the opposite direction of her room number. "It's the other way," she laughed.

"I guess we're not paying much attention," Manny chuckled. "Is it me, or is there a little nervous tension, here?"

"Just a little, but I'm sure it makes sense."

"Makes perfectly good sense to me."

Tiffany stopped in front of the room door, sliding her key into the lock. "I'll wait for your call."

"Yeah, sure, no problem. I shouldn't take long."

"Okay." Tiffany took her carry-on and watched him walk towards the elevator. *Damn, that man is...* Her cell phone rang and she quickly entered the room. "Hello?"

"Girl, I'm waiting. How does he look? Is he anything like you thought?" Valerie inquired.

"I just got to the room."

"Is he with you?"

"No, he's gone to his room."

"*His* room? He isn't sharing a room with you?"

"He suggested we not share one, and I'm okay with that."

"Tell me: is he anything like you thought he'd be?"

"Handsome, sexy, and most of all, a true gentleman."

"Is that it? Come on, Tiffany: tell me if he's worth it."

"I haven't had time to find out, Val. I'll let you know."

Chapter 36

Manny returned to the elevator, pulling his carry-on behind him. He pushed the call button and stepped back to see which of the two elevators would arrive. *We can go to Caesar's Palace tonight. I know there's a show, for sure. If not, we can dance on Cleopatra's Barge.* Manny nodded his head. *Yeah, we can do that. She likes dancing*, he thought. The elevator arrived, and Manny got on. He pushed 16 and stepped to the rear. At his floor, he got off the elevator and turned left, following the room numbers.

Once in his room, he put the carry-on near the bathroom, and hung up his shirts and slacks. He pulled out his travel bag and grabbed his scented soap, shaving cream, and cologne, then positioned his razor next to the sink's faucet. Manny looked into the mirror, rubbed his face, and didn't like feeling the stubble of his afternoon beard, so he took his shirt off, hung it on the door, and put some shaving cream in his hand. He turned the water on and, with his left hand, splashed his face, then applied the shaving cream and carefully shaved.

He'd only been in his room ten minutes when the phone rang. He splashed his face with warm water and toweled dry on his way to answer it. "Hello?"

"Hey, are you ready?"

"Almost. Let me get my shirt on and I'll be right down. We're meeting in the lobby, right?"

"Where in the lobby?"

"I don't know." Manny paused, remembering he hadn't paid much attention to the hotel's layout. "How about near the check-in counter."

"Good idea. I'll be ready in five minutes."

"Aye, aye, Skipper," Manny laughed as he placed the phone on the cradle.

Tiffany put her phone on its base and stood front of the mirror. She changed into a skirt from the pair of blue jeans she had worn during her flight. "This works," she smiled, looking at her reflection in the tall mirror next to the door.

***

Manny returned to the bathroom, sprayed the expensive liquid in his hand and splashed his chest with cologne (after spraying the inviting chemical on his face), and then sprayed a mist of cologne onto his shirt. "This is good," he grinned while pushing his arm through one sleeve and quickly following with the other. Manny didn't tuck in his shirt, but let it hang freely over his torso. It wasn't tight, but it did give a hint of what would lie beneath, if someone was lucky enough to pop the buttons.

After a quick once over, standing in front of the mirror, he touched-brushed his hair with his hand and nodded to himself, confirming that he was ready to move on. He walked to the elevator doors, pressed the 'down' button, and waited. Standing there in the hall, he remembered her tender voice during those nights of long conversations on Skype. He imagined knocking on her door and waiting for her soothing response to come from behind the doorway.

Manny smiled just as the doors of the elevator opened. His smile evoked greetings from other guests already riding the elevator. He walked in, but instead of pressing the button for the lobby, he pressed 9. The doors closed and the elevator began its descent, stopping just once more before Manny's exit. He paused in the hallway, reading the room number map, after failing to remember the way to Tiffany's room. and turned right, into the hallway. He walked slower than usual, yet his heart was beating as if he had started a cardio session. He counted the steps to calm his nerves. *I've done this a lot of times in my life, so why is it so different?*

Manny stood at the door to room 909 and raised his hand to knock on the door, but first he took a breath and allowed his hand to touch the cold barrier between him and the woman he had traveled across the country to see. He knocked two times and waited. He heard the faint tone of an angel on the other side, calling out to him.

"Be right there." Tiffany closed her toiletry kit and looked in the full bathroom mirror, smoothing her clothes and touching her hair. She clicked the bathroom light off as she pulled the door closed, then opened the room door without looking through the peephole. "Hi, I thought we were meeting downstairs?" she smiled.

"I thought it was better if I came to get you. Am I too early?"

"No, you could never be too early," Tiffany winked.

"Are you ready?" Manny stood in the hallway and waited for her to accompany him to the elevators.

"Let me get my purse." Tiffany turned from the door, grabbed her purse and room key from the dresser, and turned to join the waiting hunk of a man. She stepped into the hallway and locked eyes with Manny, smiling from her soul.

"All set?"

"Yes, I'm ready. I don't know what we're doing, but I trust you have something planned."

"No worries. I do have something planned." Manny allowed her to move first. He followed her, glancing at her body and admiring her mature physique, imagining the touch he yearned to enjoy. He increased his pace until they were walking abreast towards the elevators. His hand brushed hers, and she grabbed it without hesitation. They didn't speak, yet their smiles said a million words.

Heading to the ground floor of the hotel, they didn't break their bond: the connection that joined their spirits and embraced their friendship's transition to a love interest. When the doors opened, they stepped forward in unison. Their walking together gave Manny a positive sign: it indicated a natural connection. And Tiffany didn't want to let his hand go, realizing she liked what she saw after many nights of imagining being by his side. Her acknowledgement and his proof gave both an internal vote of confidence.

They arrived on the hotel's ground floor and walked towards the casino. Manny directed her to the right, passing the dance club and a small restaurant. They walked on the main fairway to a hallway that held restaurants and stores. Tiffany grabbed his hand as she looked at the surroundings, window shopping, and glanced at their reflections in the store windows.

Tiffany slowed her steps and Manny quickly responded. They stopped in front of a clothing store and she took a step forward. Manny didn't hesitate to follow and didn't let her hand part from his. He stepped lively, shadowing the full bodied, curvaceous woman he'd gotten to know. Manny tapped her with his free hand and suggested a top that he hoped would fit her style. Tiffany was surprised when she saw his taste in clothes, and nodded her head in agreement. She released his hand and held the garment against her for a full view. Manny stepped back, looking at another, and selected one that he thought would suit her. "Here, try this one."

"Okay." Tiffany took the top and walked to the dressing room. "I'll be right out."

Manny nodded in response and stood in the aisle near a garment rack. He kept a close eye on the dressing room door while glancing around the store. . When Tiffany appeared, she didn't have on either of the tops he had handed her. "What happened?"

"They didn't suit me." Tiffany shook her head. "I can shop later."

"Yeah, okay…. but I don't mind if you want to do some shopping now."

Tiffany looked at Manny and gave him a soft smile; one in which her message was of appreciation. "Thank you for that, but we need to see Vegas."

"I have something I'd like to show you." Manny looked at his watch and estimated how long their walk would be, to take them to get to his planned destination. "Let's go out here." Manny led the way into the hustle and bustle of the Las Vegas strip.

Tiffany noticed the heat of the afternoon. It was much different than San Francisco. She'd heard about how hot Vegas is during summer, but she had no idea that the heat persisted into the early fall. Though the heat touched her skin and made her perspire, she walked beside Manny, keeping up with his stride as he led the way.

"Look over here; watch this," he said as he pointed to pirate ship replicas, complete with crews, moving back and forth in a shallow pool of water. *Boom! Boom!* Smoke billowed as cannonballs were shot between a Galleon and a Schooner; beautiful reproductions of 17th century ships. A narrator's voice identified the scene and onlookers enjoyed the acrobatic dives and jumps the crew performed from the sinking ship.

Manny noticed Tiffany's eyes, luminous in the evening light. He had seen this show the last time he'd visited Las Vegas, so his attention was on Tiffany. He watched her reactions to the reenactment and deliberately touched her shoulder with his. It was a gesture of confidence that she responded. She moved closer, without a second thought or any hesitation, and waited for him to put his arm around her.

At the end of the show, Manny gently grabbed her hand. "Let's go this way."

"Okay." Tiffany tightened her grip as the crowd dispersed. They moved safely onto the sidewalk and headed south on the strip, walking into the shopping forum of Caesar's Palace to escape the heat. . They window shopped, visiting interesting stores and unique boutiques. In one specialty store, Tiffany grabbed a purse and walked to the mirror. She waited for Manny to press her into leaving the store.

It wasn't his first dance; he knew exactly what to do. Having been married to a fashion-driven woman and then with a young adult daughter, it was second nature to him to allow women to shop and dream. "Nice," he smiled.

"You think so?" Tiffany turned to her side for a full view, with the purse on her shoulder. She nodded her head in agreement. "It looks very good." She pulled the purse off of her shoulder and opened it to see the price tag. "No wonder it looks good," she laughed. "Not right now; maybe later."

"If we hit a jackpot, we'll come and get it."

"Maybe my jackpot isn't about money," she responded, glancing at Manny.

Chapter 37

They exited the store and walked further into the Forum, where Tiffany stopped at Poseidon's fountain. *They really didn't hold back on designing this place*, she thought, falling for the decor of old Rome. Thunder rolled, water rushed into the fountain, and actors rose on columns that lifted them towards the high ceiling. Echoes of verse, as told in olden times summoned the god of the Sea to bequeath his power unto his children. Flames, choreographed to perfection, shot into the air and the act continued to its end. Water rushed to the surface and the statue went back to its original position. "They really entertain at every opportunity," Tiffany smiled. "Good show."

"You'll see more, before we leave."

"I thought there was more gambling here than anything else."

"That was the old Las Vegas. Now it's more about shows for entertainment. I guess you can't gamble all day and night anymore."

"I heard was about the entertainment, but I didn't expect a mall to have anything but stores."

"Different; no doubt, it's different." Manny walked close to her as they proceeded to another court of the Forum.

"Are you hungry?"

"I think it's time. I should eat something." Tiffany looked around for a restaurant.

Manny guided them to the Trevi Italian Restaurant he remembered, not far from their position in the Forum. "I hope you don't mind Italian."

"It's one of my favorite," she smiled, and held his hand with a tighter grip. *This man listens.*

The hostess showed them to a table and handed each of them a menu. Within minutes their server arrived and asked for their orders.

Tiffany and Manny ordered wine, mozzarella sticks and calamari, then conversed

as if they were spending hours on Skype. "You never told me about your flight," Manny inquired.

"It was nerve wracking. I don't know how to say this..." Tiffany paused. "I debated all the way here, if this was the right thing to do or if I should hop on a return flight once I landed."

He straightened, unconsciously tightening his muscles before responding. "I, ah, hope you're happy you came."

"So far. It's like we've known each other for years...I'm comfortable."

Comfortable. What the hell does that mean? thought Manny as he looked at Tiffany with a raised eyebrow. "I don't follow."

"Let me just say that you're the same man I talk to on Skype. You haven't shown me anything different so far, and I'm comfortable."

"Does "so far" mean you're not quite finished with your assessment?"

"A girl has to be ready for any change, don't you think?"

"I guess I'm watching for the same thing. You could flip into a monster when you hear slot machine bells." He laughed. "Haven't you noticed I've been keeping you away from them? Just in case."

"You're joking, right?"

"Of course I am." Manny slid his chair further away from Tiffany.

"You're a joker," she laughed.

Manny pushed the chair back to its original position. The waitress returned with wine, water, and a small basket of bread. "Thank you," Manny nodded to the waitress. "Here's to you, Tiffany." He raised his wine glass and waited.

"And here's to you, Manny," Tiffany smiled while softly tapping Manny's wine glass. They each took a sip and went back to the conversation.

"I wasn't skeptical at all on my flight. Actually, I was kind of anxious." Manny smiled.

"Anxious, really?"

"Yes: anxious because we'd talked for so long and I was more than comfortable – as you said."

"Comfort is important." Tiffany glanced at Manny as she turned to scan their surroundings. She faced Manny. "And are you that comfortable?"

He blushed before responding, "Quite comfortable."

"Oh, you're so cute," Tiffany giggled. "You're blushing."

"It happens when I like someone so beautiful."

"I see; it's all part of winning my heart."

"I thought I had a piece of that before you got on the plane."

"Well…"

The waitress returned with their appetizers. After Manny thanked the waitress, he took Tiffany's hand in his,. "It's good to give thanks before eating."

"I agree." Tiffany nodded her head and listened to Manny.

Manny spoke softly, giving thanks; but to Tiffany's surprise, she heard something she never expected. "…and thank you for

Tiffany's safe arrival to meet me; and Father, give me the strength to continue making her comfortable. Amen."

Tiffany didn't move her head to look in his eyes, nor did she release his hand from hers. The world became silent, to Tiffany: she heard herself breathe, and that was the extent of noise in her surroundings. The last time she had heard someone specifically call her name in prayer was at her wedding. His action and his consideration in thanking God for her presence touched her and released a tear from the corner of her eye. "That was sweet, Manny."

"I meant every word." He took his napkin and gently touched the wet spot on her cheek. "No worries. So let's dig in; we have lots to do."

"We do?"

"Yes," he looked at his watch, "we do."

He waived for the server and handed her his credit card. "Can you settle this please? We're in a bit of a hurry."

"Certainly, sir. I'll be back in a moment." The server scurried to ring up the check and returned for Manny's signature. Manny completed the transaction and pulled Tiffany out of the booth. "We have to go."

"Okay, I'm moving," Tiffany smiled, as she responded to Manny's quick pace.

They went to the boulevard and hailed a cab. "The heliport, please," he requested as they entered the cab.

"Sure," the cabbie said.

Tiffany and Manny held hands while they rode to the heliport. "You're going to love this. Have you ever been on a helicopter before?" Manny inquired.

"I've never been on a helicopter in my life."

"You'll love the experience. Trust me, it's going to be fun."

They arrived at the heliport and arranged for the tour. She walked to the helicopter and, as directed by the pilot, climbed into the backseat. Manny did the same from the other side and helped Tiffany put on the headset. The pilot pointed to his earphones and asked, "Can you hear me?" Tiffany didn't respond because she hadn't heard anything. She looked at Manny after she saw the pilot point at his ear phones.

Manny answered the pilot's quest for a communication check with "Yes," and gave a thumbs up. He then looked at Tiffany's earphones and turned a knob. The pilot saw Manny's move and asked, "Can you hear me now?"

"Yes, I can," Tiffany said.

Manny grabbed her seat belt and pulled it across her waist and snapped it to the one closest to him. "There, you're ready." Manny confirmed Tiffany's status to the pilot. He buckled his seat belt, grabbed her hand, and held it as they took off into the sky. The helicopter moved forward and banked as it rose past the boulevard and strip. The pilot said, "Hold on and look left, and you'll see the strip down to the needle."

"I never knew it could be so exhilarating," Tiffany confessed.

The pilot spoke again on the ride to Grand Canyon West. He pointed to the Hoover Dam and Lake Mead and explained some of its history. He also pointed out the rocky mountain ranges, which looked like anthills from their elevation. The pilot flew the copter into the canyon while Manny held Tiffany's hand and said, "Isn't it breathtaking?" Tiffany nodded her head and smiled. When the helicopter reached its turn around point, the sunset was in full glory. She touched her chest with one hand, released

Manny's grasp, and covered her mouth. The sight took her breath away.

"Manny, I'll never forget this day. Thank you for sharing this with me." Tiffany's hand over her mouth hid the most impressive smile she had ever shown.

An hour or more later, the helicopter returned to the heliport. Manny and Tiffany disembarked, got into a cab, and headed for Treasure Island. They laughed as they recalled the experience of flying to the Grand Canyon, and talked as if it might be the beginning of an annual event. *I hope to share the excitement again with him,* Tiffany thought. Manny took Tiffany's arm and whispered, "If there is a reason to repeat the tour, it will be in celebration of us." Tiffany couldn't believe her ears, but smiled at him. I It was as if he'd read her mind.

"Yes," Tiffany said, "that would be a very good reason."

Chapter 38

She hadn't smiled so much since college. Tiffany couldn't contain her excitement, especially since Manny seemed to be doing all the right things. Her time with him in Las Vegas was having a positive effect on her outlook in life. After a short shuttle from the hotel, they stood in the showroom waiting area.

Tiffany went to the ladies' room, stopped at a pamphlet stand, and grabbed a few. She went inside, holding the pamphlets in her hand, and began reading them while sitting on the toilet. She walked to the sink after exiting the stall, looked into the mirror, washed her hands, retrieved lipstick from her purse, and touched up her lips. She noticed how dry they had become. She pulled her hair back, anticipating a drive in the convertible she'd seen in the parking lot. Her smile wouldn't fade, even though she wasn't making an effort to show excitement: it was as if it was a permanent fixture for the day. Tiffany left the ladies' room and walked into the waiting area. "Did I miss anything?"

"Not really, but you have to sign this waiver."

"Waiver?"

"Yes, they don't want to be held liable if we damage a car."

"Okay, I get it."

"But no worries. It's going to be fun."

"I know: I'm with you, and everything has been fun so far."

Manny grinned as he nodded his head. "I'm glad you're still having a good time."

"I am; I really am. Now, do I drive first, or do you?" Tiffany asked about the six cars: a 2012 Lamborghini, a 2011 Audi R8, a

2012 Ferrari, a 2012 Jaguar XKR, and a 2011 Ford 500. The last was a 2012 Mustang GT. Each car was over 500 horsepower.

Manny and Tiffany elected to drive the Lamborghini first and then follow through the list. They flipped a coin to see who'd drive first. Tiffany rarely drove, but she wasn't afraid to get behind the wheel of these fast movers.

"Is there a helmet?" Manny looked at the clerk.

"If you want one," she laughed.

"I think I may need one only while she's driving."

"Funny, Manny; real funny." Tiffany elbowed him. The lead driver gathered everyone there who was driving the exotic cars and briefed them on safety, the two-way radio's operation, and the trail they would be taking. Tiffany got into the Lamborghini and buckled in, adjusted the mirrors and seat, then looked at Manny. "Hold on."

Manny nodded his head and waited.

The lead took off and spoke on the two-way. "Remember, keep a safe distance, and don't push up on the bumper of the car in front of you. No passing! I'm sure you won't need to pass. I will keep a good pace so you get the feel of the car. Make sure you don't let others into our line of cars."

"I got this," she smiled.

Manny smiled back. "I trust you know how to drive."

"It's kind of late to ask me now."

They took off on the trail, driving down the street to the interstate entry. The lead car drove up to 80 miles per hour and pushed its way through traffic. Tiffany followed and cut in and out of traffic like a professional cab driver. She pushed the car (or, the car pushed her). Manny held on and secretly breathed to relax himself as he watched her cut in and out of traffic.

"You can handle this car pretty good. Do you have one at home that you didn't tell me about?"

"No, Manny, why would I own a sports car like this?"

"I asked if you *secretly* had one." Tiffany laughed as they turned into a parking lot near the national park they were driving through. The two-way sparked and the leader's voice came over the air.

"Okay, this is the beginning: we'll drive a few miles and stop for a driver and car change. Remember: no passing, and keep up. No lagging behind! Push it to catch up." The leader pulled out, and off they went down the stretch. The lead car pushed to 100 mph and Tiffany followed him without effort. She became one with the car, and Manny was thoroughly impressed. "Wow! You aren't afraid of speed."

"What speed?" Tiffany said as she pushed a pedal shifter. The car pushed them both into the seat and jolted forward. "I love this response."

"I can imagine."

They arrived at the change point and Tiffany and Manny walked to the next car behind them. Manny jumped into the driver's seat. "Okay, don't let me scare you."

"You're joking, right?"

"Yeah, I'm joking." Manny adjusted the mirrors, seat, and radio. "Music must set the mood. I'm driving."

"You're driving." Tiffany gave Manny devilish grin and tightened her seat belt.

The lead driver came on the air again, gave instructions, and took off. Manny followed the Lamborghini in the Audi R8 and stomped on the gas. He wasn't surprised at the response but he was really excited as the car pushed forward and, without effort, caught the car ahead of them. "Wow! Did you feel the power?"

"I felt it, and it's how I like my men. Powerful."

Manny didn't respond to Tiffany's comment but focused on driving instead. He sped up on the trail, maintaining a high speed, along with the group. Only minutes had passed when they came to the next point for changing cars and drivers. Manny exited the R8 with a huge smile on his face. "If I ever get a few pennies...we could share this car."

"Share?"

"I don't mind sharing with you. I think you can handle a fast-moving car."

"I can, and I will show you in the next car."

They repeated instructions, pushing each car to a controllable limit and feeling the power of the pedal. It was their last exchange on the Mustang before heading back to the office when Manny looked at Tiffany as he walked to the car. "Would you like to drive the Mustang?"

"It's your turn."

"I know, but I'm being a gentleman."

"It's okay, Manny, I've had my turns. I don't mind riding this time."

Manny got into the driver's seat, adjusted the mirrors and seat, tightened the belt, and hit the gas. He heard the roar of the Ford's super engine. "Damn nice," he nodded.

"I'm not a car lover, but I see you enjoyed doing this."

"From what I saw of you, I'm not alone."

"No, you aren't."

A Cyber Affair

The leader came on the two-way and off they went, heading back to the office showroom. Manny followed, enjoying the ride and the power in his control.

"Okay, what's next?" Manny looked to see if she had anything planned from her research.

"After lunch, there's something I'd like to try."

"Anything…I have something up my sleeve for sunset, so whatever you'd like to do is fine with me."

"Good, because I think you'll like this."

Manny pulled up to the showroom, backed the car into a parking space as directed, and shut off the engine. "What a thrill."

Tiffany exited the car and walked around to meet Manny. She grabbed him and hugged him tight. "This was really fun, and different. I never thought I'd get a chance to drive these cars."

Manny hugged her back, holding her tighter than he'd done before. "I'm glad you liked it."

Tiffany pecked him on the lips, giving him a kiss of thanks without getting sensual. Manny was surprised, and waited for a second attempt so he could take advantage of the long kiss he wanted to enjoy. Instead, Tiffany let go and released Manny from her embrace. He followed, abiding by her lead of unspoken instructions.

The van taking them back to the strip arrived and they boarded, sitting next to each other. "Treasure Island," Manny told the driver. They sat in silence until they arrived at the hotel.

"How about having lunch inside?"

"I wanted to go across the street," Tiffany nodded. "Let's do something inside that's fun, too."

"Oh, you mean the Venetian?"

"Yes, I've saw a pamphlet at the exotic car showroom."

"I'm game for whatever you have in mind."

They exited the van and grabbed each other's hands as they walked across the street to the Venetian. They walked up to the entryway and stepped aboard the moving sidewalk. At the top of the stairs, arriving at the end of the moving walkway, Manny pushed a door open and allowed Tiffany to enter first. She took a moment and stood at the balcony overlooking the bottom floor, examining the style and decor of the building. She was amazed at the sights: the high ceiling, the stores, the marble, the balcony going downstairs, the open feeling, and the impressive idea that cost was no object in the building's design.

Manny observed her inspecting the building, and without warning he touched her waist as he stood next to her. *She's impressed. Now, if I'm as impressive to her as this casino, we're onto something.* He smiled before moving to his right, and Tiffany followed his lead. She window shopped as they walked into the Grand Canal stores.

They entered a coffee shop; an Italian T*rattoria* that served chocolate Italian-style. Tiffany led Manny to the front door, but stopped to see the mannequin in the hall. She stood next to it. "Manny take this picture," she instructed him.

"Sure." Manny grabbed his phone and held it up. The mannequin next to Tiffany moved and she yelled, "Oh, hell!"

"You didn't know?" he laughed.

The living mannequin nodded his head while he tipped his hat and posed next to Tiffany while Manny took the picture. Manny tipped the guy and turned into the restaurant. "The picture I missed was the one where you were screaming," Manny laughed.

"I'm glad you didn't," Tiffany giggled. "I had no idea. No wonder he looked so real."

"He's real. He's alive."

"You get my point." They ordered and took a seat. Manny looked at his watch.

"What time is our next appointment?"

"I don't have an appointment set for us."

"Are you sure?"

"I'm sure."

Manny picked up the tray after they finished eating, walked to the exit, and placed it on the bin. He returned to the table and winked at Tiffany. "Right on time?"

"Perfect," she smiled.

Manny took her hand to help her from the table and walked out into the main hallway. They turned left, moving further into the Venetian's Grand Canal Shopping area, and strolled until they came into an open piazza where skits of old Italy were at center stage. The bridge held a bride, taking pictures. People were everywhere and that's when she heard it…singing! She looked into the direction of the music and pointed out the area to Manny. "Let's do this."

"You don't want to wait for the real thing?"

"Who said I'm going to get a chance for the real thing? I don't know if I'll ever get to Italy."

Manny leaned his head one way and closed his eyes. "I'd say your future is bright."

"You're a Gypsy now, a fortune teller. Where's your crystal ball?"

"Give me your hand," Manny giggled.

"Oh heck, no: my line is deep and I doubt you can read it."

"I can tell you the immediate future."

"Oh, really?"

"Sure." Manny grabbed her hand and held her palm up. "I see a gondola ride before the evening sun."

"You're a funny man."

"Nothing wrong with laughing," Manny laughed, and directed: "Wait here, I'll be right back."

Tiffany waited while she watched the crowd become involved in the show, and turned to see couples on the gondolas. She stopped watching the others long enough to breathe. *This man - my God, this man. He's something special and I'm surprised I don't need to try to impress him. It's really easy. Is this bad?* She looked into the palm of her hand. *I have been wrong a lot of times, but this time I have got to be right. I trust you.*

Manny returned with tickets for the gondola. "Are you ready?"

"I'm ready."

"Come on, let's go." Manny led the way to the boarding step, gave the porter their tickets, and they stepped onto a gondola. "You'll have to sit down before I can move," the gondolier instructed.

"No sweat." Manny sat next to her and off they went. The gondolier gave them a safety spiel and asked which song they'd like him to sing. Manny chose a soft and bellowing song; an Italian love ballad. Tiffany didn't know any of the songs that were being offered, so she nodded in agreement. The gondolier started softly and crescendoed into a full bellowing melody. Tiffany touched her heart at his voice, and Manny touched her other hand. The gondolier paddled the gondola up the canal and back, and in a few minutes they were back at the dock.

"That was different." Manny helped Tiffany from the gondola.

"It sure was. One day I'll do the real thing. I may not know with whom, but I'll remember this as being the best one ever."

"Memories? Are you referring to the memories I promised we'd make?"

"Memories in the making." Tiffany held his hand while they walked from the gondola area to the open piazza. "This too, Manny. I'm remembering everything about this trip." She touched his shoulder and laid her head on it after she removed her hand from his. "I like this weekend, so far. I mean, everything is perfect."

"I'm feeling the same way. Perfection is hard to come by."

"Especially for people who live so far away from one another."

"I know that tomorrow will be difficult, getting on the plane for Miami."

"I don't want to think about it. Let's do something else."

Manny looked at his watch. "I guess if we walk to the next event, we'll be there in time for sunset."

"Which direction?"

"North."

Manny and Tiffany walked out of the Venetian heading north on the strip. They walked hand in hand, and laughed as they remembered the events they'd shared over the day and a half since meeting. "I never suspected you were so active."

"Tiffany, you never told me you were a race car driver."

"Like you didn't know. I've hinted around it while we Skyped all this time."

"I didn't get it, but I'm glad it worked out for you."

"You mean for us." Tiffany put her arm around his shoulder. "I am having a really good time and it's our last night together. I should have taken a week off."

"Yeah, but we didn't know it would be like this. I never suspected my imaginary kiss could turn you into a princess."

"If you think I'm good just from an imaginary kiss, why not see what a real one will do?"

Manny looked at her, stopped, and turned her to face him. He caressed her face with his hands and pulled her slowly to his lips, moving in and connecting his lips to hers. He didn't press forward, allowing her to push him away if she wanted. Their lips touched and Tiffany turned and tilted her head to the right, and then Manny responded by going in for the kill. His tongue entered her mouth and danced with her resident. Tiffany responded and gave her best, giving him what she was getting.

They kissed and embraced as what felt like a thunderstorm blew over them, but the tender kiss was enough to get a feel for what joys they might share. Manny let go of her and stepped back as Tiffany released her grasp. "Oh, it's working. The magic is working." Manny felt his excitement rise for the first time.

Tiffany nodded in response. "It's working, all right." She grabbed his hand, "Where are we going?"

"Oh, yeah, The Space Needle."

"Are we riding into space?"

"I am right now: who needs a lift?" Manny smiled and pulled her closer.

Chapter 39

They arrived at the elevators on the bottom floor of the Stratosphere Hotel Casino and instructed the operator to take them to the swing ride at the top of the space needle. The operator pushed the floor button and they rose up, nonstop, until they reached their destination. "I never asked if you were afraid of heights. I'm sure you aren't but, I need to ask now."

"It's kind of late to ask me, but I'm okay. Is this what I think it is?"

"Another thrill!"

"I never knew you were a thrill seeker."

"Actually, I'm not, but for some reason I thought we'd enjoy this at sunset."

"Sounds like a good idea." Tiffany hesitantly followed Manny inside. "Is it safe?"

"Of course it is. If they had any accidents, I'm sure they would stop using the ride."

"I guess so." Tiffany followed instructions and buckled into the *Insanity* ride. She looked at Manny sitting next to her. "If I fall, remember: this was a really good trip up to the time I fell screaming to my death."

"You're not going to fall. Enjoy the sunset. Look at the mountain range." He reached for her hand. "Here, hold on until we start moving."

The ride rose and spread, its prongs wide, turning at 900 feet above ground. It spun and turned, giving the view of the entire sunset: the soft orange glow over the horizon and then the lights of the city below. The view was amazing and Manny didn't let go of Tiffany's hand. He held on to her while she held the safety bar in a death grip with her other hand. When it started spinning faster, she closed her eyes and breathed, without releasing Manny's hand. By the time the ride finished, she opened her eyes at last and looked at Manny. "Did we stop?"

"Yes, we stopped. We'll be back on solid ground soon."

"Nice view."

"You finally opened your eyes to see it," Manny smiled.

"It started out good, but when it got fast, I closed my eyes."

"I saw that. But at least you got to see it." Manny led Tiffany to the elevator, rode it to the bottom floor, then took the escalator down to the ground.

"I have a question for you."

Tiffany looked puzzled. Manny hadn't asked a question the entire time they were together. "Okay," she hesitantly responded. "Ah, what's your question?"

Manny stopped walking, turned to her, and looked into her eyes. "If a man was alone in the middle of a forest and yelled at the top of his lungs, would anyone hear him?"

Tiffany had never heard such a question posed to a woman. At first the common sense response came to her mind, *Of course, dummy. It depends on who's close, or the animals.* Then it dawned on her, and the response she wanted to tell him flashed into her mouth as if it led the way without thought. "If they're spiritually connected and deeply in love, she'll hear his cry a thousand miles away."

Manny looked at her and pulled her close, embracing her tightly and feeling her chest rise from taking a breath. He whispered, "I'm yelling, can you hear me?"

Tiffany held him tightly as a tingle ran from her mind to her toes. Manny had responded like a real man, a man she'd dreamed of having, a man easy to admire, to fall head over heels in love with, and one who was respectable. "I hear you," she responded. "I hear you loud and clear."

Manny moved his lips next to hers and with a gentle touch, he engaged her heart with his tongue. She reciprocated his advance, her senses dancing the tango with him, her tongue twisting and turning, encircling his as though she was giving him a combination to her most fortified chamber.

Tiffany's energy went to her feet, leaving her body weak but her mind happy. She was content being in his arms and realized that his powerful invitation was her deciding arrow for a dance with reality. Tiffany didn't move to break his embrace and the second kiss between them was indication that she'd landed on the moon. Manny made her powerless: he divided her into small pieces where he toyed with them and placed each one in his pocket for future use. She didn't mind; she didn't care to forfeit the game or raise a white flag of defeat. Tiffany had gotten to experience a tender heart for 24 hours: something she'd wanted, but hadn't expected.

Manny released his tight embrace, without letting go of her completely. He looked at her again. "Are you okay?"

"I'm, I'm...no, I'm not okay."

"What's wrong?"

"Let me lean on you."

"I'll never let you go."

Tiffany smiled and placed her arm around his waist as he moved to her side. "Don't let me go."

Chapter 40

It was on the ride back to Treasure Island that they decided to share one room for the night. She wanted to experience his touch, and felt that the time had arrived to fulfill her imagination. He wanted to get to know her more, and wanted to enter her mind through every possible channel. "Let's get a bottle of wine and escape the hustle and bustle of Las Vegas."

Tiffany smiled. "I couldn't have suggested anything better."

They got out of the car and walked to the elevator. Manny pushed 16. "I hope you don't mind my room."

"No, not at all." Tiffany held his arm while she stood next to him.

They exited the elevator and Manny pulled his key out of his pocket, slid the card through the slot, and pushed the handle to open the door. Tiffany walked in first and Manny followed. She sat at the foot of his bed. "I'll call room service for that bottle of wine." Manny called and ordered Merlot.

Tiffany took his hand as he walked past her. "I'm not always the aggressive type, but I've waited to…"

Before he could say another word, she was in his arms, kissing him and tugging at his shirt. Manny responded by unzipping her pants and releasing the button at her waist. Within seconds, they managed to undress while they continued to kiss. Manny lifted her and Tiffany clamped her legs around his waist. She held on while Manny maneuvered them onto the bed. He laid her on her back and shared his passion.

He followed his mind's intent; he kissed her lips and then created a path of gentle kisses to her breast. He ran his tongue around her nipples while he caressed her with one hand through the garment covering her chest. He focused on one and then the other breast, savoring the taste of her nipples. She exhaled in response and moved her hips towards him.

Tiffany pulled his forehead to her lips and grabbed him to feel his loins next to her moist chamber of commitment. Manny followed her lead, allowing the head of his sexual prowess to tease her lips of excitement, and then slid his erection up and down the path of her ignition. He pressed just enough, allowing her to feel the pressure for entry, and then pulled back from her seductively grinding hips so that entry wasn't immediate. Instead, he rose from the bed and went to his wallet, where Manny retrieved a condom and hastily put it on. He returned to her and kissed her lips before he said, "Where were we?"

Tiffany grabbed him and pulled him on top. "You were right here, right at this moment." Manny inched his way into her and pressed forward with interest, responding to her invitation. She tugged at his waist to aid his entry. Manny's teasing made her intensity grow. She wrapped her legs around him and tried to pull him closer. Suddenly Manny made a manly thrust and pulled her tightly against him as he went deep within her, sending a jolt of sensation through Tiffany's body.

She positioned her arms above her head and gripped a pillow while feeling her body rock from the attack on her nervous system. Tiffany yelled, "Ah!" at the peaks of sensation that ran through her body. He repeated his thrust and increased his movements. Tiffany wrapped her arms tightly around his back. The slight pressure of her nails on his tight skin drove Manny to push harder. He encouraged her to dance this tango with him until she was breathless.

And she did, panting wildly and moving her hands to his hips to slow his pace. Manny, surprisingly, flipped her on top. She tried to catch her breath and take control, but his strength restrained her movement and caused her to buck in rhythm to his upward thrust. She was ready to explode, but held on. Tiffany bucked until her pace matched his and her body broke into a sweat. She closed her eyes and screamed, "Stop, oh my GOD, STOP!!!" and held her breath from the intensity. She saw stars from the lack of oxygen when she looked at the ceiling. She felt her blood rushing from her extremities, which made them insensible. She felt numbness spread throughout her body unlike anything she had experienced in her life. An orgasm ravaged through her, draining her energy. Her skin was prickled with goosebumps.

Manny released his grip and she fell onto the bed. He repositioned himself to enter her again from the side, placing one of her legs straight on the bed with the other knee bent at 90 a degree angle. He caressed her butt, straddled her lower leg, and pressed his love muscle into position for entry.

Tiffany didn't resist and waited for her breathing to slowly return to normal. She allowed him to continue in spite of her better judgment. This new sexual experience had her body screaming for more. He pressed and pulled, and she didn't know what to do but enjoy the experience. Tiffany felt the growing sensation of another orgasm building up.

She put her face into the pillow and screamed at the top of her lungs while she experienced the strongest climax of her life. With tears in her eyes, she lifted her arms and tried to push Manny back, but she was weakened from the number and intensity of her orgasms. He pressed forward with an odd, rhythmic stroke until she stopped responding. Manny pulled out, watched her body rise and fall with each breath, and then reclined behind her, spooning with her. Tiffany didn't move and didn't utter a word, nor were her breaths labored. Her body was fully relaxed and Manny threw his arm around her. When she finally moved, Manny gave her a gentle kiss and suggested they crawl under the covers.

"There's more where that came from. I'll wait for my big moment," Manny said.

"I'm okay with you waiting." Tiffany smiled. *I've never had a man focus on me so much.* She took control and pushed Manny on his back, placed her rear deltoids onto his chest, and faced the ceiling. She rocked her butt up and down, moving as she slid on the strength of his reproductive magnetism. Manny caressed her breast, kissed the back of her neck, and responded as he pressed upward to her movement. One of Manny's hands found her spot of no return, which he massaged while his erect reproductive muscle moved in and out of her tunnel of commitment.

Their pace increased as she led the advanced interchange and he responded to her heightened feelings, which brought her closer to climax. When she screamed and exhaled before going limp, Manny finally relieved himself of his contained pressure. He shook from its intensity, holding her tight.

"I want to stay like this forever." Manny said.

"Nice thought, but I think we should face each other, especially if "forever" includes talking."

"Yeah, you're right," he chuckled in agreement.

The night continued and they cuddled while falling asleep. Periodically Manny awoke feeling frisky - and Tiffany responded with unbridled energy. They made love three times that night. Tiffany couldn't believe how her body responded to Manny. She experienced having multiple orgasms every time he touched her. Exhausted, they finally dozed off and slept in the spoon position.

Chapter 41

Early the next morning, Manny woke to the sight of his beautiful woman still asleep, exhausted from the physical demands of the night. She didn't budge until he brushed her hair away from her face. "Good morning," he greeted her. "I'm sorry if I woke you."

"You didn't, it's my body waking me at the usual time of morning."

"I'm that way most mornings, too."

"What time is it? It's about 8, isn't it?" asked Tiffany. She smiled at Manny and pulled him in for a kiss, thinking *I could do him again.*

Manny glanced at the clock. "A little after. Don't worry about the time. I know that whatever the hour, when we're together, it's the perfect time of day."

"I like that answer."

Manny responded with another kiss, then rose from the bed.

"We fly home today." Tiffany sighed, "I really don't want to leave." She looked at Manny and watched him put his soured gym clothes in a plastic bag. "But we have to."

"I know, trust me. I woke thinking the same thing, and about the next time."

"At least you're thinking of the right thing. Next time."

"How about we get up, dress, pack, and meet for breakfast. We don't have to check out until 11."

"I need to get downstairs and pack. How much time do I have?"

Manny looked at the clock. "I think 9 is good, so how about in 50 minutes?"

"Wait." Tiffany went to the toilet, leaving the door cracked.

"I take that long just to get dressed," she laughed.

"Unless you want to wait until 10 for breakfast."

"Okay." Tiffany flushed the toilet. "I'll be ready by 9."

"Good." Manny dressed in yesterday's shorts. "I'll come and get you."

Tiffany picked up her clothes and put them on. "I'll be ready." She walked to him, grabbed his body, and put her lips to his. "Good morning."

Manny smiled. "Good morning, Love."

Tiffany grabbed her purse and walked into the hallway, heading to the elevators.

***

Tiffany's flight was two hours earlier than Manny's, so he escorted her to the airport. He didn't want her to escape his arms until the last minute before she needed to board the plane. They did everything in their power to make these moments last, until they reluctantly poured themselves into a taxi headed for the airport.

"You don't have to come with me," Tiffany suggested. "I'm a big girl."

"I want to be with you as long as I can. I've got you here and I'm holding on until you leave me."

"I'm not leaving you. It's temporary, remember? We agreed we'll see each other again."

"Yes, I know; and believe me, I don't want to lose the best woman who ever came into my life."

"I'm only a flight away and we can see each other in a few weeks. I have vacation days. I'll come to Florida."

"And I can come to San Francisco. We have to work something out to keep this going. Believe me, I'm not letting you go. I'm only delaying what I think will end up happening."

"What do you think that is?"

"Need I explain?"

"Please do, Manny."

Manny didn't want to speak of commitment so early, but he'd had enough of being single. He wanted to win Tiffany's heart. This had been the best weekend since he'd sailed the seven seas. "You have to understand," Manny said as he looked away for a moment. "I'm not a simple guy, and finding a companion whom I enjoy is a difficult task." He looked into Tiffany's eyes before he said, "I've found you, Tiffany, and I'm not giving you up. I can't."

"What are you saying?"

"I'm saying I'm in love with you. I know it, I feel it, and I admit it. We've talked for months, shared our lives, and I can't explain what being with you this weekend has meant to me. It's like feeling a battle cruiser rock multiple 16-inch guns at once. It's as clear as day to me."

"I'm impressed, and I want you to know that you're not alone. I feel exactly as you described. I don't want to give this up. I'm not going to - and, love? Hell, it's in my vocabulary."

"Are you sure?"

The cab stopped before Tiffany answered and they both got out of the car at the airport. She turned to Manny. "I'm sure of one thing. This is the beginning of what I want and hope for: a long-term relationship."

Manny thought it was too early to press for a commitment or a greater validation of her emotions. What he knew was the confidence in his soul, the spark in his spirit, and the strength to follow his gut. His drive and determination led him to believe he could get Tiffany to open up to him one last time before she boarded her flight. They checked in at the kiosk and went through security. He escorted Tiffany to her terminal and flight gate. She chose a seat on the front row which looked away from the gate door. "This was the best weekend I've ever had."

"I wish it would never end."

"I know the feeling." Tiffany placed her head on his shoulder.

"I'm going to miss you."

Manny didn't respond and thought of the reasons why he felt he had to return to West Palm Beach. *Suzie acknowledged she's grown enough to live independently. My job is just a job and it's not going anywhere. The material things - my apartment, car and bike - they're just stuff, and my Baby Girl can look after them.* He thought hard about his choices as he felt the warmth of Tiffany, the beautiful woman next to him. Manny pondered the pros and cons and wondered if going home was the right thing to do. Nothing else really mattered to him. His heart pounded as loudly as a Taiko drummer at a Japanese festival.

It was Tiffany, the conversationalist, the dancer, the thrill seeker, and the beauty, who compiled positive thoughts for his decision. The gate attendant announced an early boarding and Tiffany raised her head. She looked at Manny with tears in her eyes.

"This is it, before I see you again," she sighed.

"Yes, I guess you better get going."

"I enjoyed this weekend. I didn't want it to end."

"I understand." Manny got up from the chair and pulled Tiffany into his arms. "It's the beginning, so don't worry. We'll work something out."

"I hope so, Manny. This was the reason I didn't want a long distance relationship. I'm here and we're separating already. I don't like it."

"I know, I know." Manny kissed her deeply and held her close, giving her the passion his heart wanted her to believe existed. "I love you. I mean it."

Tiffany broke his embrace, grasped the handle of her carry-on luggage, and walked to the line for boarding. She couldn't find the strength to look back at him. She didn't want to leave. Another tear fell as she wiped her eyes.

Manny watched her walk into line, one small step ahead of the other, when it dawned on him. <u>Why not?</u> He allowed his heart and mind to be free. Why not? He ran to the nearest check-in counter and changed his flight to board the same plane as Tiffany. The only seat available was in first-class, and without a thought he spent the extra money to purchase it. Manny called Suzie and quickly explained his intention. He was the last passenger to board the aircraft.

Tiffany found her seat aboard the airplane. She looked out of the window again and remembered her fears of seeing Manny for the first time. She tapped her foot as she held back the tears. When her seatmate sat next to her, Tiffany held a napkin up to hide her face, embarrassed and wanting to avoid anyone who would notice her tears.

"Anything I can help you with?" asked the woman next to her as she buckled her seat belt.

"No, but thanks for asking," sniffed Tiffany.

"It's going to be all right, whatever it is. It always works out."

Teary-eyed, Tiffany responded, "I sure hope so."

She sat and looked out of the window again. To her, the sound of the airplane door closing felt ominous for her future. Though the flight attendants gave the safety brief, she didn't hear a sound. When she finally looked up, everyone was seated as the plane moved away from the terminal.

"It's a shame he lives in West Palm Beach," Tiffany whispered under her breath.

The flight landed one hour and twenty minutes later. Tiffany sent her girlfriend Valerie a text: *It was awesome, and he's gorgeous. I miss him already.*

Valerie responded: *I'm in baggage claim waiting for you. I can't wait to hear about every moment.*

Passengers left the aircraft and Tiffany followed suit. She walked up the passageway through the terminal doors. To her surprise, Manny was standing at the terminal gate with a huge smile. She dropped her bag and ran to him and they kissed with great passion. Tiffany sighed, her arms shaking from surprise and nervous energy running through her body. Her doubt and worry about a long distance relationship finally flew from her like a bird soaring into flight.

"How long are you staying?" Tiffany asked.

"As long as you'll have me," responded Manny.

A Note from the Author

Thank you so much for reading A Cyber Affair. I hope you truly enjoyed the story and connected to the characters. In today's dating world, meeting and dating online is a common event. Actually, it's more of the norm than the unusual.

It took a few years to complete the novel and especially since technology rapidly changes the accuracy was a sure challenge. You may have noted some chats were kind of out dated. But the principle of the story remained.

Please consider leaving a review. I take every response to heart, especially since I can only enhance my writing   with feedback.

Write your review on any of these websites:

www.amazon.com

www.amazon.ca

www.GoodReads.com

or   www.ElevationBookPublishing.com

or   www.LonzCook.net

Join me on facebook: Lonz Cook Author
www.facebook.com/Lonz-Cook-Author-168973854345/